# Scoffers Will Come
## short stories

I0671641

## David Porter

**by David Porter:**

*Old Men's Dreams*, a novel
Walk in My Shoes Publications
ISBN 9780993489808

*A Rebel's Journey, my life and times*
Walk in My Shoes Publications
ISBN 9780993489822

*Wild Beasts and Plague*, short stories
Walk in My Shoes Publications
ISBN 9780993489839


**Co-authored:**

*GCSE Drama Study Guide*
Rhinegold Education
ISBN 9781785581731

*AS and A Level Drama and Theatre Study Guide*
Rhinegold Education
ISBN 9781785581748

*Cambridge Technicals Level 3 Performing Arts*
Hodder Education
ISBN 9780993489846

**Walk in My Shoes**
PUBLICATIONS

First published in 2019 by

**Walk in My Shoes Publications**
11 Irex Road
Lowestoft
NR33 7BU

The right of David Porter to be identified as author of this work
has been asserted in accordance with Section 77 of the
Copyright, Designs and Patents Act 1988

ISBN 978-0-993-48984-6

# Scoffers Will Come

## Contents

# Introduction

While preparing my book of short stories, *Wild Beasts and Plague* (2018), I found I had too many for a single self-published volume.

So I put together this second collection, *Scoffers Will Come*.

**Scoffers Will Come**, 2018, from a story originally conceived in the 1980s and using an idea from an old unsuccessful play of mine, *The Beach Map (1970s)*.

**Nobody Will Dance With Me,** 2017, a story about a sufferer of the condition I have and his 15 minutes of fame.

**Pleasing the Crowd**, written during the early 2000s and reshaped after my hernia operation, December 2018.

**Lonely Hearts**, 2006, was an entry in a short story writing competition that went nowhere. As I reworked it in 2016, I realised some connection to my novel *Old Men's Dreams* (published 2015).

**Approximately Charlie and George**, a story that went thorough several versions in the 1980s as part of a show, revisited and reworked in 2017.

**Something for the Weekend**, 2007, another entry in another unsuccessful story competition. Also part of a series of episodes I planned for a TV series on stories from the Palace of Westminster.

**A Theatre Empties**, from poems based on a real theatrical experience in Soho, 1971, made into a story in 1976 and revamped 2018 for this collection.

**Queue This Side for Hatred**, from a short play of 1970, slated by the BBC radio drama people and revamped as an example of stories with weird titles about self-focus with off-beat introspection that were once all the rage.

**Stop That Laughing**, from a short play of 1972-1974, following experience in a challenging teaching setting in the East End of London.

**Breath-Play**, 2018, from a scene in an unfinished novel of the mid 1970s and updated. Horrendous ideas, but there they are.

**Timeslips**, my first completed novel (early 1970s), sent to a few places but then languished in the loft till redrafted as a short story in 2015.

**Gone Away for Good**, also from poems composed in 1968, revised several times and finally restyled in 2017.

**Backstory Writer**, an original story idea from 2015-16, remodelled and updated in 2018.

**Plain But Adequate**, 2108 from an old idea, in essence going back sixty years.

**Ghost of Christmas Shopping**, from a series of blogs and ideas from 2004, updated in 2018.

**Cages for Laughter** from a play that was meant to be a Happening which sums up so much about the hippie, performance art scene and how I coped with it. The play caused some controversy which I embraced at the time.

**The Blue-Arsed Fly**, 2018, revised idea from a story of loathing stretching over decades with unexpected developments.

*A Chorus of Hallelujahs*, 2018 from a story first dreamed up in 1968 and subsequently re-imagined many times over.

*Howling Darkness*, first written in the very early 2000s as the Millennium began and adapted in 2017

*Time to Stand and Scream*, written 2017-18 about an increasing problem for the western world with longevity on the rise.

*The Alcatraz Stretch*, imagined in the early 90s following our first Californian family holiday, revised in 2018.

*Cedric Has left the Building*, 2018 from a story first drafted in 2011 and updated to bring this collection to an end.

# Scoffers Will Come

His view of the prom grew fainter as afternoon gave way to evening. Wind picked up, offering his lips a taste of gritty sand. For a final moment, he sat enjoying her sketching, perched on that wobbly stool, awkwardly clutching the pad and a pencil stub in cold, arthritic fingers.

Her determination was palpable; he was no longer sure she understood what she was trying to do.

He loved her. Or at least they'd been together so long and through so much that, yes, it was long-standing love. Yet it went beyond that.

Most of the media was jumping up and down about dementia and how almost all old fogies were predicted to degenerate into drooling, vacant husks of their former selves while gently rotting into release with the occasional lucid outburst of sanity.

It was nonsense. As far as he could make out, he was fine. Several old buffers he could think of were similarly able to function by making small but useful contributions to life.

Selected images from their past, separately and together, appeared in his oft used mental slide and video show. Their children's and the Prime Minster's names he was certain about; his birth year was secure.

Of course, she was not quite so aware, but he looked after her, so it didn't matter overmuch as long as people left him to get on with it.

With deepening darkness came stronger wind, whipped across the restless North Sea, now trying to snatch the pad from her, but she clung on grimly. As she became engulfed in late autumn darkness, it was time to leave the beach for today.

He'd have to pack up and guide her back home. He usually tried to delay it as long as possible as evenings were so dreadfully interminable and pointless, shivering in their flat.

She'd probably fall asleep soon after they'd eaten, still in her day clothes, rather worn blouse, three out of shape jumpers and a pair of thick woollen workers' trousers that had seen better days. But she could wake at any time, distressed about whatever was in her head.

He used to love to read and owned hundreds of books. They filled his mind, his soul and the evening hours even before she was taken with her condition. He never missed the TV they'd had to let go after the children grew up and moved away.

But his precious library had gone up in smoke a decade ago. This was when they still lived in a decent house in a marketable area, the home where they'd raised their two children.

She was then just a few steps along the journey from the mild eccentricity of her youth and middle age towards the stumbling confusion and absent bits of her old age. She'd been alone that winter afternoon while he was out sorting the shopping for a week or more.

She simply forgot how to turn the heating on earlier than tea time when it kicked in automatically.

Perished, she recalled enough to know she needed heat. She'd lit a fire in their lounge, at the side of the table. As the kindling of screws of paper files crackled to flame she added a couple of newspapers before reaching for a book to tear up and put to the growing fire.

Once his bookshelves were cleared, she felt warm, better. She remembered that fires die away if not fed; he was still not back; she needed more fuel.

In the corner behind the sofa sat four boxes of his vanity-published autobiography. The tome he'd written as a record of his career as an engineer on the railways and for the benefit of his as yet unborn grandchildren.

He'd started it even before he retired while memories were still fresh. A great work of fiction it was not; the life it described wasn't that remarkable. But he'd enjoyed writing and had laughed and wept over different memories. It was important to leave something.

She'd ripped and tossed most of those books into the fire with an increasing urgency, unaware of anything but the drive to keep the warmth. The table was well alight; the carpet caught and before long the floorboards were charring and the curtains went up with a whoosh.

It was a miracle that a neighbour called the fire brigade as soon as she smelt smoke and knew that a batty old woman was momentarily alone. It was a mystery how she suffered from neither smoke inhalation nor skin burns. She survived.

Their house didn't. Parts of upstairs were untouched, but the insurance company wanted the place rebuilt rather than patching up. Their family insisted they move to a smaller and more manageable home. That's how they were in a tiny top floor apartment of the big old house facing out to sea on what was locally called a 'cliff', though visitors from away laughed at that.

Home. Well, it was a place to be. A largish room was for their sitting in, their bed in one corner and a tiny kitchenette in another. There was a pokey bathroom and toilet off, adjacent to the stairs. With the accommodation built into the actual roof, it was always cold.

As long as they could both drag themselves up the four staircases, it would do. All their remaining worldly possessions were piled around the spare walls of the main room. The grand pair of windows rattled in the wind, but afforded a dramatic view of the sea and the beach they spent days sitting on.

Colder than hell in the winter, spring and autumn with a good few chilly summer days, too. As she got worse, of course, they'd have to move to a more suitable place. Perhaps a care home.

It was five years before the fire when she became obsessed with her ill-defined beach map project. So, every day they possibly could, rain or shine, high summer season or short bleak winter days, they'd sit there. A gazebo they took when he could carry it was finally blown to tatters, so they simply carried a bag of drawing junk, some snacks and a couple of flasks with two old mismatched stools.

While she sketched her beach map, he kept himself sane with one way conversation, her body fed with occasional food and made sure they were safe. He'd read from a library book – he never bought books any more.

By nature, he was a careful man and they lived on his works pension that had seemed adequate when he retired, but now never quite met their outgoings.

The beach map itself was meaningless, as the wind of the North Sea removed anything she got down. And her whole original plan had been long forgotten. She'd just taken it into her head that the beach needed mapping in a cross between cartography and imaginative artwork.

As the idea swirled slowly round her brain during the hours they spent there over the years, he went along with it. Could it prove a useful map combined with expressive arts? Even if nobody grasped the point, would it sell?

Years back, when their children were still at home, they'd rented a wooden council beach hut and spent happy hours inside while wind and rain swept the prom. Or sat in front, just enjoying the beach, the grey sea and boundless fresh air. The kids had grown with it as a home extension. After the fire they had to give it up – too expensive.

Every time they sat on the beach now, in the same spot in front of the hut that used to be theirs, the attack from which he'd recovered, but still hurt inside refreshed itself in his head.

He, partly to match her activity with the beach map, had begun to practice tai chi, slow measured exercises of the body to calm his soul. A doctor had recommended it to him at a check up, waxing lyrical about how it helps to reduce stress, improve posture, balance and general mobility, and increases muscle strength in the legs, particularly in the over 65s.

He'd built a circle of sand mounds, which evolved into spirals of engineering complexity, using them to inspire his movement and controlled breathing routines of the tai chi. The structures were high up the beach away from the tides, just below their row of huts.

It had been an early autumn Saturday, as he did his last session and she was starting to gather their stuff that they wouldn't safely leave in the hut overnight.

Four young men, rather the worse for wear with a long night ahead of them to get properly tanked up, suddenly spotted him in full sweep as they wandered down the prom passing time till the evening pubs opened and the talent would be out on stilettos, sporting short skirts.

He ignored them, which they took as offence, so they swarmed off the wall and faced up to this strange man doing weirdly dodgy stuff. What was he, they demanded, some sort of dancing fairy?

Angry at his failure to respond, they shouted more incomprehensible questions in his face; he said nothing. As one, they pushed him, tripped him and goaded him. A lungful of warnings was shrieked from his wife on the prom outside the hut; the kids clung to her, agitated seeing their dad surrounded by hooligans.

Once one had cottoned on to the pattern and purpose in the sand they were trampling on, he led the others in an increasing frenzy of hostility with tripping, dragging, spitting and some nasty thumps to their victim's body and head.

Several people watched and one sent his own kid to run to the call box for help. As the violence gathered pace because he resisted in no way at all, enough bystanders finally found concern enough to intervene, seeing off the youths who staggered down the prom on their way mouthing obscenities at everyone.

The later consequence was he abandoned tai chi, drew no further attention to himself and confined his future efforts to helping his wife fulfil her dreams and plans. However crazy others might find them.

Among the people who'd intervened, were four from a local church, one of the more radical places of worship in the town. Neither he nor his wife was interested, but the group explained they were on a prayer walk around the immediate area, talking to people, offering help and above all, praying for them, if they agreed.

They hadn't preached. They'd just listened, nodded and smiled a lot, checking that the man was fine. Nice people who wanted to show interest and offer real, tangible help. One of the men, a mid-ager who'd worked on oil rigs most of his adult life, gave him a small Bible.

The three versions he used to have on his shelf had perished in the inferno. So he took it, flipping through while the man went on, using the taking and opening of the book as a sign.

Near the end, the page settled at *2 Peter 3*. He read it silently; the man waited so he read it aloud. 'In the last days scoffers will come scoffing and following their own desires...'

The kind man explained the passage, saying it was about those who scoffed that Jesus would return. His listener nodded, well aware of that.

People scoffed when Noah built the Ark on God's instructions. There was no sign it was needed at all. So they scoffed. And they will scoff again in the Endtimes when this world starts to collapse...

The Bible was slipped into a pocket; the four church people were enthusiastically thanked. It was blowing chilly, so time to take the family home for their tea and let her husband recover.

Later, or perhaps it was at the time, he forgot, he recognised that those who knew of the beach map and the other things she yearned to do but couldn't, were scoffers indeed. One day she'd be proved right, somehow. The beach map would find its purpose, scoffers or not.

The people who prayed for strangers called several evenings after that, each time pushing a little further, inviting them to church and praying openly for them. He took it all, quite happily; she smiled but made little sense of their words.

All that seemed long ago. Beach routines had occupied them almost every day since. Tonight he felt more chilled than usual and made a big effort to get off the stool, stamping his feet to restart circulation, gather their things and start that homeward trudge.

She followed along, still clutching the drawings. Today's work would join the reams of paper she'd covered, heaped, stuffed and spread over the other things in their flat.

Pulling the scruffy overcoat he'd bought in a charity shop in the mid 1970s around his shoulders, drawing breath and as much energy as he could find, he took firm hold of her arm to guide her.

That action always gladdened him that his caring love had kept her out of an institution where so many had wanted her incarcerated, especially after the fire. He would look after her till either he couldn't any longer or she passed on.

Scoffers indeed. Let them all scoff. He was indifferent.

Tonight it seemed they needed more steps than usual up to the prom, across it and over the road. The stairs to their floor seemed particularly onerous, the worn boots he'd kept in his car as an engineer felt as heavy as lead. He understood that it couldn't go on. He had to find a new home for them both, without stairs.

It wouldn't be easy, but he'd battle on, resisting the opposition. Looking after her, because he loved her.

It was a relief to get inside; the place felt warm compared with the chill their bodies had absorbed over the past few hours and the walk back. Gradually, though, that benefit wore off. He sat, just for a moment in the single arm chair, perching from habit to the left to avoid the spring from the seat.

He needed to concoct their tea from what they had in the noisy fridge. He couldn't go out to the shop; he was tired. He just needed to rest his weary bones for a few minutes; then he'd cook.

Playing among her drawings like a toddler, she was absorbed in the revelation that they gave her. Her long, grey hair kept getting in the way. He hadn't washed it for a few weeks. He ought to do that. When it fell in front of her eyes, she sometimes pushed it away; sometimes chewed the end.

He smiled at her fondly, pleased that the drawings meant something to her. Dimly aware that the smile didn't reach his face, he rested his eyes a moment.

Without pausing her exploration of the drawings and partial maps, she spoke, quietly but coherently. 'I'm cold, John. I'm cold, John.'

He knew she was; he should stand up and fiddle with the thermostat. But he couldn't move. A few more minutes of rest, then he would.

Forgetting she'd already told him she was cold, she scooped up a few drawings, found a matchbox in the sideboard drawer, twisting it as she opened it. She lit a drawing. And then another.

'John I'm cold.'

Soon sheaves of drawings were merrily blazing and she began to feel warm. He struggled to find his feet to stop the fire spreading, but his body was shutting down, refusing to respond to brain signals.

'John, I'm warmer now,' she yelled triumphantly as the fire licked out, taking in more of their junk, furniture, floor coverings and John himself.

The beach map had found its purpose.

# Nobody Will Dance With Me

Nobody will dance with me. He says. Aloud. Speaking his thoughts to the ubiquitous cameras around has become second nature.

How could anyone dance with a person with such poor mobility? With ankles that could give way at any moment, twisted on the slightest lump or indentation in the floor?

Who would risk being brought down dancing with a man suddenly losing balance and clutching at anything and anyone in range as he crashes to the floor, often in agony?

And even if I could stay upright and move around a little, it would be like embarrassing 'dad dancing' times ten, he says. Aloud.

No, I quite understand why nobody will dance with me. He says. Aloud. Thoughts made flesh for the cameras.

A man with advancing nervous disease is not fit for dancing in public. That's a fact. He agrees.

And what would I wear? I wouldn't want people to have the same universal revulsion caused by middle aged and older men wearing shorts unless they're on a Mediterranean beach.

He still loves to respond physically to music. It's an emotional thing, a visceral, psychological, animal thing. And besides, it's like laughter, the very best medicine.

Of course, he can still sing. Nobody needs to move about much for that. And singing is good for the soul as a solo exercise or in a choir. I'd like to teach the world to sing in perfect harmony and all that.

But more than one listener, wearing a pained expression, has indicated that those perfect tunes inside his head emerge from his mouth as mangled, discordant, tortured cat, wince-inducing noise.

So Jacob Marley, still daily cursing his parents Stan and Ethel Marley for naming him after the Dickens' character, decides to do something about it. No more talking to himself as a substitute for action.

People will dance with me if they're afraid. They will sing if they're terrified – hell, they'll sing in tongues if they're truly shitting themselves. People will take note of a man with a gun if they think he'll use it.

Marley becomes obsessed with researching how guns might be used, how his physical inadequacies could be set to one side with a gun doing the talking. He looks up how to get hold of a gun. How to make an untraceable gun using an affordable 3D printer? Samira says she knows someone who could fix that for him. She's the most junior member of his team; the one who's grown closest to him, the one who helps him, who seems to understand his needs.

Nobody will dance with me. Now they will.

Then one day he reads an online news item about how everything searched for on the net is there permanently. It never goes away. He learns how trigger words like bomb, gun, victim, terror alert the authorities and put him under surveillance.

It would be a matter of seconds for Them to put together a case against him. He isn't planning to spend the rest of his days in a prison hospital as his mobility declines to almost nothing. That would lead to the end of the series, unless he was handed a very long sentence, of course.

And who would dance with him then? Nobody will dance with me.

It was the phrase and the linked ideas that had got him the job when he pitched to Channel Unvarnished nearly four years ago. They liked the central plank of a man, getting on a bit but not too old, a man who has missed so many opportunities through a crippling illness that is gradually taking hold of his feet, his legs, his hands.

A man, indeed, who suffers fears and panics, speaks thoughts aloud that make a convincing twenty minute programme. A man with some serious anger issues.

'Nobody will dance with me' has become a catchphrase, summing up the deep feelings the disability engenders; the frustrations of trying to live life with it and despite it.

It's ticked a lot of fashionable boxes. He insists in his contract that he gets to play the straight white man version. Other people – or avatars for all he knows – play different and mixed races, women and the full gamut of trans versions for the wide range of their audience target groups.

The show has become a major hit, winning two campaigning awards and one for innovative docudrama. A *Truman Show* for the 2020s, but without duping the central character, it's most popular among the 40 plus demographic, many of whom still watch it on their old TV sets.

All the executives and many of the public have admitted that to them the dancing is a metaphor for perpetually unsatisfied sex. For them it's a comedy. For the old, sick or those paranoid about getting old and/or sick it's a fine piece of social-documentary soap opera.

But for Marley it's his way of campaigning on disability, minority issues, earning a living and perhaps finally being able to dance.

He just wants to get a life and extract what he can from it before his body gives up, presumably some time ahead of his mind calling it a day. Samira alone in his circle encourages him to think bold, to challenge barriers and to take risks.

He's dreamed up and performed episodes on false-hope medics, trying to hold down a job with the disease, moving about a community, excessive tiredness, genetics, previous generations who lived and died with the condition and grudging public funding for research.

Most have been inside the small apartment he's managed to find to live in, with occasional entries from social workers, family (one who also suffers the condition), a few failed relationships and an aged parent.

He's also created episodes in shops, at a job interview, crossing a road, in a hospital and being robbed in a street. One was simply him in bed because he was too physically exhausted to get up and do a thing, even feed himself.

As long as he keeps coming up with the ideas and developing the character, Jacob Marley is doing well. Invites for chat shows, appearance fees and a stream of communication flooding social media from the weird, wonderful and woeful who inhabit the digital world.

The time is coming when he needs more for all he gives. He thinks. He discusses it with Samira. Indeed, he isn't sure that she didn't plant the idea in his mind anyway.

He decides the best way to air the matter is through an actual episode of *Nobody Will Dance With Me*. Audience pressure and feedback should shame them into giving him a better reward for his work and ideas.

So, following the purchase of the 3D printed gun, he takes it to the Channel Unvarnished headquarters, asking for a meeting with the exec in charge of his show and makes his pitch for an increase in his pay cheque.

When the woman, caught unawares by the request, turns him down flat, knowing he is contracted for years ahead, he threatens her with the gun. She manages to press an alarm under the desk and it finishes with the building surrounded by armed police, helicopters overhead and Marley squeezing the trigger.

When he puts it up as the next idea, all the team who bring the show to life say it's marvellous, brilliant darling, a winner ... but how will he progress the next episode?

Marley has an answer. We have two choices. I wake up in my bed and it was all a dream, so I get dressed and go off for the meeting, the audience knowing how it's going to turn out.

And the second way? I shoot myself under the chin and the series ends.

When they stop laughing, it dawns on some that he's serious. Contract, old boy, you can't end it yet.

Stalemate. Samira pipes up with three alternative suggestions. One, he shoots the executive. Two, they use the meeting itself as an episode. Three, he shoots himself and continues as a ghost, unable to break away from the nightmare he is in.

Jacob Marley, the ghost, yes? Brilliance. She will go far, that girl!

As the meeting descends into shambolic discussion, the exec in LA on screen shouts for calm and asks Jacob Marley what he really wants now?

A payrise. Nothing more.

Again, there's shoulder-shaking laughter, many concluding that Jacob Marley really should give his inner comedian more scope.

The meeting ends with platitudes about giving it some thought, but times are hard, advertising revenue is not growing; the show may need new blood anyway….

Samira catches his eye and smiles warmly, conspiratorially. Yes, she is certainly a friend. She'll never dance with him, of course, but he feels more alive in her company than with anyone else.

With a week of filmed episodes in hand, they next make the one about the meeting between Marley and the executive, climaxing in him demonstrating that the gun is real with a shot into the ceiling. The firearms unit is arriving.

The next one is about trying to talk him out of the room, so he staggers through the open window to a balcony dragging the exec with him. She is terrified and promises the earth, including a substantial payrise.

They follow that with a sequence in a hospital where he is explaining to a doctor what he'd been thinking when he threatened public safety with a gun he had illegally laser printed.

After that comes one with a court appearance where he is committed to a series of mental health check-ups, with some allowance for the mental pressure he's been under through his physical condition, blah blah blah.

That story thread is coming to a natural ending. Audience reactions indicate that it's a let-down. Some want him to have thrown the executive or himself off the balcony. They certainly don't want it all to be forgotten as a bad dream.

Jacob Marley is generally perceived as in need of punishment, as if his condition isn't punishment enough. The matter of the payrise agreed under threat is quietly forgotten, though Samira keeps it alive when she and Marley chat over coffee between takes.

What happens before he can come up with a plausible new development is that real life takes over. Marley is attacked as he exits his apartment to get some air and hobble about a bit by way of exercise, clutching at his walking stick in one hand, the fence in the other.

There is invariably a fan crowd outside, eager to catch a glimpse, some convinced he's just an actor and there is nothing really wrong with him.

A woman steps into his path, a big shouldered, mean-faced creature with anger spitting from her mouth, hatred clouding her eyes.

'Why should you get a payrise? I haven't had one in years? Who do you think you are?'

She slides a length of polished wood from inside the sleeve of her tattered coat, some sort of bat. With three rapid blows she fells him and sets about his legs till she is dragged off by two shocked celebrity crowders and the Channel security guy who has been very lax.

Samira smiles happily, and whispers into her device, 'And roll the credits, but keep filming.'

It's good that she said that. One of the crowd, white-faced and appalled, says in total disbelief, 'Nobody will dance with you now, old mate, nobody.'

It is the perfect opener for the next episode that Samira has already decided will feature a very talented but overlooked junior programme team worker who promises to look after Jacob Marley until his sad death, about three weeks from now.

# Pleasing the Crowd

It was one of those strange and unfortunate coincidences that Fulmer and his grandson, Louis, arrived at the hospital just as the celebratory events for the re-opening of the new foyer were getting under way.

He'd noticed the car park was rammed solid with red-faced motorists, aware that their appointment times were approaching with nowhere to park their vehicles. He'd been glad they came on the bus. The charges for parking where available were something else, too.

A steady stream of people poured through the swish new entrance doors. Fulmer, wiping sweat from his forehead, took a firmer hold of Louis' little hand and concentrated on keeping his feet steady.

No more than twenty seconds passed before he decided to back them outside again to wait for space – he was as early for their appointment as he was for most things in his life – but their exit was blocked by the ceaseless crowds piling in.

Heart rate rising, that old sense of no-escape gripped his throat. But there was no way through the solid tide, only forwards. Several were there for their own medical appointments; some clearly for the free snacks and drinks and a few because they had nowhere else to go. But nobody was yielding any space to anyone.

Fulmer had an appointment for the 10-year old lad's asthma to be checked by a specialist. Fulmer's son and his partner were both too busy at work and Mrs Fulmer was desperately unwell. So Fulmer had volunteered to shuffle the boy in for his check up.

*Ladies and gentlemen, welcome!*

The Chair of the Hospital Board was a big woman; powerful, oh yes. Defying any worm even thinking of challenging her and booming into the hand-held microphone, she dominated a raised platform specially erected for today which temporarily sealed off the only free toilets on the ground floor.

She'd dressed up in a big summer flowery and fruity dress, topped by a large Eton mess of a hat with artificial feathers, and paced about engaging with her audience, smiling at cameras and enjoying herself as anybody does when a plan really becomes reality.

*Welcome to the grand opening of these wonderful hospital facilities. Oh, I should say, these wonderful foyer facilities. We're bringing destination retail into a new dimension and using redundant space in this public building.*

*We do hope we'll have sufficient funding in the next three to five years to upgrade the surgical wards, all the operating theatres and the recovery suites. We confidently expect to plug medical, ancillary and clerical staff shortfalls the year after next.*

*We have big plans! And in the meantime, what have we created here?*

Her big white handbag swung round dangerously as she used it to reinforce her message and warn anybody even thinking of rushing her to think again.

*Our old drab, unexciting foyer has been transformed into a sharp new, state of the art shopping opportunity and a spectacular, one-stop entertainment hub.*

*This makes Liverpool Street Station and Gatwick Airport look like 3$^{rd}$ world museum pieces, let me assure you all!*

People in the crowd strained and oohed and ahhed a great deal as she pointed, gesticulated, shouted and excited herself at the futuristic vision she had breathed into being.

*Here we have every food and drink outlet known to humankind. From fast food to luxury dining, from every corner of the world comes cuisine and cooking magnificence to satisfy every palate. It goes without saying that all our menus are fully vegan-compliant.*

*Don't forget to check out our nostalgic themed restaurant called Hospital Food 1965, for a real taste of the past.*

That particular pitch meant something only to those over 60, really. They would have felt the same about a reminder of British Rail curled sandwiches and spoon-supporting tea.

*We have set aside a tiny seating section for those unfortunates who are still carnivores, where you can watch an environmental movie about pollution and habitat destruction caused by eating animals.*

*You can do a week's grocery shopping here while waiting for your medical appointments. Drone deliveries are available of course. By the way, we have taken over half of the rooftop helipad for retail drones as it's silly to have that resource just sitting there waiting for accidents and emergencies to come in.*

As far as Fulmer could see from those tightly around him, she was holding them well; they were neither restless nor disagreeing. She had them and could have said almost anything.

*Clothes, lingerie, toys, games and sportswear – we have them all. Health related outlets like glasses, hearing aids, mobility appliances, artificial limbs – they're all situated on the second floor.*

*Musical treats and Grade A shows? Why go elsewhere – it's all here? Hair salon, nails, dental services? Yes, we have them!*

*We have a tattoo parlour – get yourself inked up with the latest must-have designs. Our new armpit tattoo of a bleeding heart valve is proving very popular. And right next door, the tattoo removal parlour. If you go for removal within 30 days of the tattoo application, claim your 25% discount!*

Fulmer needed to shift his weight, to stretch the legs, just had to get the hell out of there. He began to push on the back of the closest smelly blob of flesh right in front of him. It resisted. He pushed to the left and right to meet the same immovable forces.

*You know where the term 'theatre' comes from in hospitals? Well, in the bad old days, people would come in and watch operations in progress and lunatics being treated. Great fun!*

*And we've brought it back! Yes, you can now watch a live liver transplant from the safety of a screen or you can pay a little more to sit on the operating room floor among the blood-splattering details!!*

*If the government ever decides to bring back public executions, we will apply for a licence and have identified the old medical records department as a perfect setting to carry out executions on site.*

*That'll make the trip to the morgue quite short. And yes, we have a morgue display area where you can buy tickets to enjoy post mortems and commentaries as they are carried out. The real life ones are slightly more expensive than the robots, but for relatives we're offering a 25% discount.*

Louis' body twitched under the pressure. Fulmer sometimes wondered if his grandchildren had inherited his loathing of crowds. This one had. He was whimpering, his hand was burning, his little body shook as he looked up at his grandfather. 'Please, Granddad.'

Not without difficulty, Fulmer reached down to hoist the lad up into his arms, to give him some air. The space where the boy had stood closed up.

*Mental health is one of the buzz-phrases of our times. Who doesn't have mental health issues, hey? Well, mindful of that we have converted the geriatric wards into a new mental health resource. By the way, don't worry, our elderly loved ones are now treated off site in a selection of homes and bungalows where we used to house human nurses.*

*The Mental Health Zone is full of caring and sharing, soft lights, gentle music at one end of the scale right up to visual and aural shock therapy at the other.*

*If you're depressed and suicidal, don't do anything till you have talked to one of our trained counsellors. The first half hour is free. If they don't talk you out of ending it all, then don't do a thing till you have taken advantage of our Will and Last Wishes Bequest Service.*

*You can pick up a range of medications to assist you in departure, and a list of suitable places, all near the transplant unit where we can salvage something to sell on. Do please, even in your most selfish hour, think of those of us left behind.*

Fulmer was no longer absorbing the gist of the endless speech with its myriad offers and advice. He got 'suicide' and 'last wishes'. He was ready to shriek out that he was the man to sign up right now. He couldn't draw sufficient breath to make any sound.

26

*And for those of you poor specimens who are still nicotine addicted, we have a smoking cupboard along this corridor, which is free to use if you permit real time monitoring of your lungs and brain for future entertainment shows.*

*There is a similar space for alcohol obsessives, who similarly can use the padded rooms for free in exchange for some raw material for our archives.*

*Feeling aggressive? Well, mosey on down to the gymnastics area where you can do traditional exercises before fighting with someone bigger, smaller or the same size as you. Don't forget to sign the waiver and know that should you be smashed to a pulp, your main organs will be put to excellent use.*

*Just dip into our Organs Directory if you don't believe me, and look at the discounts we're offering this week – family deals and special offers. You'll think Christmas has come early!!*

The boy was heavy, even with some weight taken by the crowd. Could Fulmer punch and kick some space around them? Could he shriek that he was having a panic attack? Would any real medic be on hand to get them out of the crowd?

*One or two of you may have already sampled the services of our latest generation of Autonomous Medical Bulk Unified Local All-terrain Neo-Care Empowerers – what we used to call ambulances. These offer the very best of human and robotic healthcare and are winning awards for us all over the world.*

*In fact, we have invested this year's cancer research budget into purchasing a facility in Derby to convert into a robotic factory making these Empowerers to sell on the global market.*

*The Board has recently approved a plan to branch out and use the same revolutionary technology to make autonomous hotels on wheels - AutoHots. Travel overnight across the country, sleeping, washing and working in AutoHot. Drones drop food and medication at agreed points. Save time and money with your vacation on AutoHot.*

*We're revolutionising the tourist industry, my friends! And all that puts more much-needed revenue back into this great hospital so that we can upgrade the old multi-faith chapel and bereavement areas next year to produce a Faith Suite for you to buy in and out for whatever belief system takes your fancy.*

She bowed, her handbag waving across her frame, her smile revealing gleaning white teeth that reflected her pride. Surely an official honour beckoned now?

Applause was muted, as only those at the very front could extend their arms wide to bring the hands together to clap. But it was over.

Now he had simply to hang on, grit his teeth and surely soon the crowd would begin to evaporate down corridors with some exiting the front door? Just be a bit patient, a fraction relaxed and it would surely pass?

What Fulmer didn't know was the entertainment and archive department team at the screen end of the banks of cameras installed in the foyer had picked him and the boy out some time ago.

Now his struggles were being recorded for posterity and future medical training. Dr Flanikoss spoke warmly in the control room. 'Ah, classic case of Demophobia, Enochiophobia or crowd phobia, if you prefer. This social phobia is surprisingly common and the crowd doesn't have to be very big.'

Fulmer was observed a moment longer. Sweat ran into his eyes, smearing his glasses. The boy was rested on his grandfather's neighbours more than the old man. Fulmer strained ahead but there was no indication that the floodgates holding the crowd were being released.

'Many sufferers fear being trampled in a crowd, getting deadly diseases, getting lost within the crowd or feeling insignificant, if not invisible. This one is showing signs of rapid claustrophobia on top of that crowd phobia. Very interesting,' the overjoyed man rubbed his hands.

As the clip was relayed to the medical training department, students began to watch dispassionately, grateful for a real live case to examine on a day they'd been told to expect little but being on their best behaviour at the buffet.

The Chair reached her office suite, acknowledging the fawning praise from her team of nineteen assistants. Wonderful! Marvellous! A winner! We are off and running now. She knew how to please a crowd, and oh boy, had she pleased that one!

Someone asked, 'shall we release them now for the food?'

'Not yet, give it ten minutes more till the VIPs clear most of the best from the tables.'

Like the boy pointing out the Emperor's New Clothes were a sham, one of her junior staff had the temerity to tell her in a soft, almost apologetic tone, that she'd forgotten to mention the Hypnosis Block where for sessions starting at £300 an hour, they could have themselves hypnotised out of every addiction and affliction known.'

'No, did I forget?' the Chair gasped, in mock horror.

'I'm afraid you did, Chair. And therefore, you didn't draw attention to our special bargain for hypnosis *into* any and every addiction and affliction known.' The soon-to-be-redundant employee sat, rather pleased with herself and looked at the Chair.

'No matter, my Chair, no matter,' gushed Dr Flanikoss, as he darted into the room, scattering staff to grin broadly at the Chair, just a short distance from her face..

'We have a classic panic in the crowd, an elderly male suffering Enochiophobia and best of all - he is trying to hold onto a small child. Priceless medical training!'

'Oh bless!' chorused several of the more emotional younger staff in the room.

'And priceless entertainment,' shrieked the Chair, clueless of what Enochiophobia was but fully awake to what made good television. 'Get it on the news channels, all social media and get that man out of there and into Hypnosis. Now!'

A poorly rehearsed fumble began with staff repeating orders at each other, into mikes and phones, some clicking madly online and everybody waiting to enjoy a parting of the waves through the crowd and a dramatic rescue of Fulmer and the boy.

In the foyer the crowd was dispersed by six uniformed officers in full riot gear wielding batons and barking orders to stand aside. Make way. Give us some space. Casualties in the crowd.

The Chair was spot on. It made superb television and allowed the Hospital to promote its Hypnosis Block with some real time docu-drama of Fulmer and the adorable little Louis being dragged from the crowd, fitted with oxygen masks, slapped and strapped onto trolleys and wheeled to salvation.

The touching little moment when a staffer relieved Fulmer of his wallet, swiped his card and replaced it, was a particular highlight, especially as the man kept fighting everyone, tearing his mask off, gasping for air and shrieking blue murder at all and sundry.

Hypnosis worked brilliantly for the little boy. The parents being brought in by an Autonomous Medical Bulk Unified Local All-terrain Neo-Care Empowerer warmed many hearts. He was pronounced cured and a credit to medical science within the hour, when the advice given to the Chair was that the story had been milked to its limit.

Fulmer wasn't quite so fortunate, being older and more set in his ways. Hypnosis failed but was presented as best medical advice to transfer him to the Mental Health Zone where a huge program of self-discovery, shock awareness and personal insighting swung into action.

It was so popular that the Chair signed a huge contract two days later for the global rights to the daily broadcasting of Fulmer transforming himself through the medical aids provided at the Hospital into a normal, healthy, functioning human employed as Hospital Phobia Demonstrator.

The Finance Department reported that they now were Number 1 Hospital in the country, top of the waiting list league. People were so keen to come that they paid a premium, were content to wait for months and knew they'd be better for it.

In the end.

When Fulmer fell one day shuffling round a hospital corridor and twisted his hernia badly, necessitating a genuine emergency operation, the public didn't take to that quite as much and wanted him replaced with some visual wizardry so they didn't have to watch his face actually suffering.

31

# Lonely Hearts

Jim knew that killing her was drastic. Did she deserve that? She'd only slighted and humiliated him all those years ago. But actually killing her? Depriving another human being of life?

Even Jim accepted that murder was way beyond reasonable. However, he hadn't found himself so absorbed with a project since he worked out a perfect way to escape detection three years ago when a TV programme put up a handful of clowns who tried to escape the forces of law and order in the digital age and he came up with a foolproof plan to win.

The fact that he'd discovered her by apparent chance just reinforced his view that it was meant to be. He'd never completely forgotten Penny Hampden, even after all the long years since.

He'd fancied her for weeks, and once he'd bucked up courage and asked her to the Sixth Form dance, everyone knew all about it. It wasn't every day that a tall, elegant beauty like Penny agreed to go with a small, awkward, spotty youth like him. I know; I was there, I saw it.

He'd half expected a crowd of friends outside her house when he pulled his classic silver grey Lambretta Li150 onto its stand and knocked. Or even as he emerged from the indifferent stares of her parents and curious gawping of her younger sister.

Arrival at the school had occasioned some smirks from mates who noticed them arrive, standing around smoking in the carpark. Even more observed him as he stood waiting outside the girls' toilets in the hall entrance foyer. Talk was impossible against the appalling crashing of an imitation Liverpool sound coming from within the hall. All the rage.

Lonely Hearts Club night, a themed homage to the Sgt Pepper's album and George, John Paul and Ringo, ten years on. The hall was meant to be a journey from Penny Lane to Strawberry Fields via Eleanor Rigby's funeral. The art department had done its best, given the aging trendy who ran it would have preferred something more beat or jazz than hippie.

But nobody knew how many holes there were in Blackburn or could fill the Albert Hall. Yeah, yeah, yeah. It was the 70s, but hey, everyone still loved their images of the 60s.

People came and went, in and out of the fun. Girls went into the toilets in pairs and came out. Penny didn't. What the hell was she doing in there?

In the space of four songs, his anticipation of someone to talk and dance with, someone to take home on the back of his scooter, evaporated to be replaced by cold rage. She simply failed to materialise.

Even if she'd died it wouldn't have taken as long as that. People were definitely noticing and whispering now. By the time a fellow student from his English class took pity on him and told him Penny was in there sobbing because she didn't want to see him, dance with him or go home with him, he could have strangled her.

But that was a very long time ago.

*******************************

Jim had an elephant's memory for slights, frustrations and setbacks that had shaped his character and led him to a life wasted mainly in his own imagination. He'd found a woman –

Lettie – to take him on and settle down with him. But when she was knocked off her pushbike twenty years later and never recovered, Jim's life took a parallel road.

Last month when he'd spotted Penny Hampden – older but still very definitely her - in the supermarket with a younger woman, obviously her daughter, old obsessions and memories seized hold of his thoughts, like wildfire. All were way out of proportion.

Working his way as close to them as he could, he joined their queue. He was sure she'd not recognise him. She'd hardly looked at him even when she agreed to go to the dance with him.

'Look Mum, there are some lonely hearts ads in this magazine, maybe one for you?' The daughter was clearly being sarcastic, but the mother took the magazine as they shuffled forward closer to the checkout.

'Your dad has been gone for three years now. I think I'm ready to try again.'

It all clicked into place for Jim. The father was Rob Bowles, his old mate, so-called. Jim followed mother and daughter to the carpark. Not for the first time he'd followed her out to a carpark.

Having endured a long evening of total 1967 lonely heart misery watching Penny dance with lots of boys, he'd followed her and Bowles out after the last dance. He'd stood shivering in the bushes while Bowles' parents' car rocked in response to what Bowles was giving her.

I don't think rational thought shifted the deep dark that swamped Jim at that time. He was moody for days before finding another one to obsess over.

When she could hide it no longer, Penny left school to have her baby and never returned. It was the swinging sixties, but still, something of a local scandal it was. That Bowles married her after he'd secured his degree was what Jim called rubbing salt in his wounds. They'd done it to spite him.

Penny had aged well. The daughter – 50-odd – must be the child of that post-dance activity, Jim calculated, noting their car number as they loaded shopping into the boot. They were still talking about Penny dating and the daughter's main concern seemed to be she should avoid a 'desperate, dirty old man.'

He watched them drive off before returning to buy the same magazine.

*****************************

By the time she answered his ad two months later, he'd discovered her weekly routine, the highlight of which was shopping with the daughter – Dora, from Pandora (a mistake waiting to trap any man who didn't do his research) - who didn't work but lived in a nice house with her husband and three primary school children.

Penny lived alone in a large old house that had been the family home, close to the golf course. Bowles had clearly done well over the years. Besides the shopping, her week seemed to comprise little more than gathering with a bunch of like-minded same-age women for lunch and playing the odd round of golf with another woman who looked like an older Selina Dawes who'd once laughed out loud at Jim when he suggested they go to the pictures.

With few friends, her daughter was the focus of her life, even more than the three grandchildren. Jim hadn't made the study of women in gruesome detail his life's work for nothing.

35

Dyeing his hair, borrowing an engineer's uniform and acquiring a passable British Telecom ID pass was child's play – he worked for the company on the admin side.

Penny had to ask Dora to report a fault once he'd cut her line in the middle of the night. He'd learned enough to tap into the daughter's line and intercept the request call as if it never occurred. The ease of arriving at Penny's house, showing his card, getting right in and looking around almost made him smile as he took in everything.

Up close, Penny looked her age. That didn't stop her flashing him a few warm smiles and a glimpse of cleavage with a quick smoothing of the skirt on her leg. She didn't recognise him, plainly.

While she made coffee there was enough time to slip into her handset the phone-and-room listening device he'd bought from a company he'd met on the internet. As he sipped the coffee – not bad, actually – she gave him half her life story in a friendly and charming openness that he would have found quite agreeable if he'd fallen for it.

He learned that her husband Rob Bowles had gone permanently missing after being diagnosed with testicular cancer three years ago and now she realised she still had needs, still wanted the company of a man, a real man ...

For a moment he was tempted. She'd have led him upstairs to the marital bedroom and have given herself to him in a releasing passion that would have done her good. And he'd have enjoyed it too. Past child-bearing age, no risks. Sweet revenge; Rob turning in his grave.

Reality returned. There was work to be done. He cited other jobs and made his escape to the garden to repair her line.

When Penny rang him on the number he'd given the magazine to go with his ad, he hoped she wouldn't link the voice with his face recently seen. But she showed no signs of anything except a keenness to talk to a stranger and fix a date with a widower who allegedly shared her background and interests, having 'lost his wife to breast cancer three years ago.'

'He sounds perfect, darling,' Penny told Dora on the phone, unaware Jim was recording them from the comfort of his own house five miles away.

'No man is perfect, Mum,' warned Dora. Penny protested and they had the excited teenager and worried mother conversation in reverse – Penny was the excited one.

'Relax, I can take care of myself.'

'How are you going to do that? Hell, he could be a murderer or rapist, an escapee from an asylum, you just don't know! A perfect stranger ....'

Penny cut in, 'we're all strangers aren't we, at first? You get to know people. I'll follow all the codes and advice – I'll tell you where and when, meet in a public place, have my phone handy, take a taxi not my car, he won't have my full name and address ....he's just a lonely heart like me.'

'I'm coming with you!'

Penny spluttered, 'don't be ridiculous.'

'No, I mean, I'll drive you there and wait in the carpark.'

'The Swan' at 8.30pm on Wednesday evening. Instructions quite clear to the stranger who she was told to call Jim, just Jim. And clear to Dora, who'd shared her fears with her husband to get him to babysit while she chaperoned her mother.

She'd told Jim she'd be wearing her dark business suit and gave him a generalised description of herself. He said he was almost six feet, sandy hair, thinning from the temples and he'd be in a sports jacket sitting at the main bar. He'd be there early and would be drinking gin. She'd find him.

Dora watched her mother disappear into the pub, a few reservations still swirling around. It was already quite chilly, with the nights pulling in. She settled to her wait. At least Mum knew she was just outside. And for Dora this was better than chafing at home getting on her husband's nerves.

She flipped through radio channels and then opened the glove box to sort the CDs. Beyond the kids' stuff, there was only her husband's *Inspector Morse's Opera Favourites* that she could bear to listen to so on it went. Half an hour, then Dora'd peer in the pub window.

Showing few of the nerves she actually felt, Penny looked ahead as she walked in. She prayed nobody knew her and called her over wondering what she was doing meeting a stranger.

But nobody matched Jim's description. Too young, even allowing for male exaggeration. Too old, even for a mature woman. No tall stranger drinking gin at the bar.

The barmaid stood waiting for her – how often did that happen? She ordered a glass of white wine and sat on a vacant perch, hoping nobody thought she was a prostitute.

After a few sips, she looked around the bar. It was busy enough, people coming in and going out. Definitely no man for her. Nobody made eye contact. Nobody showed any interest in her whatsoever.

She glanced at the bar clock – she'd give him till 9 o'clock. He might have broken down, been injured in an accident, gone to the wrong pub or changed his mind. She had neither messages nor texts.

Another half hour and that was his lot. She swallowed the first taste of anger that filled her mouth. She'd been made a fool of. No, she'd give him a reasonable chance.

*********************************

Dora didn't hear her killer approach. The music was too loud; the heating too high, she was probably drowsy.

He must have opened her door, grabbed the surprised woman by the hair and smashed her face into the steering wheel.

Then, while she was stunned, he slit her throat and made what the press called 'thirty three frenzied stabs' before running away, taking the murder weapon with him.

*********************************

I looked across the table. The Inspector shook her head, almost sadly. 'You expect us to swallow all that crap, Rob? Oh yes, we know your name and who you are, make no mistake.'

She looked at me, waiting. I said nothing so she continued. 'I put it to you, that you met up with your old friend Jim Spiller awhile back, after you went AWOL with the testicular cancer story and he told you some of what you've just put into this bollocks story.'

Still I said nothing.

'And you killed Dora, the girl you brought up as your own because as you talked to Jim, you realised who it was with her in that rocking car all those years ago and you wanted to pay Jenny back by killing her and Jim's daughter, didn't you, Mr Bowles?

# Approximately Charlie and George

Gradually, piece by little, joke by gag, Lynette felt that her husband of thirty five years, George Farrier was in danger of becoming his own alter ego, Charlie Marshman.

George was an everyday sort of guy – a retired landlord by trade. Raised in a rural village where his father kept the local pub, The Dark Ferry, he'd taken over once his father passed on, and had staged stand-up comedy nights to please the regulars and himself while pulling in a few punters from further afield.

As George toiled on the little stage in the corner of the lounge, Lynette pulled pints behind the bar. In the mid 1980s, their comedy nights were popular and successful. The only trouble was that the seeds of the destruction lay in that success.

Farrier created old Charlie from a wise old Norfolk boy who'd once actually existed when he was a lad – a coypu catcher on the marshes. The name Charlie Marshman was a tribute to that old boy, a legend in the village for trapping and killing more coypu than anyone for miles around.

Coypu are orange-toothed South American beavers originally bred in the UK for their fur. A group of them escaped from a fur farm in 1937 when corrugated iron collapsed during heavy rain.

They quickly became Public Enemy Number 1 in Norfolk and Suffolk as they voraciously damaged reed banks, sugar beet, cereals and riverbank defences.

41

These giant three foot long sewer rat lookalikes bred with a horrifying rapidity - five times in 24 months with up to nine in every litter. There was disagreement about just how much habitat damage they caused; but in the end their destruction was ordered and paid for with a nice bonus for results.

In the early days coypu trapping was very profitable; there were so many to be shot on sight. Into the second phase of extermination, the creatures were trapped in welded mesh cages and rafts baited with carrots, before being shot by .22 pistols.

George secretly felt a soft spot for them. He smiled whenever he heard of one who'd suddenly appear in front of somebody, unexpectedly. Like a good joke, the unexpected punchline was always best.

Gradually over the long years, they were found less frequently until finally they were declared extinct in 1989. A bit like his brand of rather misogynistic, partly sexist stand-up comedy, George suspected as time went on.

His material became exclusively built round clever old Charlie who city slickers thought looked stupid and so therefore must be. Charlie always had the last laugh. He layered the Charlie stories with regurgitated gags from bygone eras.

*I know you're out there, I can hear you breathing!*
*Why don't I get English speaking audiences!*
*I'll finish now; I want to allow time for the applause.*

George painted Charlie as a good ole Norfolk boy, happily out of fashion, obtusely out of kilter with the world but sharp as a swing flail, with rare moments of consideration for others.

*When his wife, Daisy, was ill, he carried her downstairs so she could cook his dinner!*

And the child of a tourist family asking Charlie all sorts of questions about village life and Charlie responding with nothing. Not a word.

*You don't mind if Peregrine asks you all those questions?*
*Oh no, if he don't ask, he won't larn, will he!*

George described a village community with a healthy suspicion of officials and mistrust of strangers. They kept their own closed social life. Take the Marshes and Shrublands Scrutiny Area Committee Rescue Enterprise (MASSACRE) that used the willingness of volunteers to preserve their local marshes.

*Morty said to Charlie, you weren't at the last MASSACRE meeting, Charlie!*
*Blust, if I'd known that was the last one, I'd a been there!!*

The local doctor was a shining exception as he came from Norwich which was only ten miles off, though that didn't count as 'local'.

*Doctor, doctor, can I get a second opinion?*
*Yes, come back tomorrow.*

At that time, there was a village hospital where the surgeon said to a patient,

*We've got some good news and some bad news for you.*
*Oh I'll have the bad news first.*
*We cut the wrong leg orf.*
*Blust, what's the good news?*
*The other one's getting better!!*

There was a variant to that scene that George quite liked.
*We've got some good news and some bad news for you.*
*Oh I'll have the bad news first.*
*We cut both your legs off by mistake.*
*Blust, what's the good news?*

43

*Bloke in the next bed wants to buy your shoes!!*

The little village school had one teacher.
*One father asked the mother, how's my little clodhopper doin'?*
*She say, he's doing alright, that teacher ent no good though.*
*Why, what's wrong with him?*
*He keep trying to teach them all to write taters with a p.*

And in the little café, a stranger arrived when it was crowded and had to share a table with ole Morty. The stranger ordered a steak, but he couldn't eat it as he'd forgotten his dentures.
*Morty pulled from a deep pocket in his long coat a big bag of false teeth and offered him a pair.*
*Didn't fit, so Morty kept offering different teeth till the stranger felt OK to eat his steak.*
*Thank you, are you a dentist, then?*
*I'm not a dentist, I'm the undertaker!!*

Morty, Freddie, Ebenezer and Charlie became real as daylight to George. Any situation, any fragment on the radio or their little black and white telly set him off being creative.

A news story about a modern highwayman stealing from people in dark woods became a joke about ole Freddie and his daughter riding home from market in their pony and trap.
*A highwayman steps out - stand and deliver, he say.*
*He searches them, but finds nothing of any value.*
*So he takes their pony and trap.*
*Father and daughter are trudging home on foot, daughter opens mouth and pulls out purse full of coins.*
*Hare yew are father, she says, you allus said I had a big mouth and thass come in handy.*
*Yis says ole Freddie, an thass a pity yar poor dear mawther wunt here or we'd have saved the hoss and cart!!*

His core routine was based on one first performed by actor Bernard Miles and set in a Wiltshire accent. It soon transformed into Norfolk and became George's own, in a manner of speaking.

*Oi, was born in the village of Barnham Thorpe, that's what they call hinter denominational. Thass got a church, a chapel and a Salvation Army Bethel with a corrugated iron roof. That don't half rattle when that rain. Still, thass nice soft water.*

*The church, thass Parpendicular, built by the Vikings afore the railways come.*

*They got a crusader lay inside, they put his likeness on top so he recognise hisself at the second coming. He won't recognise hisself cause we been sharpening our flagglehooks on him since I can remember.*

*The old vicar he say this statue was defaced by Holiver Cromwell at the time of the Revelation. I never told him.*

*Nice old boy, the vicar. We didn't know what sin was till he come to the village. I say to him one day, I can't make it out, how you parsons get your dirty great skulls through them titchy collars!*

*He larfed but he never told me.*

When Charlie and his ole gal first met it was at the crowded village dance held in the decrepit village hall, built after the First World War. Young Daisy sat waiting to be asked to dance.

Up comes Charlie.

*Are you gonna dance, young gal?*

*Oh yes, thank you, I am, says young Daisy.*

*Oh good, says young Charlie, that means I can sit on your chair!!*

When they were courting, he took her to the pictures. Half way through the film he had to go to the toilet. *They were mid row, so he pushed past some fifteen people and as he left the row he trod on the toes of the woman sitting on the end.*

*When he came back, the film still on, he say to the woman, was it your feet I trod on?*

*Yis she said, waiting for an apology.*

*Ah good, I found the right row!!*

And when they married, the village clubbed together to give them a weekend in a posh hotel in London.

*Two o'clock in the morning, the night staff got a phone call. It was a drunken Charlie, what time does the bar open?*

*It opens at midday, noon. Goodnight.*

*Just after 3am, they got another call, from an even more drunken Charlie.*

*What time does the bar open?*

*Well, as I told you, sir, 12 noon. Goodnight.*

*At just after 4.30 there was a further call from an almost paralytic Charlie.*

*What bar, does the time open?*

*We've already told you, it's 12 noon. You'll have to wait till then to get in.*

*Oh no, says Charlie, I don't want to get in. I want to get out!!*

One day the BBC, intent on making a documentary about rural life, came to the village. One of them asked Charlie, *'have you lived here all your life?'*

*'Not yet, I int!'!*

The camera crew went in the totally empty pub where ole Ebenezer behind the bar was playing dominoes with himself.

They ordered a pint each and while being served one asked how on earth they managed with so few customers.

*Oh we do alright, don't you fret.*

*OK, how much is the beer?*

*Fifty quid each!!*

*There was a notice over the bar, reading 'a pie, a pint and a friendly word.'*

*They'd got the pints, so they ordered the pies and asked for the friendly word.*

*Ebenezer leans over the bar to them, and says don't eat the pies!!*

*The rabbit pies used to be legendary, but after a time they didn't taste so good. Ebenezer told Charlie he just couldn't get the rabbits, so he put in a bit of hossmeat.*

*How much?*

*50-50; one rabbit, one hoss!!*

*Charlie and Daisy used to keep pigs and this television lot admired his pigs and saw there was one with a wooden leg.*

*Well, we had a fire about a month ago, that old pig rushed indoors, grabbed the fire extinguisher, got the flames under control, dragged Daisy outside, called the Fire Brigade and cleaned up the mess.*

*That's amazing. But why has he got a wooden leg?*

*Well a week later a burglar come, pinched all our stuff and was about to attack Daisy when the pig heard, rushed in, hit the burglar over the head with a table, tied him up and called the police.*

*That's fantastic, but you haven't said how he got a wooden leg.*

*Oh come on now, be fair, says Charlie, you don't think after what that pig has done for us we can bear to eat him all at once!!*

*Ole Daisy decided she wanted to go to Norwich for the day. They go down the station, there's this blook behind a pigeon hole.*

*We wanna go to Norwich.*

*Yis. Fust class?*

*Yis thank you, how are you?*

*They sit in the train and ole Charlie puts his pipe in his mouth.*

*An ole gal up the corner start on at him, you can't smook in here!*

*He says, I int smooking.*
*You got your pipe in your mouth!*
*Yis, I got my shoes on my feet but I ent walking am I?*

*They get to Norwich, they go to Pardy's, best place in town.*
*We can't go in here, Charlie...*
*Yis, come you on, gal.*
*Feller come along, tails, side parting and bad breath. What you want?*
*We'll have a cup of tea and a bun. We dint touch the cakes.*
*When he come back later he say, that's a pound each.*
*Charlie say, blust, pound?*
*Yis he say, there's all that other stuff there, you could a had it if you wanted it.*
*Well, when he come back with the change, ole Charlie catch him such a one across the kisser.*
*He say, what was that for?*
*That's for touching up my ole gal, Daisy.*
*He say, I never touched her!*
*No, Charlie say, but she was there, you could a had her if you wanted it!!*

As Farrier took to reciting the gags he'd found, overheard and stolen from old films, music hall, collections of humour and pantomimes while he moved about the pub, filling his everyday life - basically talking to himself - it was clear it was all getting too much for Lynette and everyone around them.

Crowds thinned; soon the weekend comedy nights melted away to nothing. Once the brewery doubled the rent on the pub in the late 80s, the Farriers decided to call it a day and retire not in the village where they'd been so long, but to be near their three kids in Norwich.

They hated it, but Charlie kept old George going, in his head, secretly, quietly. He probably kept Charlie sane. Working a small village pub for decades is a challenge to the grey cells.

48

Psycho problems, he had a few. Nothing he couldn't handle. They had notices up around the pub that people asked them to display. Sexual diseases in the gents; ramblers and darts playing in the lounge. They had a Samaritans notice for anybody contemplating suicide during a comedy night right by the payphone in the hall.

Lynette hoped somebody might bring in a poster for people suffering alter ego anguish issues, problems with separating a fictional joke from the realities of commercial life. But nobody did.

A new rep from the brewery visited and assumed that George was the landlord till he called himself Charlie Marshman and shouted for Lynette to come over and take care of business.

George said it was either his harmless imagination or he'd take to drink. Lynette knew there was nothing worse than a pub landlord with an alcohol problem, so she eased up on George. When two consecutive comedy nights failed to sell a single ticket, George had to agree they'd use the space for video horseracing and another slot machine.

Two years after they moved to Norwich a group of city businessmen decided to hold an inaugural annual dinner to celebrate St George's Night on 23rd April. This was in an era when a group of businessmen could keep themselves as all males and nobody made any fuss, though a couple of them had their wives in tow since they ran their businesses.

George was asked to do a turn, simply on the strength of one of the committee who'd heard him when he'd taken his girlfriend out to the pub when they were courting donkeys' years ago.

A delighted and flattered George retrieved his old gag sheets and visual aids from the loft where they'd been dumped when they moved in, along with the kids' school reports and paintings, old music records and the presents the regulars gave them when they gave up The Dark Ferry.

George decided that the dinner would see the rebirth of Charlie Marshman, despite the reservations of his now adult kids and downright opposition from Lynette who found in her diary a meeting of the Retired Victuallers' Association that she hastily organised.

In the closing days of their time running The Dark Ferry George had been advised, then pressurised into getting rid of all his Charlie material.

So he held a big burning in the pub garden of the contents of an old shoe box – a few handwritten notes, some typewritten sheets, lots of paper and magazine cuttings, a couple of photos…

After that he made a conscious effort to leave Charlie as a fading memory.

The fact is that the box was filled with bits of junk he scraped together after secreting his Charlie life in a different box labelled, 'bank statements' and as nobody was close enough to note exactly what he was burning, when he rediscovered his Charlie, he was ready to inhabit him again and at once.

Smiling, he read through his notes. When gigs were at a dinner rather than a slot on stage in a pub, George always began by thanking the organisers for inviting him.

*He'd single out the one who'd done the most and carried the biggest responsibility, and said he or she was like a film director, making sure everything flowed to the best effect.*

*Like Cecil B de Mille, who set up a once-only shot of a car going over a cliff. He put 8 cameras on it from different angles.*

*The car went over!*

*Then he called to each cameraman in turn, Camera 1?*
*Sorry, Mr de Mille, hair in film gate, no good!*
*Camera 2? Broken sound, boss, no good.*
*Camera 3? Back focused, unusable, sorry.*
*And so on, each one with a sorry excuse. He was left with the last one, his last hope.*
*Camera 8? Yep, ready when you are!*

He'd laughed aloud at the one about some VIP visiting the village hospital and meeting three local men in a ward.
*What's the matter with you? he asked the first one.*
*Venereal, sir.*
*Sorry about that, what's the cure?*
*They gives me a brush, they gives me some ointment and they tells me to paint the affected part.*
*Splendid, and what's your ambition?*
*Get back to work, sir!*
*Good man and what's the matter with you?*
*Piles, sir.*
*Oh dear, what's the treatment?*
*They gives me a brush, they gives me some ointment and they tells me to paint the affected part.*
*Marvellous and what's your ambition?*
*Get back to work, sir.*
*Glad to hear it and what's the matter with you?*
*Laryngitis, croaked the last man.*
*And what's the treatment for that?*
*They gives me a brush, they gives me some ointment and they tells me to paint the affected part.*
*I see and what's your ambition?*
*To get the brush before the others!!*

That one rather depended on his audience, though the ladies weren't always fond of it in any setting.

Occasionally, he'd get some open mike opportunities in quick succession.

*I'm telling my jokes three nights running.*

*Well, I daren't tell them standing still.*

*I'd be the funniest man if I was as well known as my jokes.*

*Someone asked Charlie about the rumour that a woman in the village had given birth to piglets.*

*Yis, he said, an they're looking for the swine that done it!!*

When a conversation struck up in the pub about how we all have to use metric, continental measurements, *Charlie reported he'd been into Hammer Toes' hardware shop and asked for 6 feet of copper pipe.*

*Oh you can't say that, we're all metric now. Do it in metres.*

*Alright, give me two meters.*

*That's better. Now, do you want, inch, inch and a half or two inch pipe?*

Charlie was nobody's fool; *a little known fact about ole Charlie Marshman is that he was a great inventor.*

*One day, shuffling through the village, minding his own, a stranger stopped him as he wheeled two heavy suitcases.*

*The stranger asks him for the time, Charlie about to say dew yew think I'm a copper, but he's had his moments with the law.*

*Like as a boy caught fishing in the river with no permit.*

*Copper say dew yew come along a me.*

*He's pushing his bike walking by the lad when Charlie say, Blust I left my hat on the bank, can I go back for it?*

*Go on then says the policeman.*

*Charlie scarpers right off away, don't he.*

*Next time the policeman catches Charlie fishing and he says he left his hat behind, the ole cop say*

*Yew ent catching me out on that one again.*

*You hold my bike, I'll go an get it.*

*And another time, policeman say to Charlie,*
*your dawg chased a woman on a bike*
*He say that weren't my dawg*
*He say how do you know that weren't your dawg?*
*He say my dawg int got no bike!*
*Any rood, the stranger asks him the time. Oh that's a nice*
*watch he says, it tells temperature, humidity, time in Thailand,*
*high tide times, sunrises and sunsets, stock market prices,*
*world train times and global recipes – remember this is the*
*60s, probably.*
*Bloke says he's gotta have it. How much do you want for it?*
*£10? £20?*

*Now Charlie knows about money.*
*He went to the pub and ordered a pint.*
*Barman say, that look like rain.*
*Yis and you still charging five shillings for it!!*

Charlie also maintained a healthy respect for his parents.
They used to joke about their Charlie.
*His father say to Charlie's mother*
*this here new baby is cross eyes.*
*I can't make it out. I int got crosseyes, you int got*
crosseyes,
*where do that come from?*
*She say that must 'ave been that time in the woods when*
*you say you look that way and I'll look this way!*

*While Charlie was a baby, his mother say to the grocer,*
*this here bearby of yours, I can't feed him, can't afford it.*
*So the ole grocer say, dew yew come in every week and I'll*
*give you free groceries till he's 15.*
*That went on for 15 years and Charlie got to be a big boy.*
*Grocer say, how old are you now, Charlie?*
*15 say Charlie.*

*Blust he say, dew yew tell your mother no more free groceries.*

*She had them for 15 year and watch the expression on her face.*

*So orf he go tell his mother. She larf.*

*She say, Charlie, go back and watch the expression on that grocer's face when you tell him he never was the father in the fust place!!*

*Back to the stranger and Charlie's watch.*

*They shake on £100. The stranger takes the cash out of his wallet and goes off with Charlie's watch.*

*But as he moves away, Charlie shouts out, pointing to the suitcases –*

*don't forget the batteries!!*

*Leaning on his gate one evening, big posh car comes down the lane and blook winds down the window and says, Excuse me my good man, where is the White Horse Manor?*

*Charlie scratches his head, blows out his cheeks, 'Blust, I dunno.*

*Off the car goes.*

*Freddie joins Charlie at that moment and as they're talking blook looks in mirror and sees Charlie waving him back. So he reverses.*

*I just asked my ole friend Freddie about the White Horse Manor of yours.*

*Yes?*

*Blust if he don't know neither!*

For St George's Day he decided a few good foreigner jokes would go well. This was when Irish, Italian, German or French jokes could still be told without causing mountains of offence and lead to grovelling apologies that rendered the humour pointless.

He decided to say that he was proud not only to be British, but even more proud to be English. No, he'd go further and say he was most proud of being an East Anglian, a part of the nation comprising Suffolk and Norfolk.

He'd talk in glowing terms about good ole St George and his heroic rescue of a damsel in distress as if it was recorded fact. He'd also, a bit controversially, stiffen their backbones by affirming it was fine to be a man.

About fifty city businessmen, stuffed variously in tight or hired dinner jackets, enjoyed drinks and nibbles in the lounge bar of the Airport Hilton, a new, contemporary designed hotel adjacent to the city's link with Europe and beyond.

George was welcomed and while not exactly feted, he was given some respect in anticipation of a rattling good after-dinner performance.

Only one man wasn't in a dinner jacket. This one was dressed in a flowing woollen kaftan revealing working men's boots and sporting a technicoloured turban which set off his long golden earrings perfectly.

He looked like a hippie. But in fact, Marcus Berry, according to Marcus Berry, was a millennial entrepreneur, more into work-life balance and health issues than money. However, for all that, this laid-back, bi-sexual 30-year old had done very well for himself with his vegan café, natural crafts with yoga classes and art courses in the back room.

He'd also just started selling his own home brews of craft beers and had a licence, so what he was running, he informed everyone, was a modern day pub. George didn't rise to that bait, being now retired from his.

He wound old George up further by calling him Grandpa while they stood in a huddle of blokes gauging if there was time to grab another glass from one of the schoolgirl waitresses or pause their imbibing till seated.

Don't you think the nature of humour changes? demanded Marcus of everyone but looking at George.

Of course it does.

Look at how people back in the day used to laugh about blacks, foreigners, Jews and the Irish, the handicapped, women and gays. Remember that?

Well, of course I do, but –

There you are. What was funny in the 1980s is unlikely to be comic today. And going forward, there will be different jokes ahead, not the same old stuff.

Blust, I hope you're going to enjoy my set, then? George laughed, but nobody joined in.

Before the awkwardness escalated further, the gentlemen were invited to sit down, dinner was served. Amidst the hubbub, as places were found, George was directed to the top table, set facing the rest of the dining hall.

To his dismay, Marcus Berry was on his table, as he'd served on the organising committee. The man made a big point of drawing a waiter's attention to the fact that he'd ordered the vegan option with Norwegian Spring Water, home-ground bread and a sugar-free, low calorie dessert.

The starters were a choice of homemade vegetable soup or a mini-platter of meat pates, followed by seasonal roast turkey (it was April) or some pasta concoction in a bowl that made George sick just looking at it. There might be a joke about a dog returning to its own vomit there somewhere.

Marcus Berry made a song and dance about the poor quality bread accompanying the 'home' made soup and when

56

all but he were served with the roast he hoped a number of times that the retro-carnivores among them would enjoy their meal and not worry about their hearts or the air quality.

It did cross George's mind that the man should hear about roasting coypu when people were hungry enough in those days and if they wanted any fancy food, they starved. But he didn't.

The man amused himself by needling George about old jokes and changing humour and what was unacceptable these days. George stuck by his guns that there was humour in simple things, faintly nostalgic and slightly un-politically correct.

Marcus' claim that George was practically guilty of hate crimes – or it may have been thought crimes, or both – was somewhat mitigated in the increasing volume of the guests as they washed down the poor food with liberal quantities of alcohol.

By the time desserts were dished up, with a spectacular choice of spotted dick with custard, Eton Mess with double cream or a cheeseboard of local varieties, most were far down the road towards oblivion, just before ugliness and violence arrived.

Marcus' criticism of the full fat cream, the cholesterol in the spotted dick and the sexist title of the dish was given little credence. It just made George want to joke about spotted dicks all the more.

After a five minute comfort break, the gentlemen settled to listen to a passable and witty talk from the Chair (more literal jokes in George's mind, thinking as Charlie would) and then a little pep talk, appeal for funds to do it all again next year from a little man who looked like a 1970s' bank manager.

Then with a big flourish the MC stood and boomed an invitation to George Farrier, former landlord of The Dark Ferry, well-known stand-up comic and good all rounder, to address the gentlemen there assembled and propose the toast to St George, patron saint of England.

George stood in his place on the top table as a round of boisterous applause died down. Looking round at his audience, ignoring the sneer on Marcus' face, he smiled, his nerves evaporating as he poised before launching his still well-remembered routine.

He took a big gulp of sparkling water before carefully placing his little stack of prompt cards on his glass, just to raise them a little closer to his eyes. He resisted the temptation to take off his watch and place it on the table to reassure people he'd not be speaking too long.

No, Charlie would speak as long as the crowd lapped him up, yet still finish with them wanting more.

They'd kitted him up with a little box on his belt and a tiny microphone looped round his ear, so he had freedom to move about as he brought Charlie Marshman back to his old, irascible, Norfolk life.

*Oi, was born in the village of Barnham Thorpe, that's what they call hinter denominational.*

The order of the gags flooded back to him, which was just as well when a gesture swept his cards off the glass and he knew he couldn't shuffle them back in sequence again.

After no more than five minutes with the jokes never really rising above flat and groan-worthy – they needed time to warm up and acclimatise to his accent, George thought – pockets of unrelated conversation began.

He'd experienced a fair deal of that in his pub comedy nights. There were always a few wisecrackers in who liked to lark about. When the drink got to some of them, there was sometimes more noise and interruption, but Charlie handled it all in character.

This was different. He sensed he was holding fewer of them, even out of politeness. Marcus certainly did his bit to disrupt from the top table with cries of shame about the dog, the pig and other animal jokes. He sputtered that the men were all misogynists and the women all stereotypes in Charlie's stories.

When the remains of the cream from the Eton Mess, some custard from the spotted dicks and a few pieces of cheese began flying across the room, spoon-catapulted by grown boys in evening dress, George knew the game was nearly up.

He made a fatal error. He allowed Charlie – or Charlie, equally despairing, allowed himself – to snap peevishly, 'I suppose what you lot really wanted was a stripper and a porn show to round off the evening? What would St George say?

That was the trigger to fire off the less sober guests, banging the table for the strippers to come on and the porn show to start. Management flapped about removing the waitresses from the floor, fearing for their well-being and one or two expected the police would be called.

Mustering what dignity he could, Charlie rapidly ended his talk, bid everyone a good evening, raised his glass to good ole St George, God bless 'im, and left, stripping the pegs of garments in the cloakroom till he found his own.

By the time two police cars arrived, reports of a riot were clearly overstated and gentlemen were being ushered into taxis while those who'd had the foresight to book rooms in the hotel were quietly being urged to find them.

A local newspaper reporter had been among the guests but as he'd invested time and energy offering to wipe cream off the blouses of waitresses, his report was of the outstanding success that the dinner had been and the comedian Charlie Dark Ferry had made an amusing comic retirement speech.

A month later George and Lynette went into the City centre to find a birthday present for one of their grandkids. She had resumed speaking to him after his St George's Day gig and had extracted a promise on pain of castration that he'd bury Charlie Marshman in a lead lined coffin under two tons of rocks.

To cement the deal, she'd stood beside him while he slowly destroyed every last memento of Charlie on a shredder she borrowed from a tidy neighbour. If he fed the sheets in too slowly, Lynette pushed his hand down to encourage him to get on with it.

His protests that his material may have future social, historical or cultural value fell on her deaf ears. She'd had enough of the alter ego.

Charlie was no more. Of course, he still lurked in George's mind. Somebody you've lived with for decades and known better than yourself isn't forgotten with the snap of fingers.

George was reminded of the dinner in several ways as they walked past shops and offices where owners and managers had witnessed his performance and he theirs.

Behind the market and City Hall, in a third tier shopping alley, was 'Berry Good Food', a vegan café, natural crafts with yoga classes and art courses in the back room, with an offer of home brews of craft beers and had a licence, so it was clearly a modern day pub.

Except it wasn't.

Berry Good Food was a little greasy spoon, old fashioned cheap, fast food outlet with a few wobbly tables, lots of unhealthy snacks and drinks and a young man rushing about serving in an every day clothes far removed from his hippie image.

Lynette stared as George pointed out what Marcus had looked like and pretended back in April, compared with the reality of this. She spotted a healthy corner, where vegan foods, wholesome, home-baked goodies were on offer.

That section seated no customers; the cheaper, unhealthy side was heaving with obese, hungry people from all walks of life.

Just shows you, doesn't it Lynette?

What does it show you, George?

Never take people at face value, hey?

She looked at him. Don't you dare make an old joke about that. Let's go find something to eat somewhere else.

# Something for the Weekend

Emily accepted his offer. She needed a break. While the prospect of a weekend in a second-rate hotel playing mind games in the back end of East Anglia with Barry Nettlewood wasn't the most thrilling prospect, it would get her out of London for a bit. Take her mind off things and people. Well, off one person, actually.

For his part, Barry was over the moon when the very attractive Emily Barlow – tall, slender, long strawberry blonde hair, comfortable in her late 30s – declining another glass of Californian pink she'd taken to absorbing by the gallon, agreed to the murder mystery weekend with him.

He barely contained his excessive delight through the coffee and mints, settling the bill, recovering coats, finding an empty taxi and the peck on the cheek before she got out at her flat and another long night on his own imagining what it would be like to take her in his arms.

He sat at the screen and booked a double room in what was billed as 'Skeletons in the Cupboard', a murder mystery weekend at the Nag's Head, a haunted coaching inn in high Suffolk.

*******************************

They'd been seeing each other for months now in a regular and predictable pattern - dinner, a few drinks, sometimes a film or a play and occasional lunches at work in the canteen.

Not that he was much of a film or play buff, but he knew she was and he always advance researched what they saw so he could hold his own in their long talks afterwards.

Nettlewood was a researcher for several MPs in the Palace of Westminster who collectively paid a reasonable salary. Not much of a career for a man in his fifties, he knew, but he had his police pension to fall back on, loved the work and was actually good at lifting the rocks on the dark monstrosities Government ministers, toadies, bureaucrats and minions wanted hidden.

Besides, it was in New Palace Yard as he walked towards the gates past Members' Entrance and the taxi queue where he abandoned hope of a sneaky place with an MP as none there knew him, that he first saw Emily. He'd never have met her if he didn't work there.

She was being escorted by Tom Bradfield, a distinguished, tall, early fifties medium ranker in the opposition cannon. He assumed the woman was Bradfield's new secretary, a special constituent or even a relative getting a tour through the back way rather than the cramped St Stephen's public entrance.

'Lucky bastard,' he muttered to himself of Bradfield. As he looked back at them he saw the Honourable Member for Oldsham's hand touch her back fleetingly.

It was enough to tell a man with years of observation under his belt that they were lovers.

*******************************

From that moment, his fantasy about sleeping with her, owning her began to take hold. He asked around the Palace and learned that Tom Bradfield had smartly kept his wife and three little angels in Oldsham, where they attended schools, shopped locally and were the lives and souls of the place which gave him a high rating on the positive perceptions chart among his voters.

Bradfield toiled in London all week and seemed to survive the ordeal with a succession of reasonably sophisticated, unattached ladies to get him through the nights. Emily Barlow had filled that job for a couple of years, almost since the last election brought Bradfield in, disappointing his ambition at once by being able to sit on only the opposition benches.

Emily was a Commons' secretary – or constituency caseworker as they were known these days. She worked for one of the few remaining knights of the shires who'd clocked up thirty years of service and was his fifth secretary.

Their affair had been as discreet, private and exciting as all Commons' affairs are in the Westminster-Whitehall bubble/village. Barry learned that Emily was unmarried, had had offers over the years but had cut loose before matrimony, she shared a flat with another secretary and word was that she was cooling on the smooth Tom Bradfield.

A former detective sergeant found it a piece of cake to ascertain her routines. To be in the salad queue at Bellamy's, Number One Parliament Street over the road from the Palace where she was several lunchtimes in a row was child's play.

He struck up a conversation with her and gradually, without pushing it, keeping it casual, Barry and Emily became canteen chums. After a time, people would leave them alone when they sat together.

He shared a few police stories with her. Routine stuff like traffic work, witnessing in court, breaking bad news to relatives, tracing stolen goods interested her – none of it a million miles from her casework for her MP.

She was less keen to hear some of the blacker stories. 'Unfortunately I was first on scene when that woman was stabbed outside Pimlico station and it turned out to be the first of the works by that lowlife the Evangelist Ripper – remember him?'

Emily shuddered. That had been a scary time for women travelling alone – he'd taken another five lives before he was caught. 'That look in the woman's eyes as the life drained out of her, quite literally...'

She put her hand on his. She wanted him to stop. It was the first time she'd touched him and told him she didn't like gore.

Occasionally he'd threaten in jest to share snippets from the gritty street life he'd known intimately. She always stopped him by touching or moving closer to tell him to change the subject.

***************************

The man who'd grilled some of the underworld's second tier finest encouraged Emily to talk about herself and open up some of her emotional baggage in a way that made her feel safe.

She liked that he was a good listener and was happy to talk. She had few close friends in the Commons and had been glad when she'd started up with Bradfield. Her own family were distant – her two siblings were roaring successes (they claimed) and her parents were getting beyond being interested in much outside their house in Arnos Grove.

Barry was non-threatening, supportive and he liked her as she was.

'Kill him!' snapped Barry one lunchtime as she was talking about Bradfield.

'What?' She was startled.

'Kill him. Do away with him. Pay to have it done. Do it yourself. Whatever. Threaten him with it. Wake him up – he can't use you like this. Leave him. Gut him.'

She'd just told Barry she'd reached the end with Bradfield. This was out of character. Barry pressed on, less viciously. 'Of course, he'd just get someone else, we know that.' Barry wondered for the millionth time in his life why some women fell for life's bastards.

'You could write a novel, Emily, that's what I mean. Kill him off that way and you'll feel better, especially when the publicity gets out.' He smiled at her, back to his sympathetic self. She smiled in return, feeling reassured again.

'Oh I can see you're wondering, as I used to be a cop, hey? Well, I'm into those murder mystery evenings and weekends, where actors set up an apparently so-called great mystery and guests have to crack it. I'm usually quite good at it!'

Eyeing the clock, aware how strict she was on lunch and coffee breaks so she'd be free if Bradfield called after a late night sitting or during the evening if a vote wasn't expected for an hour or so. 'Another coffee?'

She shook her head and he smiled. 'You know tonight, it's Education orders which will drone on till 10pm. Any chance of a drink early evening, with me?'

She wondered why he was changing their routine. 'I reckon, though, Emily, a drink will not be enough. I reckon you need a weekend away with me. A murder mystery weekend. Solve everything!'

'Barry, I hope you're not making an improper suggestion!' She gathered her tray, ready to go back to letters about a constituency she'd never even visited.

But the seed of Barry's idea had been planted.

\*\*\*\*\*\*\*\*\*\*\*\*\*\*\*\*\*\*\*\*\*\*\*\*\*\*\*\*\*\*\*\*\*\*\*\*

Emily spent time examining her relationship with Bradfield. She sat waiting once again – perhaps this evening? If the high and mighty man could fit her in. He hadn't been near since their rut a fortnight ago. He'd turned up in the early hours, straight from some function, turned on by other women there, and satisfied his lust.

The trouble was that even the furtive meets satisfied a hunger in Emily, albeit briefly. She didn't want to hurt his wife and kids; she just wanted that desperate, hopeless thrusting. She loved by giving, totally and fully.

That's what Bradfield took advantage of. However sordid she felt afterwards, however secret they had to be (fooling few), she clung to it. He'd suggested she go to Party Conference in the autumn, but how would that ever work out?

Barry Nettlewood on the other hand had asked her for a whole weekend in a hotel! OK, it was part of a theme she knew would be a pain in the arm. But would it make Bradfield jealous?

Barry was fine. Lots of guys his age with a lost or forgotten wife and kids somewhere would be more pushy, cynical or freaky. Barry was none of those. He was a straight guy, she reasoned.

As she wiped her makeup off for bed, she was unable to escape a crossroads feeling. She determined that if he asked her again, she'd damned well go with Barry on his murder weekend.

**\*\*\*\*\*\*\*\*\*\*\*\*\*\*\*\*\*\*\*\*\*\*\*\*\*\*\*\*\*\*\*\***

The drive out of London was novel for them both. Ahead of the worst of the Friday afternoon traffic through the dreary East End (where Barry had worked for years) to the A12 - not one of the nation's finest achievements. Barry cruised comfortably inside the limits pointing out speed cameras as they chatted, like kids on a school outing.

'Anyone know where you're going?' he asked, casually.

'Lisa knows, if she remembers.' Emily frowned at the notorious absent mindedness of her flatmate. 'Why, am I going to disappear without trace?'

He laughed, not unpleasantly. Just feeling like a teenager near his dream. He rehearsed in his mind his plans as they drove; she imagined how Tom would take it when he read the note she'd left on his secretary's desk. 'Mystery weekend away' would both irritate and intrigue him.

Barry's sequence was clear to him – arrival, spooky hotel, beams and hidden passages, their room, double bed, perhaps four-poster, dinner, stories of the haunting, first part of the murder mystery, drinks, more drinks, more stories of ghosts, bed.

Then it got interesting. Cuddling up to him out of sheer terror, giving herself, needing him … He eased the window a little and readjusted his seating position.

The pace of life was discernibly different once they left Ipswich, off the A14 and onto the B1078 at once archaic to their London eyes and slowed to a crawl in a pied piper queue lead by an ancient tractor returning to base.

To take her mind off Tom bloody Bradfield – where he was sure it was in the silence – Barry said, 'I've been doing some research. The hotel is an old coaching inn. There's a story about a couple of young lovers who got married with the blessings of both families and settled in the village as people did.'

Emily wondered where the story was going. 'The man was a labourer but was offered work at the inn to look after horses.'

'The nag, presumably,' Emily smiled.

'Presumably. But the innkeeper took a shine to the wife and when the man was at work, he went round their cottage and had his wicked way with her. She was very upset, naturally, and told her young swain when he got home for his tea.'

Getting into his stride, Barry went on, 'He flew into a mighty rage, the story goes, went back to the inn and beat the landlord with a hammer to such a pulp that his head came away from his body in full view of everyone present. For that he was hanged at Ipswich gaol.'

He'd just reached the limit of Emily's tolerance for violence, but had to finish. 'Sometimes the bleeding body of the landlord is seen at night, looking for the girl, her demented husband or his severed head!'

Emily wasn't going to swallow that. 'Sounds like a great marketing yarn for a murder mystery weekend,' Emily grinned, pushing him in the ribs as they reached the outskirts of Fettlesham Tye. The Nag's Head was unavoidable.

As the sky darkened with rain clouds and night, Barry knew she'd be scared into his arms spot on cue.

\*\*\*\*\*\*\*\*\*\*\*\*\*\*\*\*\*\*\*\*\*\*\*\*\*\*\*

Their room was every bit as dark beamed and with a sloping floor as he could wish for. Emily took in the bed, looked at him, raised an eyebrow and opened the drinks cabinet, implying she'd need something if she was getting in that with him. She'd wondered if he'd book separate rooms.

He unpacked his tiny case, slipping a small clip of A4 sheets out before moving to the little desk, where he leafed through the brochures, fire instructions, menus and 'discovered' the papers he'd typed at the Commons.

'See these, Emily. Let me read. Some of the ghost legends associated with the Nag's Head and the village of Fettlesham Tye. Number One – the Body in the Attic. When the inn was used for coaching purposes, once a day in its heyday and once a week as it declined, this was the scene of a real life murder to make your hair curl...'

'Mmm. I'm listening, Barry. Don't read too much out,' Emily cautioned, heaving her case to the bed and sipping her drink.

'In the 1950s the almost total remains of a body was found embedded in the thatch by reroofing contractors. Tests showed that the body dated from the late 1700s and –'

He was cut off by a shrill scream as Emily opened the door of the wardrobe to allow a large human skeleton to topple out towards her before cascading to the floor.

Even Barry was stunned for a moment. He put his arm round her shoulders. 'My God, Barry, it had better not be like this all the time or I shall need booze or therapy. Or both.'

This was going well. That plastic skeleton was a bonus; she'd be so scared she'd need his comfort and his therapy. He held his arm round her a moment too long; she bent to pick up a note attached to the skull.

'Welcome to the Skeleton in the Cupboard Weekend at the Nag's Head. You have been given a new identity. Please use it for the duration of the weekend, as it will enhance your pleasure and participation in what is about to unfold.'

Emily handed him the paper as there was a knock at the door. She hoped it might be room service so she could get some California Orange County special. There was nobody there; just a note on the floor.

She tore it open it and read aloud again, 'Dear Mr and Mrs Basle-Higham, you are invited to dinner at 8pm in the Fettlesham Room. Dress tonight is informal. You're urged to be there for drinks at 7.45pm to meet other suspects, er excuse me, I mean other guests, signed Sir Michael Buckman.'

Barry nodded. 'So, it's begun. You often pick up the clues to the killer at this very first event. Not bad so far. Remember that everyone is a suspect at this stage. The skeleton was clever and the note under the door. Reminds me when I was on stakeout duty on the Eltham rapes. We were watching this house, when –'

'Not now Barry. I just need another drink, if you don't mind.'

He didn't mind at all. She could drink all she wanted. It would make her more pliable as she flung herself into his arms for protection. About six hours from now, he reckoned.

***************************

Barry and Emily mingled with 15 other couples, all at least middle aged and one old pair celebrating their golden jubilee. They loved being thought special, and why not when fifty years was a long time. They had a patent recipe for survival – never sleep on an argument – but after regaling the company with it

71

three times, Lady Buckman, in character asked them to stop telling it.

She was a weary thirty-something, Essex born and bred judging by the roughness of her accent. Sir Michael Buckman, her 'husband' was more refined, commanding the Queen's English and was faintly reminiscent of an old theatrical luvvie.

Emily grabbed a third glass of bubbly and smiled at Barry, the alcohol warming him in her eyes. He saw no point in mingling, especially when he clocked an unlikely character called Chief Inspector Grimshaw who'd been created for the benefit of an American actor in his mid-sixties. Why was an American playing a British cop?

He was so clearly going to be the killer and his truly awful New York wife with the obligatory pitched-nose twang the victim that Barry almost felt disappointed. Except, having sussed it, he now had more time to anticipate the night with Emily.

Dinner was served by a handful of local women of a diverse set of shapes and sizes, cramped into tight black skirts and frilly blouses plus one stunning but moody teenager bored out of her mind doing the graveyard shift. Barry knew if the girl had lived in the parts of London he was familiar with, she'd earn more in five minutes on her back that in this backwater all week.

The Buckman character tapped his wineglass as the soup bowls were being cleared to welcome everyone again to the Skeleton in the Cupboard event. There was some laughter to acknowledge that several had been shocked at their own skeletons in their wardrobes.

He explained it was a German tradition for speeches after soup, but this was an English weekend. In the Christie,

Cluedo/Colonel Mustard genre. Or, for our friends from over the pond, Al Capone or Fat Sam style. People warmed to him.

After the main course, they were given fuller instructions on what to look out for. A page lifted from the sergeants' pre-shift briefing guide, Barry whispered to Emily, not wanting anyone to know he'd been a police officer.

Emily finished the bottle and wondered aloud if they'd manage another. He suggested a half-bottle compromise but made sure she drank most of it. Once the sweet dishes were cleared and the teenager was clattering coffee cups down, Buckman stood again.

'You may have heard all sorts of tales of strange goings on in the night. Sightings in the dark. And some nights, when the wind is straight from the marshes twelve miles away....'

He waited with a professional pause. The noise from the public bar struck loud. 'You may be wondering about the ghost of the Nag's Head. Let me tell you. The nag is not a horse, though this was a coaching inn. It refers to a wife of a keeper in the late 1600s.'

The Yanks seemed unaware that a woman could be styled a nag and looked around, puzzled, at the laughter. Buckman was enjoying his star turn. 'The wife, Susan Chartis, was a shrew, a nagging woman straight from Shakespeare who drove everyone in the inn completely mad, especially her poor husband.'

He licked his lips. 'The story goes that the husband and some regulars butchered her like a side of beef in the kitchen –'

Above the suitable shrieks of horror, Lady Buckman chimed in with, 'good job you lot had yer dinner already.'

And the climax from him – 'they hung her severed head on a pole outside the inn and that's how the place was known as the Nag's Head. Oh and by the way, they ate her remains over the coming days.'

He raised his hand to quieten the hubbub as this nonsense was digested. 'The husband regretted what he'd done – '

'Missed her nagging!' came from the woman.

'So he put the head in a large pot and anyone on payment of a farthing could take it out and gaze upon it.'

It was a good warm-up freeing everyone into talking openly to each other then until the evening ended with an impressive warning to stay in the bedrooms 'whatever people heard.'

*****************************

The gathering broke up with lots of laughing and well-oiled swaggering from the bar and up the stairs. Emily and Barry entered their room, saying nothing. Barry was thinking how best to clean the devilled chicken off his teeth, get into bed and undress to allow her to get undressed however she wanted.

He felt he should keep the pressure on her fears by one more anecdote from his previous career. Between mouthfuls of paste and water he shouted through from the bathroom, 'Emily, that story of the nag's head put me in mind of the bloke in Fulham who we found had three heads in cardboard boxes.'

She was scarcely listening. 'Turned out to be the family of his girlfriend whose mind he'd mixed with some strange dope he'd been sold in Brixton. We searched his place and found the heads. He'd told her they'd all be safer in boxes, and she believed it ...'

As he came out of the bathroom, he finished with, 'While he was doing a life stretch she paid people to get two blokes inside to do him in the prison workshop, so his head was in a box an' all. You must remember the case?'

She was reading the information he'd prepared on gruesome stories. To his dismay, she seemed neither merry nor phased by the horrors he'd filled her head with. Even heads in boxes didn't work.

She lay on the bed, still dressed. He wrapped his dressing gown round and lay beside her wondering how to get her under the covers. She wanted to share.

'Ever since I first realised boys were different in a nice way, I've wanted to be loved, to find a man I could give myself to in every way. And do you know, in some way, big or small, every man has let me down. Robert my first love in the 6$^{th}$ form... and Alan, I nearly married him for God's sake.'

She smoothed the duvet with a rhythmic finger. 'It's me who is at fault. I just expect the same passion, loyalty that I give to come back to me as I need. But it never does. I realise that I give in order to be given in return.'

Barry said nothing. 'And, you know, Barry. The worst thing is, I give the most of myself to those who take the most. Tom is the classic. I'd give myself to him for years, in the hope that one day he'll give to me instead of taking. So, it's fear of never being able to achieve that, not fear of scary stories as you –'

She looked at him for some understanding. But he was crashed out, dead to the world. Even the 2am screams and running down corridors laid on neither woke him nor terrified her into his arms.

**\*\*\*\*\*\*\*\*\*\*\*\*\*\*\*\*\*\*\*\*\*\*\*\*\*\*\*\*\*\***

Barry felt irritation and disappointment in equal measure when he woke on the Saturday morning. Emily made coffee from the little sachets and he sipped his in silence.

'I'm sorry, Barry. Sorry about last night.'

He felt obliged to mumble 'Oh, it's alright.' At least they had tonight.

'No, I shouldn't have laid all that on you. I'm not sure when you fell asleep?' She leaned over and gave him a wet kiss on the cheek before going for a shower. No invitation to join her.

Mismatch of expectations. She was talking about her monologue; he was thinking of his unfulfilled desire.

Breakfast was lively, as the dining room filled with guests beginning to warm to the spirit. The talk was of last night's noises. The Yanks didn't show.

Before they drifted from their tables, Buckman appeared looking sombre, his sidekick behind. 'Ladies and gentlemen, I hope you slept well.' He silenced the wave of laughter and comment.

'I'm sorry to have to tell you that Mrs Grimshaw, the wife of Chief Inspector Grimshaw, was brutally murdered last night. The group responded with the required shock and horror. Barry smiled to himself at being right; the husband did it, too.

'Chief Inspector Grimshaw is resting in his room' – the Yanks were breakfasting privately. 'He will be questioned and one by one, you will all help with enquiries this morning. Any helpful clues will be gratefully received. I hope your alibis are watertight and none of you went walkabouts last night ...'

Oohs and ahhs from the group showed they were enjoying it immensely.

'One last thing, my friends, none of you may leave the hotel this morning or attempt to communicate with any third party outside till you have been questioned. When you're called, come at once to the managers' office.'

The morning dragged. People talked less about the story, more about themselves. Most were trying a themed weekend for the first time. A couple from Doncaster had been on a Wild West one before – he'd loved it; she found it ridiculous.

When the sun came out from behind the early drizzle, a few wandered the gardens. Vegetation had grown – the place needed tidying. Barry felt they should have worked the garden into the story.

Emily was called first. The woman helping Buckman sat at the desk, pretending to take notes. The centrally placed hard chair she was invited to occupy allowed Buckman to circle Emily, making her uncomfortable.

'And is that really all you can tell us, Mrs Basle-Higham, about last night? You heard nothing, despite the fact that there was apparently noise going on loud enough to wake the innocent?'

'To wake the dead?' asked Emily, in a fit of levity.

Buckman's performance was good. 'Not quite madam. If you find murder comical, I shall have to ask you back for further questioning.' His eyes bulged as they stared at her. 'You don't add up, Mrs Basle-Higham.'

Emily decided then she'd had enough of the game. No longer in the mood for improvising herself into the fantasy, she itched to know how Tom Bradfield had reacted to her note.

Buckman let her go with a warning not to talk to her 'husband.'

She strolled casually to the garden where she located a side gate, cut back down the side lane and sprinted up the road a few yards, praying she'd not bump into Barry. She sat in the bus shelter and rang Bradfield's London flat on her mobile.

It rang unanswered. Two nearby school age kids kicking a ball in a garden reminded her it was Saturday. He'd be back in the constituency playing dutiful husband and family MP. She'd forgotten.

She was annoyed she'd forgotten it was Saturday and now his phone in London would show she called. And she didn't know how he felt.

Yes, she did. He didn't care less; she knew that in her heart.

*****************************

Saturday afternoon they were given a task and shown into the old laundry room and cellar below where the murder was supposed to have taken place. The gloom, damp and smell enriched the atmosphere perfectly.

On the floor, separated off with police tape, the American woman lay feigning brutal death. Her husband, allegedly grieving, caught it all on video. Barry could just see the folks back home – 'gee, Betty, you played dead!'

Issued with notebooks, rubber gloves, specimen bags they were asked to think like SOCOs – scenes of crime officers. Clues of any description could lead to the killer.

Buckman switched into the role of a laid-back, overworked, seen-it-all cop, with a jaundiced view about the human race. Holding all guests responsible, he kept asking why she was in the cellar.

Emily realised that some aspects of the story were taken from snippets of conversations yesterday evening. Barry enjoyed himself, despite last night and despite knowing the whole plot at once.

From the cramped cellar and inch-combing they all went to the garden to brainstorm, which by now was bathed in agreeable sunshine. Buckman re-questioned several of them to help shape the story. One of them had already confessed.

Everyone laughed but it made Emily wonder why some people confessed to crimes they hadn't committed, while others couldn't even confess their own shortcomings. Tom flew straight back into her mind. She whispered to Barry, 'back in a minute' and made for the toilets.

Out of sight, she veered to the stairs and their room. She sat on the bed and thought it through. Saturday mornings for constituents' surgeries; afternoon for family activities. If they could be tied in with something newsworthy like a football match, a fete or a charity do, so much the better.

This would be a good time as he'd be home before they went out for some political or civic event this evening. His home number had not been given out by him – she'd lifted it from his pocket notebook when she was curiously going through his jacket while he was showering after love-making.

She pressed the numbers, her stomach churning. Her thumb hung over the call button – what if the wife answered? If one of the kids picked up?

As her thumb went down, the door flung open and in strode Barry, taking it all in. 'Emily, don't call him. Let him go.'

She froze. She could hear the ringing from her phone in her lap. They waited. Someone picked up and said 'hello?' It was a child or a woman.

Barry moved across the sloping floor, grabbed the phone and pressed red. 'Emily, you have to let it go. It's a drug and you're cold turkey. Trust me; I can help you through this.'

She drew a deep breath, looking at him directly. 'Oh Saint Bloody Barry Nettlewood. How dare you, oh so clever cop. Stop interfering, stop controlling me. And by the way, Mr Plod, who are you really? Did they throw you out of the force? Did you really retire early? Are you still a cop on some undercover shit? Are you just using the Commons to give you some credibility? Speak up, Barry; I can't hear you whispering advice to me now!'

Their open door was unnoticed by either as Barry felt his blood beginning to boil. 'I'm not going to be spoken to like that, not by you.'

'Oh, not by me? Why not me? Because you have been so kind to me? Is that it? Took me under your wing because I was vulnerable, yes? I have lived all these years without you telling me what to *think*. Why do you presume to tell me what I *want*?'

'Because what you *want* is a man you can't have and you know that. What you have right here is a man –'

She cut him off. 'Is a man with condoms in his jacket pocket hoping to get lucky with me?' His jaw dropped – she'd been through his pockets.

'Barry, I think you're missing the point here.'

'I am? So you tell me what the point is then.'

Blissfully unaware that their loud voices had drawn other guests to the corridor and then into the room itself, including Buckman, they paused, weighing each other up.

When Emily noticed the audience they'd drawn, she started to get really angry – people thought it was part of the bloody show! And she only wanted to talk to Tom.

'You are just a nosy, smart arse, clever dick know-all who's got me here under false pretences. Do you think I can't see your game? I'm surprised you can look anyone in the eye. Talk about bloody murder mystery, the only mystery is how you can live with yourself interfering in my life which is doing fine thank you, when you are such a lying, two-faced bastard of a copper.'

As she paused to draw breath, Barry finally realised they'd picked up a gawping audience. 'For God's sake, you people...'

They burst into spontaneous applause for their performance skills.

Buckman interjected with some inspired improvisation, 'So, Mr and Mrs Basle-Higham are not all they seem. But then, is anyone? Just who are these people? What do they know about the late Mrs Grimshaw? You can question them this evening ...'

Emily, embarrassed, snarled, 'Just leave me alone' and pushed through them to escape. Buckman ushered everyone out, winking at Barry as he pulled the door behind him, grateful for the superb red herring Barry had just provided.

*******************************

81

Formal dress was requested for dinner. Buckshaw called all to order and beckoned Chief Inspector Grimshaw in on a wave of condolence and sympathy at his loss. He was followed by the American's wife, now as Detective Constable Haines, assigned to both the case and 'helping and caring for Mr Grimshaw through this difficult time.'

Guffaws all round as they settled to a meal served by the same crew, including the youngster, her face deeply miserable in her teenage angst. Questioning was the main focus of the continuing game. Buckman divided them into small groups, keeping spouses apart and encouraged all and any questions.

Barry's group wanted to know about his cop thing. He admitted it was true and the argument with Emily had been real.

Emily told her group she was not prepared to answer questions about the argument or Barry's former job and would only say she worked for an MP. Nothing more.

This confirmed everyone's suspicions. Ex-cop and someone who worked in Parliament? No, it just wasn't convincing.

Emily grinned and bore it, consoling herself with just one more night before she could phone Tom whatever Barry thought. She drank deeply again – several offered her drinks and she ordered a bottle for herself. This reassured Barry somewhat. She needed to be completely relaxed.

Meal and questions over, Buckman shooed them to the lounge where they perched on a large semi-circle of chairs. Without notes he gave a summary of what had been established and what was speculation. It was good, which told Barry that Buckman had once been a teacher as well as an actor.

All thought that Barry and Emily were plants, so Buckman accepted that and said, 'to finish this part of the weekend's fun, allow me to introduce my wife, Ron.' There was a laugh. 'No, Ron as in Sharon.'

His sidekick took centre stage, the lights were dimmed and she performed a passable monologue: 'I am Sharon Buckman. Well, I am now. Where I come from you better remember who you are and forget who you were. Years ago when I worked Kings Cross, you know what I mean, I was looked after, if you can call it that, by this geezer called Hazzie. Hazzie was big and mean. This high and mean as shit. When we got out of punters' cars, he took the money to look after and gave us pocket money....'

Melodramatically, she accepted a drink from Buckman before continuing her sob story. 'Hazzie made sure you didn't cheat him. He had this power; people just did as he wanted. He cut more girls' faces than I can count. Any punter got out of order he'd find him and cut him where it mattered.'

Another sip and a nod from Buckman, and she resumed. 'There was this old bill who was going places, Sergeant Grimshaw. He made a deal with Hazzie – names of the scum in the area and his girls worked without problems from the law. But Hazzie got greedy, didn't he? Moving in other people's manor. Grimshaw said no, so Hazzie found his address and cut his wife up.'

Gasps came from some of the group who'd made the willing suspension of disbelief absolute. 'His wife, I mean, not the old bat who died last night ... she died on the carpet in their front hall, bled out. By the time Grimshaw came home, it was too late.'

She couldn't continue; her emotion opened a round of applause. There was more drinking and the evening ended.

Guests ready for such sweet dreams as their minds would allow after that, sidled upstairs in dribs and drabs.


*******************************

For Barry it was set to be a very long night indeed. He and Emily said nothing. She was three parts gone, her bloodstream pretty full from the weekend's imbibing. He wanted to clear the air between them.

'Emily, I'm sorry about earlier, I truly am.' She gave a silly burp which she found hilarious. She sat on the bed to steady herself but the giggles rolled her off it. He let it play out.

It took several minutes before she dragged herself up by the bedding and forced a straight face. He got a Budweiser from the fridge and she said, 'What they got Barry, baby?' He considered her a moment before handing her the three wine minis.

'Go on, Barry, you were saying.'

His apology was done. 'You know, I was struck in that last story by the similarities between me and my wife …'

She'd known he'd been married, but no details. She was all ears. 'Some villains I knew because my first job when I went to CID was undercover to help the drugs squad out as I wasn't known. This group of lowlife had a speciality. They'd drive round in a van looking like a cop van and bundle any single men in Soho who were looking at brothels.'

Emily drained a mini bottle in one and unscrewed the next. 'They'd hide them in an old warehouse in Stepney. The poor sods were doped so hard that they became addicts in a matter of hours. They'd got their home addresses, so they dumped them back on their doorsteps. Usually nice, safe middle class areas.'

'They then fed their addicts over time till they'd bled them dry. When they ran out of money they did the same to the wives and girlfriends. They got very rich, very big.'

'I infiltrated the gang, took months. Everything was planned, ready for a take-down. Problem was my wife was pregnant. I went to the hospital to see the baby being born.'

He sat at the table, studying the liquid in the green bottle, his thoughts back then. 'My God, have you ever seen a baby born? Beyond words, trust me. Anyway, I was there just too long to explain satisfactorily to my new 'friends'. They got suspicious. They asked around. They had me soon enough – address, credit card number, the lot.'

He stared deeper back into time. 'They didn't come for me. They didn't come for my wife. No, they came for my baby.' There was silence. 'How low can you get to slice a baby?'

After a moment, she asked, 'what happened?'

'The force gave us counselling and a rest. I moved to traffic and then back to detection. But my wife, God I loved that woman, demanded a new identity, a new life. I couldn't give up what I loved doing, so like a bloody fool I let her go, I gave her and the scarred child up. So, I know about giving up what you love, Emily...'

He sighed, put the bottle down and looked at her. Emily was fast asleep.

*******************************

It was the longest night of his life.

85

While Emily, untouched, slept the sleep of the innocent in her alcoholic coma, Barry lay with the demons out of the bottles in his memory cellar; the skeletons from his cupboards raced through his mind and round the room.

It was the mother of all hauntings. Over and over again, images he'd put in a cupboard and thrown away the key. Razors on baby's tiny face and arms. Degraded, broken people. Dangers he'd survived. Lies he'd uncovered. The price he'd paid.

And it wasn't over yet.

The rotting corpses of his idealism, hopes and plans, the maggots of corruption few had seen. And above all, the eyes of his bewildered wife clutching their damaged child as he let them go. She refused to kiss him goodbye.

As dawn broke, he crawled exhausted from the bed to make coffee. The advertising for this inn as haunted and spooky was about right. The kettle boiled. Emily slept on.

*****************************

The denouement was delivered after lunch, the morning having been given over to final quizzes and a liberal sprinkling of ghost tales and further red herrings. Emily slept till early afternoon so Barry walked out, through the village past the church. A service was in full swing; he sat on a bench outside.

Absence confirmed their guilt for most guests. Mrs Buckman checked Emily was hard asleep and Barry out walking, whispered to Buckman who announced that Emily had been found dead in her bed and Barry had gone awol.

It was last minute food for thought but by the end of the morning as they handed their answer sheets in to Buckman,

86

they mostly thought Emily was the guilty one and Barry had killed her to cover her guilt and his shame.

During a reasonable Sunday roast without either Emily or Barry present, Buckman sifted through the answers and announced the general consensus, that Emily indeed had murdered Mrs Grimshaw and Barry had murdered her. His body would be found in a stream half a mile away, where he'd shot himself.

The elderly couple had an alternative. Chief Inspector Grimshaw had discovered his wife had shot herself through the neck and mouth, so took the gun and shot her in the chest as well to make it look like murder not suicide.

Mr Basle-Higham had been planted to check out the great Grimshaw who'd become a liability at police HQ. He'd discovered the truth and attempted to blackmail Grimshaw. Emily had been unhappy and argued with Barry, so Grimshaw went to their room to kill them both.

Finding only Emily in, he did away with her and then went after Barry, who he caught in the village, shot and returned to the Nag's Head for his lunch.

Buckman decided, under the circumstances that it was as satisfactory a solution as any and awarded the couple the prize, which really made their anniversary weekend.

Nobody saw Emily and Barry check out and drive back to London to resume their separate lives and jobs at the House of Commons.

# A Theatre Empties

It starts off as a bachelor weekend. When the girlfriend has to go away with family, he's able successfully to argue that he needs time to finish the opera he is working on. She knows there's no opera - at best there's a poem or two and an idea for a play that may never be written.

But, whatever the arguments for or against, off she goes; he is alone, not unlike when he was a student. Therapy all round.

She'd asked what he was really most worried about. She knew it was reality through a prism of fantasy. At twenty two he still couldn't fully separate the worlds his mind inhabited.

He replied, 'It's a dark name called by unseen creatures, it's a broken can by a dead cat in a gutter, a snowed over driveway hiding the blood drips, a tilted lamppost blinking, a window shattering, a night far away from tomorrow, an undeveloped film that must not be seen, a home for overcrowded things, a lightless world without you....'

'Then you either come with me or face up to all that. Go and see a show. The reality of a piece of make-believe may help put the unreality of life into perspective.'

She was right. So, he tubes into central London, just as he used to, feeling like a widower, before it passes. Then the realities take over.

A car slows at the curb, yards from him. A door opens and a hail of lead spews out. A man drops, dead before he hits the pavement. Nobody bats an eyelid.

Only later does he wonder if he'd dreamed it, or if it was a film. It's raining, as expected. There is an old woman carrying a battered case awkwardly in arthritic fingers. He gawps at her, willing himself to move on, away from her stink.

'I drove on a motorway with my son. Two rival gangs undertook us chasing for spurious glory; we were in the middle lane. Wheels scraped sparks of anger. The collision claimed four lives, nineteen vehicles were rendered useless and the motorway was closed for twelve hours. And nobody batted an eyelid.'

He realises she hasn't actually told him that. He'd read it somewhere. The old dear had asked for half a crown for a mug of tea and a plate of toast. He gives her two shillings, reluctant to break into the three fivers he has ready for his night out.

In a pub he downs a half of cider while two million pounds in forged notes changes hands in a holdall. Nobody finds it odd that two million pounds actually wouldn't fit into a bag that size, so nobody does anything.

Further along he watches a gang of villains disguised as mechanics clear a line of parked cars before the council removal team arrive. He looks round to tell someone, but nobody is interested.

On the street corners, past the sex shops, the upstairs and downstairs promises of girls of every age and many colours, he trudges on, getting rather wet now. A bar erupts into dust, blood, glass, shrapnel, flesh and screams bursting out across the street. A man runs away, glancing behind him to reveal his grin.

But nobody notices even this. Neither a vicious, wordless fight down an alley; nor a woman engaging a man in conversation before leading him down the same alley to do the business.

He does notice a couple of young girls, one in a mini that is more pelmet than skirt and the other in a long flowing, flowery, hippie drape slipping a big, well-dressed middle aged man what looks like a pound note in exchange for a little paper wrap of something and go off giggling.

At last he reaches the Backyard Theatre, a cobbled together performance area created from mismatched canvass awnings, half a shed, the remains of an old kitchen belonging to the pub at the side and some gravel space. It is very now – experimental in every sense, but after his journey, it's a haven of sorts.

He's bought a ticket for the full marathon, though they are available for two hour slots. She had found it advertised and pronounced it weird enough for him while she was away, so he'd have some managed stage illusion to fill his mind. She would know he'd already seen the equivalent of an epic movie just getting here.

The show is called *Clandestine and the Happiness Dream*, a Happening due to run for a full 13 hours! There will be regular breaks and some parts will be more exciting than others. But a whole night of theatrical experience? Blimey, this will sort him out.

He finds a seat that suits him at the very back from the ramshackle collection of old household and garden chairs, with a couple of school and one park bench acquired from somewhere. None is going to be comfortable throughout the night, but the breaks are for stretching cramped legs and gulping almost fresh air.

Expectation hangs, a cloud above all. He counts 38 people, including several obviously conscious hippies, a couple of blokes off a building site and a woman in smart office wear, decidedly overdressed. Five of the performers, are already interacting, juggling, joking, conversing with some of the audience, one mocking the smart office woman in character.

Oh and there is a dog belonging to somebody. It's a cross Labrador-collie, he thinks. But as he knows nothing about dogs beyond a few breed names, this one is a mix of mutt and cur.

It's well after 8pm when the thing gets under way. Nobody seems to mind – plenty of time lies ahead. Several of the crowd have come already tanked up and some clutch bags containing sandwiches and other refreshments to sustain them, though nourishing food is promised for sale later.

A song and dance routine highlighting various current political issues opens it and it's soon clear that the Happiness Dream is a catch-all phrase describing perfection or anything that is not the status quo. It's an aspiration, a hope, an ambition.

Clandestine is played by each performer in turn in Brechtian style, sporting a huge bit of velvet curtaining, the brass rings still embedded in the top stitching, that is accepted as 'the invisible cloak'. So the clandestine role can observe, comment, disrupt and alter the action.

Basically a sound idea, but spun out for so long? Well, it's a reasonable, drama school type start. Good rapport with the audience – some of whom are friends with performers – and everyone is enthusiastic and warm to it, even the builders at this early stage.

In one little sequence, he notes the dialogue and action particularly -

*You're a funny man, she said. A very funny man.*

*You don't wear a funny hat but your nose is a hoot.*
*You have long green straw hair but I know you're as bald as*
*a coot.*

*I love your sense of humour,*
*both the realistic and the rumour.*

*You're a funny man, she said. A very funny man.*
*Your face is in my wildest dreams*
*and your eyeballs are still intact*
*I see your lips are rouged*
*to hide where your mouth was cracked.*

*I love your sense of justice, and wake up screaming.*

*You're a funny man, she said. A very funny man.*
*You bring out fragments of paper and begin to write,*
*You work in the dark because your sense is light.*

Just before 10pm, the first break comes. Performers – eight in all and multi-skilled in acting, singing, dancing and playing instruments – are showered with applause and general appreciation. It was a satisfying show and two hours was the right length for it. He wonders what they'll do next.

A few gather round the stall offering cakes and sandwiches of uncertain vintage, no sense of queue. The dog laps at a dish of water conveniently placed that somebody will kick over soon. He weaves his way through everyone.

Outside, workmen dressed in wet-weather oilskins are attempting to thread a hose down a drain, so blocked that the rain and roof droppings are overflowing from it. The pathway is flooded. They struggle to get the piping down.

'Blimey, it's someone's brains!'

They peer down; he stops to listen.

Yes, someone has had his or her brains blown out and disposed of down the drains and now the drains are blocked.

'This is the worst case of fly-tipping we've ever had to deal with!' smiles one.

'A real brain drain,' quips another with a gallows grin, looking round for applause that doesn't materialise.

He leaves them to it, circling round their work and makes for the last bookshop still open at this hour.

He browses. There seems to be nobody around, yet a pair of eyes is watching him through a gap in the shelves, between social history and transport, in fact. The elderly gentleman has grown used to sizing customers up over the years of burning through his inheritance to run this beloved bookshop of second or third hand masterpieces.

He concludes that this one is just sheltering from the drizzle. He will not buy, he may read bits; he could even try to steal one. He is unstable. He doesn't yearn for a rare volume of Greek poetry in the original tongue. He doesn't even want a postcard of the Russian greats, authors and composers.

And sure enough, the theatre-goer wanders around, picking up odd volumes, some in poor shape, others in good nick, slotting them back and wondering why he feels uncomfortable in the shop. Then he spots one that appeals.

*A Lunatic Tried* – interesting title. Tried what? Parachuting? Basket weaving? Free love? For insanity? As he skims the covers and opening pages, it turns out that a lunatic tried to kill himself last year. In a bookshop.

Something makes him look up. The eyes; there are eyes. He replaces the volume, slowly and carefully steps back towards the door like a clown waiting to be yah-booed. 'Goodbye' comes out of the dust and gloom, a film of horror while being an idiot show simultaneously.

He thinks the eyes are for sale or rent. He doesn't want them. He has his own and they are perfectly fine. As he proves to himself once outside with a sigh of relief and witnesses two men carrying a woman out of a basement flat, like she is a roll of carpet. Perhaps she is.

At the Backyard Theatre in good time for the 11pm restart, he counts up heads and it seems that only two people have taken the opportunity to leave. Perhaps they just paid for one session. The dog has taken a position in front of the acting area. Maybe it's part of the show.

Between now and the next break at 1am, he takes part as a reluctant active audience member in what can best be described as a shout show. They are invited to behave like kids, to see the world as ten year olds and respond accordingly.

Some of the same material from the opening is reprised with this in mind. He finds it far more fascinating than he expected. The dog gets quite excited at one point, deciding a girl's leg doing a child-like jig was the ideal aid for a bit of canine pleasuring, much to the amusement of the audience.

He loves the exaggerated human Punch and Judy, the circus clowning around, physical theatre and the use of cracker jokes that kids might enjoy retelling, badly.

One comedy sequence he finds particularly funny, due to his second can of lager as much as anything else.

*1. Ha ha, ha ha! Thump.*
*The man laughs his head off.*

94

*2. Skivvy kneels to pull off Maestro's boots.*
*The right boot comes off, Maestro's leg with it.*

*3. Woman sits down; a spring coil pushes her to the ceiling.*
*Her head embeds. Body weight pulls her down, leaving the*
*head in ceiling.*
*She should have minded her seat when leaving her head.*

Just on 1am arrives sooner than he thought possible. A
smell of soup reinforces his hunger as about twenty assorted
people shuffle round the makeshift stall outside offering
homemade lentil and barley soup, wholemeal bread, beer,
salads and baked oatcakes on two plates. On one they're a
reasonable sixpence each; from the other they are half as
much again because of the added substances to help people
get through the night.

Everybody seems to be talking to each other like real old
friends. He passes a comment about the bread to a couple of
long haired, bearded, sandal-shod guys but they don't give
much back. He wanders off, after eating alone, standing, just
listening to the talking and rain outside. The dog watches him
go but doesn't follow him.

Time before the 2am section to survey a team of refuse
collectors cheerfully humping West End detritus into a slowly
moving lorry. In their wake is a gang of street sweepers. One
seems remarkably old, a poor geriatric thing, struggling with
numbed, white fingers to wield a long-handled broom in the
drizzle, inadequately dressed and trying to whistle through
three teeth in a mouth lopsided from too many encounters with
fists and boots.

He seems focused on his task unaware that the rain is
taking most of the dirt off his shovel as he works. In a sense
he takes pleasure from tidying up the locality, though nobody
cares. Nobody notices. And even when a car over-crammed
with some out-for-a-lark girls, windows open to share the

thumping radio rock music, clip him on the shoulder as he shuffles out of their way, it's not worthy of note.

Except by the driver, who, seeing the man off balance in the rear mirror, stops and reverses to give him a good smack with the rear bumper which sets her and all her mates off into hysterics before they drive on, searching for fresh fun.

In a red phone box he absorbs myriad postcards advertising personal services, some with lurid photos of well-bosomed ladies and all with phone numbers for customers to make contact. There are also the remains of a woman, well past her prime, slumped against the phone and coin-box.

He looks closer. If the cord round her neck is any clue, she's been strangled. Mascara-drenched eyes stare unseeing out at him through the grubby glass panels. He will not be making a phone call there. But then, who would he ring at this hour, he wonders aloud?

The 2am to 4am slot, what the actors called the graveyard shift, is shared with an audience of just eleven hardy people and one blokey newcomer who wants to tell anybody who'll listen that he went up the stairs at one of the places he passed to find a 'young model' who turned out to be neither young nor what he'd call a model but had sufficed for a tenner.

The dog is nowhere to be seen. People are white faced and most look determined to push through the tiredness barrier. A youth under an afro hair style gives himself a chance by heavily dragging on a succession of roll ups, offering them in turn to others.

Some of the material is dark, intended to keep people awake, though several finally succumb to sleep, one very loudly, even on that seating. He remembers one bit of dialogue, with masks, grotesque puppets and distorted voices.

*What have you got to say for yourself?*
*A rubber face squashed, insane,*
*half a mouth*
*moving vacantly, one eye backwards*
*one eye nearly missing*
*no air intake*
*the whole thing in shadow*
*moving through a siren*
*of breath coming*
*through a plastic bag*
*here comes the distorted*
*no voice no speak*
*no light no squeak*
*no move no shriek*
*wait*
*it passes*
*and now its behind me*
*the room is still stifling*
*outside frost recalled*
*but lost*
*distorted*
*it moves away*
*again*
*insane*
*a rubber face squashed.*

*The theatre is quiet, the lights dim*
*they come up*
*there against the backdrop so grim*
*are my technicolour clowns.*

*There, my clowns have clapped*
*The audience realises the performance has ended, all must*
*go away now*
*they go*
*they know*
*they'll see the clowns again in life*
*especially those most offended.*

97

He recalls no more of it because he wakes at 4am to the desultory applause of a single pair of hands to find himself and the three others present being urged to get some air before the 5am session starts. He relieves himself in a bucket, already overloaded, round the back and wonders where the women are supposed to go.

Munching a roll stuck around some unknown spread, and stretching his legs with a decent walk, he observes an ancient crone in a mangled fur coat dragging herself, her feet unresponsive. Her teary eyes look around, as if for the last time, at the theatres, the clubs, closed and dark for the night. Remembered applause, matinees, the laughter, the moans, the old hits, the near failures, the first nights and the superstitions of the world she inhabited when she was half human.

A sound emerges with some difficulty from her dry and rusty throat. It could be a line of Ibsen or Shaw, or pure gibberish. Either way it's lost in the rain and a passing car's horn. A lamppost stops her falling to the ground as two well-lubricated blokes dash for a late taxi.

With a monumental effort, fuelled by a glug from a bottle from her pocket, she begins a dance, the last reprise of what was once a fantastic routine on stage in the dazzle of the spotlight. Tonight it's a shambles, a stumbling off the pavement to the road and to the other side where a shop doorway beckons.

At 5 in the morning, three more people dressed as lounge-abouts have arrived and during the next two hours four previous hippies return and are joined by a few newcomers. The dog is back, with no explanation as to where it's been.

Another sequence that sticks in his mind is based round a prolonged song, as he fights harder to resist nodding off. The space is warm and fuggy. The dog gives up the fight and sleeps. The man with the smoking stuff is on a higher level but has picked up a young lad in what was once recognisable as a cheap suit for a quick cuddle.

*I heard the milk bottles cracking*
*I heard the road signs banging*
*I saw the corner quaking*
*and the pebbles hanging*
*I heard someone say*
*COME AWAY FROM THE DOOR*

*I heard the neon signs moaning*
*I heard some clocks grating*
*The staircases groaning*
*and the toys debating*
*I heard someone say*
*COME AWAY FROM THE DOOR*
*YOU'RE LETTING IN THE RAIN*

*I heard the dustmen laughing*
*I heard the organs whining*
*I saw the suits shaving*
*and the traffic's grey lining*
*I heard someone say*
*COME AWAY FROM THE DOOR*
*YOU'RE LETTING IN THE RAIN*
*NOBODY NEEDS MORE OF THAT PAIN*

*I heard the library reading*
*I senses harbour lights falling*
*I saw what the dogs were needing*
*and I heard forecasts calling*
*I heard someone say*
*COME AWAY FROM THE DOOR*
*YOU'RE LETTING IN THE RAIN*
*NOBODY NEEDS MORE OF THAT PAIN*
*YOU'RE DRIVING US ALL INSANE*

*I heard the rage of a long time ago*
*I heard the cardboard walls bending*
*In saw why the lonely countryman*
*steps back from any lending*
*I heard someone say*
*COME AWAY FROM THE DOOR*
*YOU'RE LETTING IN THE RAIN*
*NOBODY NEEDS MORE OF THAT PAIN*
*YOU'RE DRIVING US ALL INSANE*
*BETTER GET BACK IN THE DRAIN*

*I heard medicine following*
*I heard sunshine jangling*
*I felt a lump swallowing*
*and saw nerves inter-tangling*
*I heard someone say*
*COME AWAY FROM THE DOOR*
*YOU'RE LETTING IN THE RAIN*
*NOBODY NEEDS MORE OF THAT PAIN*
*YOU'RE DRIVING US ALL INSANE*
*BETTER GET BACK IN THE DRAIN*
*YOU'RE LEAVING QUITE A STAIN*

*I heard undertakers hammering*
*I heard sand dunes unswept*
*I saw a forest stammering*
*that it had never slept*
*I heard someone say*
*COME AWAY FROM THE DOOR*
*YOU'RE LETTING IN THE RAIN*
*NOBODY NEEDS MORE OF THAT PAIN*
*YOU'RE DRIVING US ALL INSANE*
*BETTER GET BACK IN THE DRAIN*
*YOU'RE LEAVING QUITE A STAIN*
*SO I SHUT THEIR DOOR. AGAIN.*

The 7am break is to be the last. The outside bucket, the need for something other than a bucket, the end of the food and drink, the stench in the awning and the beginning of a feeling of having been in that location forever, speak to the natural end of the event.

On the corner beyond there is a small workman's café just opening. He sits to a mug of tea and a bacon sandwich and looks around to see he has been joined by others he now regards as friends from the night, though he's spoken to almost nobody.

After using the café toilet with a sense of real gratitude he makes back towards the theatre, not wishing to give up now, although the tubes have started running again and he could just go home. She'll never know.

To his surprise a pale red light is still shining from a top flat. He stares, and moves aside as a skinny woman stumbles down the rickety stairs, clutching a big plastic bag of rubbish to be left on the curb.

As she places it next to others, he knows that they'll be there all day, till the next refuse collection in the middle of the night.

She gives him a quick up and down and tells him she is still open in more ways than one if he'd like to come up, also in more ways than one, to her flat three floors up.

He mutters about not having the time and she snorts, 'blimey, most of them don't last above a few seconds. Please yourself.'

It's only when she goes back up the stairs and he takes in the condoms and tissues in the untied plastic bag that he wishes he'd gone up. But then he moves on, and back to the show finale.

This is just one hour. High energy, fast paced. bringing all the flimsy plot strands together, adding in more music, more manic improvisation, more bizarre props (a noose, a mannequin, a clothes roller and a box of fresh cabbages) in a sequence that makes little sense but is fun for the performers and most of the audience.

At the start they pick on a girl with backside length straight light brown hair and persuade her to join them on the stage, at the side. He wonders if she is a plant. She is furnished with a chipped enamel bowl on a three legged table, pointed to some shampoo and given a couple of cups. She starts to wash her hair on stage.

The action continues and fresh water is brought to her for the second and third rinses. The music reaches a crescendo, the shouting and high range singing is at fever pitch. It all excites the dog to bark a bit and wag its tail a lot.

And there is the climax of the entire project. As soon as the girl's hair is washed and dried in towels and combed out beautifully, she is given several sacks of flour and invited to scatter them alongside a joke and sequence about flour power.

At first gingerly, gradually encouraged to apply it liberally, the audience and all the company are covered with a fine coating or an absolute wad, depending on their proximity to the stage.

It all makes as much sense as anything that went on before during the night. The accompanying song seems to be called GRAPES – *I've just eaten grapes for Easter* - with every instrument brought into play and a pile of ceramic saucers being stacked for added effect on the chorus.

It ends abruptly with the girl with clean hair being stood on a chair with the noose round her neck. The latest Clandestine character attempts to tighten the rope to a beam from the main building and most of the rest of the cast rush in wearing white coats.

No further speeches. Applause is fulsome, as much from relief it's over. And suddenly the marathon is run.

He leaves with the others, brushing flour from his head and shoulders and wiping his glasses on his pink corduroy shirt. He stands a moment as the crowd disperses around him into the dry, bright morning, everyone with places to go suddenly, things to get done. The dog has made its own way somewhere else.

He thinks like a poem. A theatre empties. The audience has gone. The platform is empty and the players have vanished.

Their last speech is already as forgotten as last week's obituaries. An old tradition has been given due deference. People with ideas devised and rehearsed and performed. On with the next one.

There was laughter, several choking pauses for thought and some sleeping during the long night. But it was all worth while.

He turns back to the little theatre wanting to say thank you, or if not quite that, to make some sort of contact. He's spent a night with these people, in a way and he feels some words may be needed from him to them. She will want to know that he learned something from them as well as watched them.

But they've already scarpered, cleared up almost everything except the food remains and the flour, some of it well trampled. The cast got something from it, a cool event to make them feel alive. But now the carnival has moved on. The dead are dead, in fact.

And while a theatre has emptied, the stage of his mind is more alive than ever as he watches a flying saucer land and the aliens inside indicate they have come for him.

# Queue This Side for Hatred

Standing with a slightly flat beach ball in his hand, he remained in the spotlight but seemed unaware of where he was, what he had to do.

A voice, an announcer's voice, clear but with intonations in all the wrong places like so many voiceovers are, spoke down to him.

'There, there young man. Young, little man. There. Oh dear, now no need to cry, is there?' He looked around – he hadn't been crying. 'Mummy will be back, I'm sure. In the meantime, just get used to things here; find out what little boys may get up to. And, more importantly, what you may not. And in the meantime, curb that temper of yours, will you!'

A woman sat at a microphone on a table just beyond the edge of the spotlight that the boy hadn't noticed. She boomed at him, 'I don't like nasty boys. Boys, yes. But not nasty ones. You seem to be good, but deep inside you're cunning and nasty, aren't you?'

'You screwed Mervyn's book up under your table and pretended somebody else did it. Didn't you? You worked up a temper about it so we would believe you were innocent.' The boy looked, again unaware that he'd done that.

'You're wasting my time. You're wasting everybody's time. Who do you think you are? You seem to hate other people, I find it extraordinary. What's wrong with you, you have everything you could possibly want.'

The sharp thwack of hand on bare knee caused an instant sharp intake of breath; he determined not to show the effects any further than that.

'You should be thoroughly ashamed of yourself. Don't start whimpering, spare us that. Be a man. Accept it, don't show it. Real men get angry inside when it genuinely matters, but not over everything and they don't just lash out at people in hatred and disgust. Next time, it'll be the palm of your hand with a ruler. Now stand in the line outside my room.'

A person – could have been man or woman - appeared in a white coat and tiny glasses and exchanged the ball for a folder, patting his head as she did so. The announcer resumed speaking from above, 'Sit, sit down. We've considered your application, carefully. You have been accepted, subject to a medical test, of course.'

The young man sat on the floor as there was no furniture. 'Liberal Arts, that's what you want to study? Very fashionable. Very useless. But still, it's your funeral. The panel was a little concerned at your small circle of friends, a thin reference from your school and thousands of recorded instances of loathing of others and some intolerance. We think the arts may help you.'

The young man looked around, trying to see beyond the circle of light. The voice continued, 'Oh, no it won't be your funeral. You've missed out on conscription, it stopped just in time. Instead you will be free to experiment with all those drugs and shit and fool around with girls. Or boys. Or animals, I don't care.'

'There is some student protest stuff around, but it won't concern you as you'll be too preoccupied with your head up your own arse. You will find that you have to do things you don't like, well, tough! Now stand in the queue outside dining room C3...'

As he struggled to his feet, a girl joined him, long hair to her shoulders. She smiled and caressed him and he responded warmly, before a man a little older joined them, smiling in a polite, not over friendly way, showing no teeth.

'I liked your essay. I liked your fiction of the queues for overflowing toilets and for grease-swum burgers at what was some kind of festival of strangeness, music and noise, a grotesque theme park. I liked your rejection of the orthodox, which is interesting for a person who is so conditioned by his habits. You'll probably end up being a politician and finding you have to toe the line, toe the line, toe the line ...'

He turned back to the girl who was starting to undress, but the man put out his hand, 'No, not now. She'll keep. You have a career to think of, Get in the queue outside.'

The man retrieved the folder and left the circle, followed by the girl who looked back sadly at him. He made a step in her direction but she shook her head.

The door crashed open to admit a trolley on wheels being pushed by a large, getting-on-a-bit woman, long greasy salt and pepper hair cascading over her shoulders. The girl and the man slipped away through the door.

'Here you are; shopping is your least favourite thing,' the old woman shrieked. 'You hate spending money, yet you support capitalist retailism. You hate spending any money till it is beyond necessary yet you want commerce to succeed. You are a strange mixture. You need clothes and food. Go shop.'

She turned to go as he was still thinking about the girl who'd started to take off her clothes. As he put one hand on the trolley the woman raised her voice to a higher shriek level, 'Oh there's a queue to get into this shop; it's very popular, trendy, in fact. And there is a queue to get out, of course. You once told your wife that you hate to queue as the ultimate hatred because other people in their stupidity are wasting your precious life and time with their agendas. Is that so?'

107

The announcer echoed from above, the voice tightening a little as if helium had been added or an old fashioned tape had been speeded up. 'Your application to represent us on the council has been accepted, congratulations. There are things expected of you, like witty speeches and clever answers to trick questions. But it's all good training for a career in politics. You don't have to like the voters to be elected anymore than a teacher has to like children or a doctor has to like lunatics. Now get into the queue for training for training, and a meeting about a meeting ...'

As he turned, rather confused, the girl returned to his circle from the other side, behind him with the flat beach ball. The older woman positioned herself and the trolley close by. 'Your daughter, well, our daughter. She hardly sees you, you're working so long. Oh I know, I know. A career to be made. People to see. Plots to ferment. A world of wrongs to put right. I know. Anger management courses to do. Hatreds to come to terms with. But even so, what do you want us to do? Queue to make an appointment to see you?'

The door swung back, revealing an almost totally bald man in a white coat, holding a clipboard. 'Contents of your wallet – four pound notes, two membership cards, one out of date, some foreign money – German, I think. A poem written in what they tell me is Dutch. And some French letters. Quite the internationalist, aren't you?'

The girl walked slowly to the table, just beyond the spotlight circle. She playfully picked up the microphone. 'Remember when you sit and write the story of our relationship that I was happy to be the subject of it, that you just stared at me, you watched every move to write with. And when we made love, you used to try and make it better for me and it took so long I was screaming ... but you didn't write that down, did you? It was all about you.'

108

The subject in the spotlight opened his mouth to protest as the clipboard-holding doctor came closer. 'Going to speak? Don't bother. Your twenty eight days of assessment are over. We know what's wrong with you. Hatred. You hate everybody, including yourself, probably. No, don't interrupt me – '

He wasn't.

'You've been queuing for the wrong toilet all your life and now you're old, it's too late. I want you to join the lengthy queue for medication to take home, then a short one for a final scan, then one for biometric records to be updated and finally the very long queue to leave us.'

As the white coat left the spotlight, the man asked his back, 'And where do I queue to get into next?'

There was a shocked pause. He had not only spoken, he had asked a question! The girl, woman and doctor approached him as if to an alien species never before seen. The woman laughed aloud, 'Oh there's no queue where you're going next; your place is ready and waiting.'

With his hand he shielded his eyes to look out into the darkness beyond. And waited.

The spotlight dimmed and the houselights came on. The Director walked towards the stage. 'Thanks, guys. Good in parts, but I'm afraid it's a bit abstract, people won't know what's going on, it really can't be fully effective, too generalised, I mean what is his problem really? We can't get into any involvement with him, which is after all an essential for a successful drama, you know?'

The performers burst into applause and smiled warmly with genuine affection at their Director.

The man who had played the central character shut his eyes for a moment with a smile still on his lips. It had been quite an effort.

The girl who played his wife said to his imaginary children, 'I think he's gone. After the years of impatience and anger and hatred, he died with a smile on his lips. Amazing.'

The critic stood up, fumbled for his coat, his fedora and his tatty camel scarf his late mother had given him for Christmas when he was in school, and with an embarrassed smile left everyone to it.

He had a review to write. A life outside to live.

# Stop That Laughing

The office of the head of some sort of administration. Could be a prison, a school, a training centre for the delinquent, an asylum or some place where people are sent against their will.

The big cheese was Mr Whalley. He loved it there. He filed his thumbnail slowly, meticulously. A tall, painfully thin man in a black suit, his grey hair plastered perfectly over his skull. His face a travesty of warmth and affection. Dickens would have made much of this man.

His black-rimmed glasses were close to his eyes. He neither sweated nor appeared flustered. However, Mr Whalley could, and frequently did, switch into a violent, frenetic impatience with others and situations.

Mr Whalley also had a habit of drawing his breath in through his teeth in a rigidly fixed jaw. His love of routine was legendary; clocks hung everywhere.

His secretary reported from a distant room that Mrs White was unwell and had gone home. Whalley, irritated, snapped down the line to the unfortunate underling, 'I'll deal with it'.

Suddenly an electronic device went off which triggered the footsteps of the many and voices raised in patches discussing absolute mindless drivel until Whalley's voice barked for silence. His office was at the foot of the staircase and at the confluence of several corridors that spanned the complex. A good position for him.

Once silence had been restored, Whalley pushed smartly through three doors to the secretary where he treated her to a lecture about moral backbones, the futility of protest for the sake of it, the laziness of certain people and the fact that he, Whalley, wouldn't put up with it.

The secretary managed to get a word in edgeways to the effect that Mrs Moxon had asked him to attend Room 14 where there was a 'problem with a window' which turned out to be that somebody had tried to hurl somebody else through it.

Whalley looked at his watch, checked it against her clock and told her, 'I can't be at Room 14 till five past ten; she'll have to deal with it.'

'Oh and the other thing, Mr Whalley, we had another of those calls. You know…' Whalley didn't or wouldn't know. 'A bomb threat.'

'Ignore it, it's a hoax', he snapped as he marched back to his room.

Another door in that room opened with a little knock. 'You're Assistant Duty today, are you?' He looked at the woman with loathing as she stood in the doorway; she was young and too well-dressed. Over smart.

'Yes, I am, Mr Whalley. Looking forward to it.'

'An unfortunate day for you to pick.'

'Pick?' she blurted out before getting a grip. 'How so, Mr Whalley?'

'We have the alleged protest demonstration today, have you forgotten?

'No, no, of course not,' she stammered as the secretary burst in – 'Admin 4 want instructions if a demonstration penetrates the boundary, Mr Whalley.'

112

'Shoot them,' he roared. He paused as the assistant stood in horrified silence. 'Only joking,' he sneered in a manner that indicated a somewhat strangulated sense of humour.

'Make it your task today to find me the ringleaders. You understand. We're not changing a thing for any of them. If I have the vermin who're driving others on, I can deal with them all.

With a nod the assistant left for the secretary's room only to return before Whalley had even sat down, 'Fire alarm in Block One, set off unofficially.'

With a sucking of teeth, Whalley ordered her to go over to Block One, find him some heads to decapitate before looking at his paperwork again.

Seconds later the electronic device signalled more footsteps and voices, this time with a lot of things to chatter about as Block One's incident became common knowledge. Whalley stood at his door and shrieked orders for silence into the melee as his way of aiding his staff.

His secretary handed him a tiny coffee cup and saucer as his assistant came in without preamble, 'Mr Whalley, some dissidents in the exercise yard, a bit of a fuss.' She sipped from a large, vulgar mug which made Whalley's lip curl in disgust.

'We'll employ the Conway Mulligan Procedure. Before your time, Mulligan … He isolated troublemakers and terrorised each one so much that they shopped the others and were told they'd been shopped by others so they, like thieves, fell out.'

Shouting had the nerve to come from outside into the building, clearly a playground-like unrest and chanting of 'fight, fight' dominated. This sent the duty assistant out to investigate, her heart in her mouth.

A knock at his door produced a barked 'come' from Whalley and in came a middle-aged, weary but anxious member of staff, whose name Whalley couldn't immediately recall. 'Sorry, Mr Whalley, a number of them say they're going on strike. Refusing to work, refusing to even come in.'

He nodded, looked the man up and down, thinking what a fool he was unable to sort out a few pieces of low-life. He barked into his phone, 'ring the police.'

She replied, 'already done, Mr Whalley. They say they're busy with some disturbances at the park and in the town centre.'

Slamming the phone down he ordered the bringer of bad news to get out there and tell them Mr Whalley is on his way. 'Put the fear of God into them.'

The duty assistant returned to report seeing Kelly beating one of them round the head. Whalley looked confused, 'So?'

'They're human beings.'

Whalley smiled, 'Don't worry, if there is any brain damage, nobody will notice the difference.' It was another joke.

'Can't we give them anything? Just a little victory so they –'

'So they take a mile. No, the victory can only be ours. I keep asking for examples, find a few – anybody will do – and the rest will follow into submission. That's what they are, sheep.'

The electronic device launched more noise and movement. There was the sound of actual fighting. Whalley filed his nails and sat sucking his teeth in.

Gradually, it subsided, leaving calm. The duty assistant returned with a 'seems OK now, Mr Whalley, all calm. Some of the staff are saying that they managed it, you didn't need to get ready to come out.'

What they'd actually said was that Whalley was conspicuous by his absence. She opened the door and ushered in a ringleader, an inmate. 'Come in, you, come and face Mr Whalley. You're the ringleader, I believe.'

The ringleader was young, like most of the denizens of this institution, but not so young he was a child. He was a nasty piece of work, Whalley concluded from a long, slow look up and down.

'Wipe that smile off your face!' The scapegoat was not smiling. 'Led a riot did you? Stop that grinning. How dare you lead a strike! Stop that laughing.'

The unfortunate young man shook his head as he was not laughing and received a clout across the side of his head for it. He staggered.

Whalley launched into a regularly rehearsed speech about moral fibre and courage, gutless people, no help to anyone, spongers and loafers and lack of loyalty and respect.

He finished by sharing an incident he'd seen last week, 'I saw Lambert being beaten up by a bunch of you, your friends. Poor mongrel that he is, do you know what you did to help him when he was outnumbered – you stood by and held his glasses for him while he was pulped!'

The duty assistant finally decided enough was more than enough. 'Mr Whalley, I must protest.'

'You as well! You're on the wrong side. What of gratitude, a last chance that we offer people here, hey? And you....' She was beyond his contempt.

'Everything is back to normal, now.'

'Good. Have this wretch chained up for a day without food, attach his thumbs to a screw and remove his hair, one strand at a time.' The inmate was afraid now. Surely, it wasn't possible in this day and age...?

'If it's back to normal now, it's only on the surface,' she said, ignoring what was presumably yet another 'joke'. They will burst out again and next time you may not be able to simply impose order.'

The woman assistant and the unfortunate scapegoat waited for Whalley to respond. He opened a drawer, sat at his desk and varnished a single thumb nail, carefully.

'When I was a boy, I resented the way we were served the same food on the same day every week. Potatoes on Friday, meat on Sundays and an egg on a Wednesday, if we had any. I didn't like it and told my loving mother so. I was a tearaway...'

The assistant and youth watched Whalley, fascinated. 'Now, my wife serves the same meals throughout each week, each day is coloured on our calendar. Today is a dark green day with sausages and a baked potato. You see, there is merit in order and discipline. The last working day of the month is Purple Day, payday.'

The assistant was vitriolic, 'I suppose you colour code the nights too, do you, with once in a blue moon a closeness day.'

With that, she grabbed the scapegoat by the sleeve and removed them both from Whalley's office.

'Why didn't you get any help from some of us who work here but actually care about you?' she demanded of him.

'We tried, but Mr Whalley came round and told us there wasn't a single member of staff cared if we hanged or drowned.'

'When was this?'

'Last week, when we held our first meeting outside about striking.'

'He lied. You see, he believes in discipline as a means to virtue in its own right. It's an old-fashioned concept, but has a lot of fans at present in high places. He and his supporters genuinely believe they're doing their best for you, that the choices you make are the wrong ones because you don't care about humanity as they believe they do.'

The lad said nothing.

'You don't know what I'm talking about, do you?' He shook his head dubiously.

'Well, can't you see that we're all prisoners here, in effect? But, your hopes and dreams can't join forces with mine and mine can't with Whalley's. It's tragic but true. So we go on wasting energy and time while all individuality is squeezed out of all of us.

Whalley opened his door, instant facial disgust revealing how he felt about the pair outside his office and almost spat at the assistant, 'I will not see you hit him; I will only see him attacking you and getting in the way of your self defensive fist. Without us trying to maintain some standards, there will soon be none at all. There will be anarchy. Believe me, I know.'

The secretary popped her head into the corridor, 'Excuse me, Mr Whalley, call from the police. They say the bomb threat is credible. They want us to evacuate at once.'

Whalley scoffed. 'What, and allow anarchy back into my institutions? No, I tell you it's a hoax. An attempt to disrupt our lives.'

As the electronic device sounded yet again, there was no movement at all. Only the thunder and the flying debris from the small bomb that had been left in a rucksack in the changing rooms.

Screams, breaking glass and in the distance emergency sirens mingled with the pungent dust that swiftly enveloped the corridors and crept up the central staircase.

Whalley coughed and spluttered but still heard the inmate tell him, 'they'll blame extremist terrorists for this one, Mr Whalley, nobody else. I see you're not laughing now.

# Breath-Play

She made the call. Specialist Cleaning and Removals (SCR) at her service day and night to take care of potentially sticky, dangerous or stupid situations. At a price. They knew what they were doing.

As did she. It was a modern day version of Sweeney Todd, really, the business operation she ran. Men arrived, paid her, did something with and to her for a few moments and some left in horizontal canvass bags at night.

And a mere observer might immediately assume she was probably some sort of psychopath. A quite attractive psychopath with sometimes red, often white blonde hair, bob-cut and always sporting heavy makeup. But a psycho, nonetheless.

However, with a target of 20 men a day to service, each parting with a minimum of £100 for thirty minutes, tops, she could just meet her financial commitments, so it was hardly surprising she was occasionally a bit tense and jittery.

The guy who owned the doss house room she rented had to be paid; it was imperative to reimburse the Russian who'd got her into this business and set her up with a few clients to get started. She'd never met him, only talked on the phone, though his heavy accent was quite hard going.

There were the ads to finance at the back of the local newspaper, cleverly disguised as 'company' and 'special events catered for'. She had consumables like condoms, wipes and laundry to buy. Oh and that SCR service - they certainly didn't come cheap.

She was generally popular so business was reasonably brisk most days. They'd arrive, often nervous, and while they talked before, during and after getting what they'd come for, she gathered what they were worth, what they did, what they might be carrying besides the usual credit cards and a bit of cash.

She knew it wouldn't last forever, but she'd learned to sort out the lonely ones and the married ones with wives who were clueless about what they were up to. The men who had no time for regular female commitment while focused on well-paid careers were her favourites.

If a man disappeared, too bad. For ages it would go unreported and even then, he'd frequently covered his tracks. Even if there was a trace of his turning up at her door, she had a good story about how he'd rushed off in a panic of remorse and she didn't know where he'd gone.

She'd do one or two of these vanishing specials a week, according to who turned up, before she cooled it a long time. A spate of localised male disappearances would excite too much law and media interest.

A few of the men became temporary regulars so she learned more about them than the one-offs. Walk-ins or regulars, she always gave them a good seeing to before she saw them off. She liked to think they appreciated it as they choked and gasped desperately for breath in the condom she'd pulled over their heads, their wrists desperately yanking at the super strength cuffs clamping them to the bed frame.

It was an option on her menu – 'condom breath-play' – but she had yet to receive an actual request for it. That surprised her because most of the guys were drawn to the perverted, the sordid and the downright weird.

Those who got breath-play didn't find it playful – it was their seventy second ticket to the life beyond. Their eyes filled with panic as their mouths sucked in the stretched rubber, lungs empty. She always watched, fascinated, but somewhat disappointed when it was over.

The SCR service entered her room in the small hours, a team of six, highly specialised and with his or own individual role in the swift exercise – about ten minutes from start to finish she'd reckoned the only time she'd stayed to watch at the beginning of her business.

One stood guard in the street, pretending to fix the 'stalled' van with black windows, logo and company name accompanied by several fake mobile numbers and a phony web address on the sides.

A second moved silently between the front door and the room upstairs, checking for noises and nosy people. A black gloved hand stayed in the dark coat pocket while its partner clenched and unclenched in silent menace.

Two carried in cleaning kits that looked at home in any office setting at night. Everything had a wipe, every surface, item, wall and doors. Even her fingerprints were regularly expunged.

The other two checked the corpse for identity-revealing materials – she'd already removed them. The cards from his wallet and perhaps his work ID were piled on the table. They took them to be credited against her monthly charges.

The corpse was swiftly stuffed into the long canvass bag and carried out, his rubber sheathed head disappearing under the zip.

They were absolute experts and specialists in their work, just as she was in what she did. She needed them, they needed discerning customers. It was a mutually convenient business arrangement.

Nobody talked, nor passed comment on her handiwork. They were paid well to get the dead men out and away. Others would process their mortal remains back at the stores, behind the shopping centre, in a unit that showed no light; emitted neither smells nor sounds.

That a man's fingers would be removed, or his head cut off and the teeth extracted, his body dissolved in the vat of pungent chemicals the designation of which excited nobody's curiosity or interred in a freshly dug hole in the cemetery ahead of a legal burial the next day was of no concern to the workers.

Some had been trained in the Russian military, a few were Ukrainians, a Serb and some were in Chinese gangs or with the Sicilians; others had escaped wars, atrocities and regimes from all over the world from Syria to North Korea. None asked questions, they raised no eyebrows, just took their payments.

She'd been told when she first made contact with the company at the advice of the Russian who set her up that one of the cleaners' regular customers required more than the usual disposal of inconvenient corpses.

Specialist Cleaning and Removals maintained good connections with some shadowy syndicates to provide personnel, so this guy's business model was to kidnap rich people, keep them in shit for days before sending a video to their families and promising their safe return for shed loads of crypto-currency.

His particular twist was that the victims he finally returned had been dead since a few minutes after they'd recorded their begging video for their loved ones to get hopeful about. What families paid through the nose for was a corpse that later post mortems confirmed had been hanged. Not on a proper gallows so the neck broke, but hoisted up perhaps over a beam and left to dangle and choke for as long as it took.

No she wasn't a psychopath, but had tendencies in that direction. Doesn't everyone, she sometimes asked herself? She also often wondered what had made her this way, was there a higher moral purpose in her way of ridding the planet of worthless male vermin?

Was she some kind of avenging angel fulfilling a divine mission? Receiving no answers, she shook off any inner thought that she was looking for redemption, theirs or hers.

Was there real pleasure in watching their final moments and knowing their end had been determined by her alone? Possibly. But more than that was the pleasure in building an enterprise and living by her own rules.

Claiming no friends, she clung to her business plan that seemed to be working. Paying into a self-employed pension scheme and meeting mortgage repayments on an apartment in Coventry that she rented to itinerant Romanian sex workers on an as-and-when basis made her daily target of men essential.

When she topped a man with resources she could sell or use, that was the bonus that made her dream feasible. She'd worked it out - at 50 she could leave it all behind, that mortgage paid off, so she'd sell it and dispose of all the trappings of this degrading work. She'd buy a decent place in leafy Essex or Hertfordshire and find some other creative outlet.

So, another eighteen years of this during which she had to keep a clear head, unlike her victims. She had that plan, like a daily catechism to recite; she was determined to stick with it.

Then her brother knocked on her door, late afternoon, final customer of her day.

He'd called himself 'Bob' for the booking but she knew as soon as she let him in that he was her brother, Simon, two years younger. A stranger for some years but now standing in the work room expecting special services.

About the same height as her, perhaps a little above average, a wiry body far stronger than it appeared. His sandy hair receding in a war he'd already lost gave him a slightly boyish aspect. Wearing a reasonably expensive suit for work in an adult world, with a broad smile on his face, he looked a likely prospect. Normally.

She noted that eyes having flicked around to take in her and the place, he relaxed a little, not sensing any particular danger.

'I'm Bob, how's it going?' he chirped, gathering smiling confidence as he noted the frame, a pair of cuffs and the rubber-sheeted bed.

'Claire,' Samantha responded, beginning to wonder if either he recognised her and was going to play along or if she was a stranger to him. Perhaps he'd been too young to remember the last time he'd seen her.

As he outlined what he fully intended to enjoy with her, he strode to the window, peered through a small gap in the curtain before checking out the toilet. Yes, he called their father to mind. This was Simon, absolutely.

She couldn't begin to provide any of those services for which he now handed her a wad of notes, offering more to dispense with the rubber.

'No, not wearing the rubber is not an option, how about some condom breath-play?' she mumbled routinely, her stock response to one she'd decided was going to gasp and choke in one. But this was her brother!

What she couldn't know was that 'Bob' was already familiar with her methods and activities. He'd done a couple of evening shifts with Specialist Cleaning and Removals – they weren't all foreigners. He'd been here before. He'd worked out that she must be making a fair amount of cash.

And Bob had plans of his own. Clearing a mortgage on a family home in Hackney he shared with his girlfriend, their two year old and her teenager from another man before they met, was merely the start.

After his stint in the army and a period of daytime working phone scams and evening shifts for SCR, he'd already branched out on his own. That high worth kidnapping and hanging the victims operation was his idea from a book he'd read when he was a teenager dreaming of wealth and fame.

He'd managed to create an identity for that sideline that SCR knew nothing about. He continued the occasional evening shifts as an ordinary worker to allay suspicion and to keep himself alive to new possibilities.

This woman, 'Claire', was one such. He admired her cool-headed approach, a good dispatch of victims, a clean disposal and money. Not too much, but enough. But it was all small beer. It could be up-scaled and operated by a number of women, or men perhaps for those with that particular taste.

Bob envisaged a franchise of her idea, run out across the nation. She evoked his admiration for her enterprise, but he needed her gone and a more pliable and compliant girl in here to act as a training model for others.

He would have to multiply the removals process twentyfold at least. He thought disposal units on the outskirts of all the cities and major towns. It wouldn't do to increase the odds on police cars stopping his vans at night, not when they were returning with a body or two. He planned some of the pick up vans to be funeral directors' collection vehicles as a variety on the cleaning company.

So, yes, Bob too had plans.

They required the removal of the key players at the top of SCR in a coup over a single night and using the first of his branch disposal units on a site near Reading he'd already paid a deposit on, in the name of Johann Klopp, a German investor.

A glance at his Rolex indicated that Bob was a busy man. She, knowing the watch was worth at least a couple of punters, swallowed while she considered what to do about him.

Still he showed no signs of recognition. Instead he provoked a row about why she wouldn't do it without protection, an accelerating argument, his voice rising in a way she hoped wouldn't be heard by the neighbours.

He strode round the room to the bedside cabinet, yanked the drawer clean out and retrieved a condom from the floor. 'Alright, sweetheart,' he snarled. 'This is what you want.'

In the spilt second it took him to close the gap to her, condom crushed in fist, she lost any illusion this was her brother. As his double-tap slaps crashed across her face she knew this was not Simon. How could she have made that silly mistake?

Gathering the strength to fight, the cunning to step back or the survival instinct to outwit him was knocked from her by an increasingly sharp succession of slaps that dizzied her and sent her sprawling on the bed, gasping for breath.

In a second he was astride her, forcing her arms under his knees that dug into her as she struggled. He sat far enough down her body to avoid her teeth or spit as she tried to score at least one point against him.

He unwrapped the sheath and with a lip-breaking, blood drawing punch to her mouth to stun her, the thing was stretched over her head and yanked down, tearing her scalp as her hair was pulled.

In those few moments of breath-play she sucked for air that wasn't there and wondered just who the hell he was. How had it come to this? What of all her plans and dreams?

Bob made the call. Specialist Cleaning and Removals (SCR) at his service day and night to sort out potentially sticky, dangerous or stupid situations. They knew what they were doing.

And so did Bob as the next phase of his business empire took shape.

# Timeslips

Cooper had another of his timeslips shortly after they told him his History department was being disbanded. If we understand the past we can shape the present to help the future. But not any more, apparently.

And he certainly understood that reorganisation of systems was a constant feature in man's history. But he thought his work was so fundamental it would be expanded rather than killed off.

Not far from the coast and his office – indeed, the offices of the regional government – he walked on what he knew was a long, long abandoned railway line. Cooper, early 30s, medium height and build, a slight stoop from years of hunching over research screens, liked to walk there as a change from looking at the sea.

And he always marvelled that people travelled in metal tubes on wheels, overground and below. He stood, resting from pushing his way through the vegetation tangles, rubbish and debris of past life. Ahead, a mutated tree stump had pushed the bridge up - the road was no longer needed.

He spoke into his monitor. 'It takes about twenty five years for a neglected structure built in the old ways to be overgrown. This line has been abandoned for less than 150 years. Yet, this growth suggests far less time.

Nobody responded to his thought; nobody on his wavelength in the department as yet. He pushed aside a strand of saltweed, felt something squelch under his foot. He'd stood on a nest of tiny, multi-coloured grang beetles – a mutation of a mutation from the dust attacks of the mid 21$^{st}$ century.

As he wiped his boot on a clump of marram grass, there was a slight trembling in the ground under him. A movement, a vibration. He reported it into the monitor and moved forward. It was growing more pronounced.

A rumbling, scraping of steel on steel was approaching. One more step and he had a foot on a hard, clean, shiny steel rail parallel with another and right angle blocks of solid wood every few units along it.

Ahead, something bright and bulky was approaching him with a large pall of what looked like … smoke! He hadn't seen smoke in his lifetime but knew from records what it was.

He also knew this was a train. Wheels drove it onward, spinning on the tracks.

He stood, fixed to the spot. The train closed the distance between them. A shrill, high-pitched whistle brought him to his immediate and innate survival sense and he jumped aside.

Cooper lay on his back, unaware of the pain in his right hand and wrist from his jump as the thing thundered past him. Rods turned the wheels, a truck filled with black rock followed the first tube followed by identical tubes with windows and heads and shoulders of people.

Then it disappeared into the curve where he'd started his walk, leaving behind evaporating smoke flumes and a vanishing smell of burning.

Copper waited - nothing but the wind - and stood, now aware of his hurt hand. He knew what he'd just seen. A timeslip into a forgotten fragment of the past.

He reported it into his device; still nobody picked up on it with any comment. He didn't doubt his mind; he'd seen and been so close to an actual long gone train he could almost have touched it. He smelt it.

That was why the vegetation was less than it should be. It was still being used. 'It was real, real as I am. It was like a shared moment in history – more than one thing going on at a place simultaneously,' he spoke his thought.

'Cooper, you're on my wavelength,' crackled a voice from the monitor.

'Fletcher? I thought you were working on inner and outer space?'

'I am. You saw a train?' There was just a hint of disbelief in the question.

'It was close – it almost crushed me, it was real. Can you do some research for me?'

After a pause, Fletcher replied, 'No, I'm busy. There is a lot of routining come in, you'd better return. I'll send a pod for you.'

'I'll finish my walk, Fletcher, but thanks.'

Cooper set off, holding his hand under his other armpit, wondering at himself turning down a pod when Fletcher had clearly been ordered to send one. They wanted him back in.

The pod he didn't want appeared moments later and stopped in front of him, leaving him no choice but to step inside.

He loved his work; the History department was so important. The lessons of the past had for too long been ignored or forgotten altogether. But now they wanted to disperse all the expertise and he himself was to go to Transitions, whatever that might be.

As the pod approached the offices it darted over what used to be shops. Cooper had looked into shops and the archaic idea that people bought and sold things for a profit. He often wondered whether to suggest they reintroduce it. Cooper was an independent thinker.

From his massive desk, Fletcher nodded to him as he entered. 'Cooper, you have a unique position in this department of being able to see both forwards and back. Don't abuse it with a lot of... er, unorthodox ideas, will you?'

Cooper decided to say nothing. He sat at his station, rubbing his sore hand. 'What did you do to your hand, Copper?' Fletcher bellowed across the area.

Shaking his head, Copper replied, 'I'll survive.'

Fletcher laughed, 'Oh yes, there's always a survivor somewhere.'

\*\*\*\*\*\*\*\*\*\*\*\*\*\*\*\*\*\*\*\*\*\*\*\*\*\*\*\*\*\*\*\*

People just accept things as they are, mused Cooper, wondering if he should share it with the colleagues. No, they knew because like him they had alternative views. What is the Now could be changed, if it didn't suit and had been in the past. This was not forever.

But it was not a view anyone outside the department could grasp. He stared out the window at the grey sea, gently heaving, restless, churning a host of rotting, disgusting forms of human created waste. From the past.

With a sigh, Cooper checked himself on the insta-health monitor. He was fine. He didn't want to do a quick mind-state check. But he did sense a restless unease. It must be his department closing soon.

He looked up and met Grimble's eyes watching him, unblinking. He never really liked Grimble, who made him feel uncomfortable. There was superiority about the middle-aged man beyond his ability level.

Cooper flipped through some routine reports to process, things found and reported from history, unexplained matters and the daily stuff they dealt with.

Reading and writing had long since been consigned to history. The machines spoke to the operators. He filed his thoughts from the train incident. A voice summarised the history of the Great Eastern Railway for his benefit.

It was of no interest, as timeslips never seemed to occur in the same period twice to him. Which was odd if more than one thing was occurring simultaneously, he thought.

As the food signal sounded he made for the feeding area passing the fat folds of Grimble's neck bent over his station and felt the same revulsion he had with the crushed grang beetles.

Fletcher hailed him again. 'I'm picking up your waves – still on a private theory, are we, Cooper?' Cooper refused to be drawn and, holding Grimble in his peripheral vision, he wondered which of the two he detested the more.

If only he could have cut them both down with something, a weapon from the past. A sword, perhaps. He was entitled to his private thoughts and if he had a worthwhile theory, Grimble and Fletcher would not stop him.

The mist cleared as he stepped aside from a pair of battling men, eyes bulging in death-struggles as they hacked at each other with maces and one with a spiked ball on a chain that he swung round at the other's face.

Nearby a small thatched cottage had sheltered the king. He wasn't the king yet, but he would be. Another day. Cooper knew they'd been soundly beaten and the final few struggles were all that remained of a day that had dawned with such hope.

His right arm ached badly from the weight of the longsword he'd wielded all day in the king's name; his hand was bleeding from the scrapes of an axe that had come perilously close to removing his limb. He'd left the sword in the neck of some poor devil stinking of sweat and the onion patch he'd hidden in before Copper found him.

Cooper was at the point of vomiting. Too much death. No, death was inevitable. There were men maimed, bleeding, howling for their mothers like babies. So many fine young men lost forever. Cooper sank down, nursing his hand.

Nearby a man he vaguely recalled was fighting off three of the enemy, until he misjudged an arcing sword and lost his entire shoulder. As he wheeled in agony, his head was almost severed by a double-bladed axe.

Night came, a relief. Cooking fires were set; men rested and patched each other up as best they could. The few with lanterns searched for lost friends. The dead would be buried in the morning, having been stripped of valuables and warm clothes.

He was invisible to them, yet he'd fought with them. He was hungry and thought of crawling near to see if there was food to be had. He didn't know which particular war this was, or the exact period – English against Scotsmen? The English Civil War?

It didn't matter. In time the stark realities of the bitter struggles would be smoothed over, summarised and mainly forgotten. The future didn't need to know all this, officially.

Yet, it did. Cooper knew that. He looked up at Grimble and Fletcher waiting for him to go to the food station to make their choices from four taps of substance, finely balanced nutritionally and washed down with enwater, a chemically-enhanced liquid that made water go further.

Cooper said, 'What do you think really happened to the survivors of the great battles in the past?'

Neither man answered for a moment. Grimble eventually offered, 'you think there are always survivors in history, don't you Cooper?'

'Oh yes, I know there are.'

****************************

After food, Cooper's screen was filled by a thin-faced woman, mean-looking with small eyes, very little hair and an unpleasant sneer.

'Cooper, come to see me in ZUB7 and explain your ideas for simultaneous activity in one place...' The screen blanked.

Once there, the floor below, the face belonged to Miller at home in a large area, no stations, no colleagues. Cooper waited while Miller looked him up and down. 'You see a chair there; sit on it,' Miller snapped.

It was a low chair, leaving Miller on hers much higher. 'Tell me your theory and then I can help you solve your problem.'

134

Cooper, very much alerted by the strangeness of Miller and her surroundings, yet realising she was in authority over him told her of the two recent timeslips, the second very quickly after the first.

'And I just wonder if certain moments, events in the past are still going on, that time is not what we think it is and occasionally we catch a glimpse of them..."

'Like a ghost?' scoffed Miller.

'Well, in a way.' Neither spoke. Then Miller smiled, 'we like your conclusions. Keep at it and do more research. Is there, for instance, the possibility that not only is the past going on but so is the future? People who will replace us in a hundred years are here now?'

Cooper thought. 'That may be a logical connection.' Miller's smile revealed unnaturally white teeth in her sallow face and Cooper suddenly didn't know if the woman was being sarcastic or genuine.

'You need to make yourself familiar with the work of Hencker, who postulated the theory that there is no future, only the past which has become the present.'

'Hencker? I'll look into him.'

Miller snapped back, 'Her. Hencker is no longer with us. You're not the first person to experience a timeslip, of course. What we are interested in is working out if we can, shall we say, how to induce one....'

She pointed at large screens on the walls, suddenly filled with images of clowns, moving, smiling, jumping, falling, scaring, being made up. 'This is my personal interest, Cooper, the ancient art of clowning. That may surprise you, but a healthy interest in something from the past is often useful and adds credibility to a career in administration.'

The short sequence ended leaving Cooper puzzling to understand what Miller was really after; something about the woman made his blood run cold. She was evil, if that was a way to describe a person, particularly as shown in the past. Cooper wasn't sure.

Miller pointed back at the screen to show Cooper a man in a striped tunic hanging upside down in what looked a medical ward. Cooper saw a pile of shoes outside and back inside a series of people lying in beds, many with their brains wired up, some open to the air.

It was a hideous, sickening experiment on living humans. Barking voices floated in, a parade ground where people were on endless roll-call till some dropped from exhaustion in the overpowering cold.

A stench hit him, a foul result of burning. And swirling at the edges of the area a line being formed at gunpoint from cattle trucks of women, children, old people, injured people, cripples, once-proud people waiting, all hope gone from their hollow eyes, their valuables stolen in front of them.

There was an escape being planned by a handful with enough energy left unbeaten out of them, but it was already doomed as they'd been discovered. Retribution was swift and violent.

Cooper clung to the only shadow in his hut. He wasn't meant to be here; he wasn't one of these people, and yet he was. A jackboot crashed down on his right hand and a voice barked at him in that language he did not know but which conveyed the loathing of the shouter all too clearly.

Swallowing, he wiped his brow and opened his eyes. Miller was staring at him. 'Just a suggestion caused by images and sound we put into you, Cooper, that's all. No timeslip. You were not there. And that's not still going on now.'

A new voice cut in, official and insistent. 'Cooper, you have been selected by the department of Life to assist the procreation program. Report to ground floor reception at once.'

This was a shock and totally unexpected. Cooper had applied more years ago than he could recall. Now they wanted him to procreate? Why?

'I shall not be doing that. I have work to do in my department.'

'Your department is closing, Cooper. Report to the ground floor at once.'

'I shall not', said Cooper, his heart beating, his breath held. Miller shook her head at him, sadly.

A sequence of a young woman with long, golden blonde hair, tied back studied him from the screens. Miller smiled, 'Cooper, take a breath of air outside. Go to the beach and we can talk. As you know, refusal of an order is not possible and it never has been.'

He opened his mouth to tell her that history was littered with people who refused to obey orders, but she vanished.

Miller snapped, still very much present, 'get on with it, Cooper. And get that hand seen to. You won't survive long in procreation if you don't pull yourself together.'

\*\*\*\*\*\*\*\*\*\*\*\*\*\*\*\*\*\*\*\*\*\*\*\*\*\*\*\*

He saw her approaching down the old steps from their building. She paused to breathe in the chilly fresh air.

They looked at each other as she came to him. 'I thought how much more agreeable it is outside. We always feel we are being watched inside, don't we?' Her voice was more musical, softer than the monitor version.

Her tunic indicated her high-rank. Almost all the senior posts were held by people identifying as women, he knew that. History had been a different story.

'My name is Ann Reeve.' He was surprised to have both the official name, Reeve, and the personal one, Ann. But then she was unusual in all sorts of ways.

'My work is related to hierarchies and acceptances so I was interested in your refusal to procreate, which you'd asked for.' When he didn't answer she talked a little of her work, asked about his, chatted about the climate, the sea, the building, the domestic blocks they slept in and a few colleagues.

For all the world it was like an old fashioned date. Cooper was smitten. He wanted to touch her face, hold her close in the wind. These were unusual feelings to him, even in his most graphic timeslips.

He wanted to tell her about his recent theory that seemed to upset so many people. He wanted to tell her everything. He wanted to look into her eyes forever.

'The individual in our world has a great deal of freedom. He or she makes choices and each one has a consequence. We are concerned to make sure those choices are the right ones for everybody. Your theory would make nonsense of how our world is structured, so it cannot be right.'

138

As they talked, they became more animated. They stood close; her eyes drawing him in, he could feel her warm, sweet breath in his face. She lay back and he went with her. Words ceased to be enough to communicate as he touched her outside, and then inside her tunic.

His right hand had a life of its own as it led him onwards on a journey he couldn't end, a road he'd never travelled before. She enabled it. This was real sex. The sex-sub sessions on offer were nothing like this; he was shaking.

An ancient instinct took over, a history repeated endlessly through time. He was moving though time; she was as one with his body.

He heard voices above them on the sand-cliff top. 'Ladies and gentlemen, roll up, see the Decadent Society Travelling Roadshow Circus....''

They were surrounded by applauding, happy people dressed as fun-seekers there to enjoy a spectacle. The man above took a double-barrelled shotgun and without looking up fired into the air. A dozen birds dropped to the ground to tumultuous applause.

A semi-circle of wagons, each sporting a grotesque display. 'Ladies and gentlemen, meet from medieval Europe, the amazing vampire bear ...' A girl pushed a stuffed bear forward on wheels but as she bowed, the bear beat her to a pulp with its fists.

On another wagon, two naked dancers were cavorting. 'From Russia, the conjoined brothers separated in an operation that went horrible wrong.' And on another, a guillotine, 'dealing with those we no longer need' and 'the blood is entirely real, supplied from the Hospital Commission.'

The crowds grew thicker, their enjoyment mounted as more people came to gawp. 'The carnival of the wind, my friends...' set off a cutting breeze which brought a fresh tableau of two men in black uniforms pumping bellows into the mouth of a thin man staked out on an insect mound of soil.

The slap of tent flaps drew his eyes - each tent was stuffed with grotesque exhibits from a parade in hell, if there was such a place. The Master of Ceremonies raised his hand, shouting, 'ladies and gentlemen, the secret of our success is to play short shows which leave you wanting more...'

As he bowed, he missed his footing and fell headlong, landing on Cooper's right hand, which was crushed and bruised.

He rolled off Ann, satiated. He looked at her. She had not gained anything, so, remembering his sex-sub sessions, he asked if he could help her. She shook her head, started to dress, 'No, you've done what you had to.

She continued, 'Report to me in KRAS90 tomorrow.' She was official, brisk. The electronic reminder from the building told them the shift was over. As she walked back, he said, desperately, 'can I see you again, Ann, to make it better?'

'Report as I told you. There is always a survivor, but it may not be you.'

***************************

The next day Cooper attracted a degree of unspoken attention by loitering in the reception area doing little but stare ahead. Cleep made himself evident in Cooper's sightline, demanding attention.

'Cooper,' smiled Cleep, patting down a brittle and wiry tuft of curly hair, 'I have been working on education – that moment when a tiny mind sees the light ..."

Cleep was an innocuous idiot and Cooper wanted to ignore this tiny man who had a habit of clinging on to somebody for hours at a time. True to form, Cleep was persistent with his raised brows, his twisted face and mouth, his standing too close to Cooper. 'I'm working on time, Cleep, time.' Cooper's face revealed nothing.

Cleep unexpectedly lost interest and moved away. Cooper was still thinking back to Ann and the beach when a voice from a screen ordered him to KRAS90.

The lift didn't move but the doors had shut on him. He wasn't afraid, but concerned. There was a panic, rising from deep inside him like bile. He'd studied panic attacks in history and was fighting it hard. There was a weight of difficult impossibility on him, crushing his chest.

He struggled to breathe. The dust swirled round him, men to his left in breathing masks, but where was his? Someone at the front of the line must know where they were going, but Cooper didn't.

They stumbled over a big heavy lump. It was a body. They turned the face to the front, cleaned the cover and saw it was the woman who was leading them. Dead. More bodies were stacked ahead, waiting in the gloom.

The dust attack was powerful and all-consuming. Cooper felt terror as a realisation that he had to escape but couldn't, gripped him. He grabbed a mask off a body and put it on but it grew arms with multi-fingered hands which slid down his throat, choking, twisting. He ripped it off and gulped air.

In a split second of absolute clarity he saw that the dust was not what was killing them. It was a poison that looked like fresh air. Man's ingenuity against his fellow man.

'I don't want to be alone, I don't want to be alone,' Cooper shrieked.

He leaped forward into space. The doors had opened. 'Get up, Cooper,' a voice commanded. He'd found KRAS90.

A large room with a single low chair embedded into the floor in the centre, one leg a fraction shorter than the others, so the occupant had to adjust the seating position constantly. The room, the space felt wrong, so he returned to the lift. There were no buttons to call it back.

He looked around, an arm on the wall to steady himself; nothing except that chair. He sat in it, glad of time to take stock of the dust and gas attack timeslip and lock his legs stiff to stop rolling to one side. Once he'd done that to a degree, he began to feel irritated he was being kept waiting. What was it, a power thing?

Then he was angry. 'Wait, Cooper, your problem will soon be solved.' It was Ann's voice, yet it wasn't. She appeared on a wall screen, smiling at him. Without instruction, he stood to approach her and was seared with a jolt of pain from a beam above.

He leaped back, rubbing his right arm that had been hit. 'Protection for a procreator,' Ann explained. 'I'm not going to hurt you,' he replied. He sat back on the chair to reinforce that he was no threat to the screen.

'Cooper, they have asked me to do more work on induced timeslips. The one in the lift was your own, from your inner mind that feels threatened by the authority of this building.'

The chair began humming, a noise from within as a mechanism started up. It spun, rendering him immobile by centripetal force. Within seconds his nausea waves multiplied and magnified.

'Cooper, you're telling yourself that your idea of simultaneous historical events has a value. We don't think it will help people to live better now. We think you need to realign your thinking to use your resources better and your skills for the greater good. Get up.'

The chair had stopped. 'Not yet,' he muttered as the chair projected him upwards and to a standing position. The floor suddenly burned hot, so he danced a crazy swirl to avoid returning to the chair and to keep his feet from the heat, desperately aware he needed to hold onto some control of this situation.

'You have researched military and criminal torture in history and in literature, Cooper. This is not it. We're not Big Brother. You will not suddenly realise you love us. No. What we want is to see if we can harness your instinctive rebellion, your thorough and imaginative research skills, your good memory and use them all to benefit society.'

He gingerly realised it was safe to sit again. His right arm throbbed. Ann entered the room in person; stood in front of him. She didn't smile, didn't frown disapproval. It was if he was an object.

However, she looked desirable, even in that mad situation he was trapped in where he was clearly the underdog.

'Come with me, Cooper.'

'Where to? To a solution to all the mystery of why can't I have whatever theory I want? Why should they tell me what to think?'

She replied, "You see Cooper, with all those attributes and individual thinking you have, that's why you were approved for procreation. You're never alone. There is always a survivor.'

******************************

Leisure time in the evenings was compulsory, of course. They had their own areas in the domestic blocks. Visitors were permitted, but were watched, naturally.

He introduced himself as Lambert. A feeble specimen, a down at mouth yes-man, a messenger of the hierarchy. He sported a white, pocked face with a rat-like expression and cold empty eyes.

Cooper took an instant dislike to him, especially when he started speaking in a whisper, sidling close to Cooper and dribbling spittle. Cooper had had enough.

So, when Lambert handed him a small grey box to 'put alongside your head to assist you to sleep,' Cooper knew it was some sort of monitor.

'They want to keep giving me visions do they, so I can call them timeslips?'

Lambert didn't know what he was talking about. 'It's from Reeve,' he offered as a sufficient explanation. 'It's from the Human Senses Department, I don't know about timeslips ...'

As a fleck of spittle hit him, Copper lost it. He grabbed the box in his right hand, Lambert under his left arm and attempted to fit the box down Lambert's throat.

144

Cooper's knuckles scraped on Lambert's teeth with a crunch as some gave way, drawing blood in the mouth and on the hand and infuriating Cooper still further.

There was a deathly hush on the floor as they watched Cooper, not a great exerciser, demonstrate a new form of physicality as he pounded Lambert till he was exhausted.

He picked Lambert up in his arms and carried him to the window, wrestled with it to open the damned thing in order to hurl the messenger out. The window didn't open and a shocked fellow resident on his floor felt he should intervene so began to attack Cooper.

Others joined in this new sport and soon a small riot was underway, overpowered by two security people who were nearly caught off guard and told them to settle, bedtime had come early.

When he went to his room, sore all over, especially his chafed right hand, Cooper spotted another small grey box on his pillow, identical to the first.

******************************

Cooper was in VM909/5, as ordered as soon as he entered the building the next morning. It was identical with KRAS90, but without Ann.

'Bladdock.' The name, slid from the lips of a square jawed head on a square body. The head tilted to the chair. Cooper sat, and wondered what they'd do about last night.

'Your problem will soon be solved,' Bladdock told him. At once a feeling of déjà-vu swept over Cooper which was reinforced by a repetition of the spinning chair game only much faster and punctuated with repeated and abrupt changes of direction.

The propulsion from the chair, the hot floor, the pain shocks into his right hand and arm – all the same, but more intense, rougher. Then Bladdock demonstrated other tricks the chair could do – rise up and turn, drop fast, push him back to a lying position, turn him over in it so he was sitting upside down.

'So, Cooper, has this been done here before in this place? Is it still going on though we can't see it? Is the future going on now?'

Cooper decided not to let Bladdock see he was upset by the chair so explained his theory at some length before she crossed to him and slapped his face so hard it clearly hurt Bladdock's hand.

'Your pioneering work has been noted and we're grateful. However, it has no further development potential; indeed, it would confuse the good people of our land.'

'Who are we? Who runs this land, Bladdock?' Bladdock grimaced a twisted mouth simulating pleasure.

This respite gave Cooper a moment to let his facial pain subside and to think of a way of distracting Bladdock and making a run for it. Bladdock had other body distortions to inflict yet, which she did with some enjoyment.

She then lowered a circular screen structure with a lid, which trapped Cooper on the chair inside a cocoon. 'Don't worry, Cooper, you won't suffocate. This construction around you will help us create more, what do you call them, timeslips?'

She explained there was a button that Cooper could press to slow or speed the chair. It was neither aversion treatment

146

nor torture, as such. The inner circle of a screen took Cooper into what he identified as part power station, part factory.

Lines of machines made what he saw were cars, 1970s' types, and despite trying to resist, Cooper was soon there in reality as a queue of people formed at the termination of the production line. He was revolving a little inside his enclosed box as the crowd jostled him.

A salesman with greasy, slicked hair stuffed into a flashy yellow and orange gaudy suit invited the first family in line to admire the sleek design, the marvellous bodywork and rich aroma of the interior while flashing a sheet of paper in their faces. The family signed and were driving off in a blink of an eye, a pall of black fumes belching from the rear.

They joined a stream of vehicles on the road outside, barely crawling, bumper to bumper. They hadn't left the yard before the salesman was repeating the patter to the couple next in line. They too signed up and drove away.

And so it continued, car after car, human beings pushing to get to the front. People were no longer listening to the sales talk; they were just signing and getting in.

Then a car drove in the gate. It was the first car he'd seen to leave, but now it was bubbled and speckled with rust, the chrome plating was red-grey sludge, a rear light was gone. It had no brakes so crashed into a wall. The man got out, bent and white – his door fell off.

As the woman emerged from her side, the door came away in her hands with the axle collapsing at that moment. The man complained to the salesman.

He shrugged, flicked the dust off his suit and muttered about small print, guarantees, pollution, traffic and poor driving. He waved him to a Complaints Unit that was bolted shut with a lengthy queue in front of it.

The anger became palpable and turned into a smell of fumes, of decay or everything that was incompatible with life. The screen around him lifted; he felt a deep sense of hopelessness, of being robbed, of missing out.

'Is this the future, the present or the past, Cooper?' Bladdock demanded. Cooper considered, shaken by the fact that despite knowing it was all simulated, he'd head dived into the timeslip and believed its reality.

For a moment, Cooper remembered the Lambert incident and wondered if he could pulp Bladdock. The woman was massive by comparison, though. He sat on the floor, then lay and started a contrived laugh.

The thing about laughter is that it's infectious to most people. It wasn't to Bladdock, but the woman came over to investigate. Cooper waited till the last minute, rolled hard to take Bladdock's legs out from under her and kept moving.

Cooper reached the console. He'd watched and knew which button to press. Bladdock was repelled by a shock. She was ordered to sit and subjected to the same treatment she'd meted out.

It didn't last long as Bladdock had a device in her tunic that nullified the system. She regained control. Cooper was back in the chair.

To describe it as revenge is to understate it. After two hours, Bladdock ordered a health scan on the comatose Cooper. All would be well after some rest.

As she walked out, Bladdock trod full weight on Cooper's outstretched right hand, pausing in triumph for a long moment to feel bones crushing beneath her bulk.

*******************************

Over the next few days, there was an air of normality about Cooper's life. They appeared to be easing up on him. He didn't understand why, but was glad of the chance for his body to recover, particularly his hand and arm.

He had a timeslip in which he was caught up with some dirty, unshaven smugglers on the coast – not far from where they were now – and a bit of treachery when it was feared one of them had told the Excisemen about the brandy and tobacco being hauled ashore at night.

There was a girl, wrapped in a shawl, her face always averted from him who had caused bitter jealousy between two of the men and it ended as a stabbing by one on the other and him being dangled on a rope in Ipswich gaol.

He had another where he and a young woman who reminded him of Ann but wasn't walked by a reedy river bank on a summer's day. She lifted her long skirt to avoid the long grass and he caught a glimpse of ankle.

They left the jalopy behind and her chaperone and walked across the stream to find a perfect green shaded area where they kissed. An eternal kiss that went on forever. He breathed her in, his soul replenished.

It took several minutes before he realised the wind had got up and it was gathering strength as their environment was swept way and the woman had become a pile of bones and fragments of clothes. The future had arrived.

It made him want to see Ann again, to touch her. So he wandered around looking for KRAS90, ignoring orders to routine work or to report anywhere. They let him wander.

It was then he entered a chamber he thought might be the one, but it wasn't. There was Fletcher, Miller, Cleep, Grimble, Lambert and Bladdock as shadows on the screens, but no Ann. Suddenly, with only those figures for company, he felt totally alone.

He had to find out who was actually in charge and talk with him or her or it. Had to.

Surrounding him was a presence that was little more than nothingness, a mere shape. Covered head. When it spoke, the blood ran cold in Cooper's veins. A soft, asexual voice that lulled yet terrified.

'You may call me Speck,' the round mouth informed him; facial skin that was visible was opaque, shell pink. Sludge from the pit of dreams and poison floating like scum on the water of damnation all at once.

'Who is in charge of this place?' Cooper demanded.

'I am. You are. Reeve is. Nobody is. We are all at once in charge as you put it. Shake hands, make peace and you will understand, your problem will be sorted.'

Suspicious but needing to get through this, Cooper held out his hand. As it touched Speck's he felt a pain shooting up his arm, which stayed with him.

'Go to the very top floor, you will see the power behind us all.'

Speck faded slowly, but Cooper needed to get away. He was allowed to enter a lift and wait for it to rise to the top,

150

unnumbered floor. He stepped out into the unoccupied foyer of a massive area, lit by myriad sources from above.

The enormity of the complex of adjacent interlocking screens took his breath away. He'd never seen the like of it. Here were moving images of every corner of this building, the domestic blocks, the area around including the beach.

This was evidence of a control hub that gave whoever looked at it absolute domination. He stood in the centre staring at it, slowly absorbing it.

He heard voices from guards entering the chamber and realised they were calling him angrily. He legged it. Cutting along the side of the area he reached a bank of steel drums holding a ladder snaking up to the top.

He waited three levels up, pressed against the huge screen and as the first guard neared him he grabbed the stairs above, kicked out and knocked her down into the guard behind; their weight took three down. He continued up.

Others came at him from the other side and along gantries that ran behind the screens. The problem the guards had was no experience of dealing with a runaway and they hesitated as they neared Cooper, allowing him to lash out at them, punching them in the face when near, hitting their terrified eyes, despite the pain in his hand.

When he reached the top, they kept their distance. He climbed across the front of the top screen and reached the safety of a strut separating the screen from its neighbour. He held on, wiping sweat off his head.

He looked down and to the side and realised he was moving, slowly, downward. It wasn't a strut but a cable and it was gradually sinking under his weight. The coils of a pipe were unravelling; he was descending.

It took several minutes, but he came straight down into their waiting arms, screens being blanked as he came, their cable pulled out.

In the lift going down to what he assumed would be punishment – Bladdock or Speck? – he thought, 'I fell for going up, the power must be down. At the very bottom. Either that, or there is no power at all.'

It was Speck who met them at the bottom. 'Will I live?' demanded Cooper.

Speck probably smiled. 'There is always a survivor. You have one more floor to go down, Cooper. But there is no lift'.

They dragged him to a trapdoor, flung it wide and dropped him into a void beneath the building, down towards the sea itself.

You're never alone.


*********************************

But he was alone. The floor was no longer uniform and smooth. He reached down in the gloom and found pebbles. This was cold beach, under the building. He knew there was no one power. The system ran on what had been set up in the past and would continue into an indefinite future.

He sat to rest and think. There was light in the distance. It was closing on him, shadows of people holding torches across the ground and walls.

'Cooper! Cooper' someone called. He knew them. They swarmed around him,

'Where in the name of God have you been, Peter?'

152

They led him to an edge with the actual beach some feet blow. Once down he looked up at the familiar skyline of the building on the cliff top at night. There was no building.

Before he could say anything he was stripped and redressed in a dirt white knee-length shirt – 'the penitent's shirt' he was told. They tied his hands in front of him, with rough hemp. He realised his hands were bleeding, the right hand knuckles bruised and twisted as well.

What happened next, if it was a timeslip, would be described as a rough interrogation by his peers and contemporaries terrified of being accused themselves of witchcraft and bringing a witch-finder here to sort it out.

They had a scapegoat – Peter Cooper.

There was a familiarity about the location and some of the crowd, despite hoods and shawls partly hiding faces against the wind and being recognised.

It was Miller who said, 'Peter Cooper, you are here among your fellow villagers to be examined by His Grace –.' He nodded to an empty bench.

'We are doing God's work carrying out this honourable examination in the night, the devil's hours where you feel at home. We have to know if you have communed with Satan or not.'

Cooper was thirsty, dreadfully so. He tried to lick his lips – 'he's thirsty', shouted Cleep from the crowd. 'Give him the water that God filled the earth with in his blessing.' They poured seawater down Cooper's throat till he retched.

'The charges have been put to you over and over. The witnesses have testified. Not a man or woman has spoken for you. You can chose now to seek God's mercy or go to hell.'

Fletcher read out some of the charges.' Blasphemy and heresy against the Holy Church, the making of numerous prophecies about the future times of men flying through the sky as birds and of talking to each other great distances, you have defiled the holy altar at the Church of St Bartoph the Martyr at Dunwyche and ...'

The charges went on. When Fletcher wearied, Grimble took over, followed by Lambert who reported being beaten by Cooper in a fit of madness. Cooper was charged with denying God overseeing the world, asserting there was nothing there and claiming to be alone as if he was God himself ...

Sacrilege, fornication, talking with devils, causing babies to be still-born and a dog with two heads and scaring farm animals and children were all laid on Cooper. Bladdock was called to give her expert advice as a man/woman of God and Speck was acknowledged as an authority on the death penalty.

It really was at this point that if it had been a timeslip, albeit a horrifically realistic one, he would have moved into another scene or setting and escaped. But it wasn't. This was real.

When Speck signed the document approving death as the only person present who could write, Copper demanded to know the date.

Speck looked coldly at him across the torch lit circle. 'Are you so in tune with Satan that you cannot remember the year? It is 15$^{th}$ October, the year of our Lord, 1599.' The crowd crossed themselves.

At that moment Cooper knew he was doomed. He had come from the future, but they thought he was the devil. He'd lived among them, but they didn't want his wild stories about worlds to come. He indicated the empty bench and asked, 'Where is the authority, where is His Grace?'

Bladdock kneed him over and over till he was sick, to subdue him. A silence descended on the crowd as the folk finished the pyre and stepped back to admire their handiwork

Cooper's hands were re-knotted behind him, with a cruel twist on his right hand from Bladdock. He was lashed to a stack set upright in the centre of the well-placed wood and faggots.

There was one glorious moment for Cooper to bring his knee up into Bladdock's stomach and kick her face as she rolled on the ground. It cost him some bones in his foot, but no matter.

His head was strapped to the stake, facing east, out to sea. As he saw flaming torches coming closer he caught sight of Ann as the crowd repositioned itself to avoid the smoke that would soon blow off Cooper.

'Ann! Ann Reeve!' he yelled.

She stood staring at him sadly. 'No one wants to know about the future, Ann, although the future is brighter for them…" She said nothing.

'Ann, are you with child?'

It shocked the whole crowd. Such outrage! Ann pulled her shawl closer and gave him the barest nod. 'You are not alone. There is always a survivor, Cooper. Rest in peace with that.'

Brushwood caught with a brisk crackle and flames soon licked up and he sweated and writhed against the rope in increasing agony. His bonfire lit the crowds' faces.

He did his best through the searing pain to keep his eye on Ann Reeve, smiling at the mother of his child, at the survivor who would take them all one step closer to the future he knew existed.

She watched his face turn white, then red, then black. She watched Peter Cooper shrivel into flaking white ashes, carried inland by the wind.

The crowd had long gone; the fire had died. Ann put her hand on her belly and turned towards her cottage. Yes, there is always one survivor, but what world would he or she be born into?

# Gone Away for Good

I'd like to describe my fellow inmates, as you have expressed some interest. At least, I like to think you have.

Me? What on earth was I doing in an asylum? You might well wonder. It was all over a three foot hunter skinning knife that my two sisters brought me back in among their dirty washing in a suitcase from a school trip to Lapland.

The blade had been thoughtfully engraved. 'Especially for our dear brother.' Now, that was deliberately ambiguous. Was the knife for me? Was the blade for me? We'll never know because as soon as I'd taken it to school to show my friends, there was all hell to pay.

Official-looking people and a white coat searched my bedroom and found a poem I'd composed, *'Knife, the Millionth Poem to You, My Love'* which threw them all into renewed panic.

So, to answer your query, yes, I was sent away for my own good (or was it the good of others?) to the loony bin because of a present bought for me and a poem that was no more concerning than almost anything else written in the nearly post-hippie era.

The others? Yes, well I was an innocent among them.

William was one of a number of people who approached me and spoke about his mind. It often happened in the asylum.

They called him Mad William. Strange, to call one man mad in a world of the insane.

He was one of a number of people who'd tried to jump off a carpark and failed. He'd had fourteen jobs in five minutes and talked to a sister that his parents never gave birth to.

I didn't know what to say except to advise him to put his hopes in oriental flowers growing in the grounds. He did that all summer, watching rain and sun on the petals and looking as contented as a troubled twenty-five year old man could look in the late 1960s.

For a flickering moment that summer, his madness faded away. His skin displayed fewer angry spots, his mouth generally stopped flecking and he put on a little needed weight to his bony frame.

Then one afternoon the grass was cut by four men with big, noisy mowers. The hope of reason melted slowly.

I imagined that soon he'd be one of a number of people who try to jump off a carpark. And do.

Mary was impossible to talk to. She was blown-out, on another plane, someone said. But don't worry, someone else muttered, she'll come back.

In her thirties – I'm not very confident gauging the ages of people. She always wore clothes that'd surely been borrowed, were ill-fitting and ill-matched. Her hair needed a wash, even after it had just had one.

The consensus was that she was actually gone away for good. So, therefore there was no hurry, leave her there; leave her, going tick, tick, bang inside her head.

She was a bulb, lit-out, so speak softly as you put your donation in the collection box, Roberto suggested, struggling to walk with his left leg twisted inwards. Once a month they check the lights and change all the blown bulbs.

Raymond filled the empty space round which we sat on a circle of chairs with a speech about how he'd dreamed of talking to the Baltic and dancing with the Mediterranean. The doors of the cemetery had opened and a voice had invited him, mistaking old Raymond for a wanderer.

He, probably in his sixties so prone to dreams and thoughts of death, saw a pair of copper scales, one holding a skull spouting prophesies and a dead hand in the other. He dreamed of a paralysed semi-foot marching over the Alps, kicking his head, breaking his front teeth.

There was plague, its dust and grime remains happily burning in a fire that sprung from a hole at the side of a statue of a grieving woman. The wall was dismantled brick by nerve as Raymond played dice with a black raven and was guillotined.

Then he dreamed that he was back where he'd started. I never saw him again after that session. Never really missed him and his weird dreams. Until I had one of my own.

Susan was an old woman, probably; they'd picked her up living among and from the dustbins of some horrendous metropolis. She kept a rat in her bedside cabinet, against all the rules, of course. It was fed titbits she palmed at the meal table.

I sometimes thought that the rat kept her, before putting on its white coat and going to work among us seven days a week.

One day a green van with yellow wheels arrived to collect Mandy. She'd told a few of us last night over the meal that if she didn't arrive in time we should ring the chime and start the party. We should definitely start the party without her; she was coming in a crate.

How nearly right she was. Except she was leaving in a crate. And none of us felt like a party then, anyway.

The twins, Tim and Babs were about middle age but how does anyone know that in advance? They'd been brought in together and were being treated as one, which was no stranger than anything else.

There'd been a playground incident they never tired of telling me. There was a splendid, expensive dolls' house with dolls locked in stubborn plastic-eyed silence. There was laughter dwelling like an icicle as they fell before ringing for a toy ambulance.

The twins had a sandpit that said, 'oh dear, I don't know' on the hour and they'd put the dolls on a climbing frame, dangling from their necks. There was some sort of fight, neither could recall how or who, but everything was torn apart in what became a game of far too much fun.

Other children upset themselves. Tim and Babs apparently enjoyed their day in the garden playground. But a philosopher with a clipboard took exception and so after legion tests during which it was found they had neither empathy nor reflexes in their knees, they arrived here.

Terrified of open windows, they were. Simon the mute discovered this lethal fact and dragged one or both towards one at every opportunity. The pair screeched and screamed, struggled and scratched in harmony till the window was shut and Simon was taken away.

We were on the ground floor.

They were at their best in the communal lounge playing with toys meant for toddlers. The nurses used to tut-tut and put them away and then return to tidy up the toys.

A single light remained on all night every night in the corridor, twisting sleep more troubled than the moans of the afflicted made it. I never really learned to live with that.

Carl the Welsh boyo thought he was a guru while little, dainty ballerina Louise screamed softly from her wheelchair. Joan, aka Joan of Arc, ran from room to room looking for somebody who either wasn't there or never had been to set on fire.

Mick was local born and bred – his great granddad had helped build the asylum in the last century. He occupied a cell, a single room next to mine. Mick recited number and periodic tables by the hour. When that got too much and people reached for his throat, he switched to spouting the sides of breakfast cereal packets he'd memorised.

Giuseppe was dying on his bed and, crucified with headaches, he'd squirm and wriggle till the sheets were a tangle of sweat and phlegm. I wondered why they didn't send him to a proper hospital for treatment.

But when a man in a dark suit was seen staring at him, everyone thought measuring him, I realised it was too late. He'd soon be back in that unheard of Italian village in the sky.

One very pretty red-haired, early twenty-something nurse – Becky - was a friendly breath of fresh air delivering medication like she was Father Christmas. I dared to hope perhaps we could meet up when it was all over and I'd be able to talk about her work knowledgeably and from experience.

It was officially disapproved – a staff member getting too close to a patient. So they laid on a moment of theatre especially for me. Five orderlies and a white coat rushed in one day, grabbed her and said, 'Becky, come along now, you are not a nurse and it's time for your medication....'

I never saw her again either, but I think they moved her to the mortuary for additional training. Or perhaps they just moved her to the mortuary.

I reiterated my mantra, sometimes aloud, often in my head: I am not mad, petrified, nervous, anxious, doubtful or neurotic. I am certainly sane. One doctor told me everyone in here thinks he or she is sane. Including the staff.

They finally set me free from the madhouse somewhat unexpectedly after a long session of sodium pentothal so powerful the white coat was overcome and blabbing about how he missed his mummy.

They let me go home, reassured. Them more than me.

Neither of my sisters was home. I learned that they too had been sent away for a bit, one for good. I walked the shoreline counting stars, stones and people. When I felt a bit wobbly, I looked for the madhouse which was stored in my memory, up to my waist in the sea. Standing was too hard. It's a strong current, after all.

After a time, the place no longer seems to exist. There is no silence like the madhouse.

What happened to me? Oh, I grew out of it and became a successful, much-feted town planner. You may have seen some of my work on your travels.

# Backstory Writer

When my school peers said they wanted to be virtual performers, techies, coders, designers or something else glamorous and up-front, I knew I'd be a backstory writer.

I've always observed the quirks of their behaviour, taken notes and stored them in my brain for future use. I imagined what people did when they were somewhere else. At home; out and about. What they'd done yesterday. What they would do tomorrow.

So it was no surprise to me when I was sent to VR Universal after education for my compulsory employment training, in what used to be called an apprenticeship, I believe.

The company made multi-media reality entertainment shows, individual games, immersive worlds so realistic that many became addicted and submerged in them so long they lost the ability to retain any connection worth calling it with the everyday 'natural' world.

I was lucky. I wasn't addicted. Yes, my imagination fed ideas to the games I worked on, but it was as if I knew I needed to keep my eyes, ears and brain open to new material, or I'd dry up.

People around me in my residential zone unintentionally gave me clues for how I could present ideas to make viewers feel sympathy, irritation or sickness in no particular order. To amuse, to question, to rebel, to comply, to bully and be bullied.

But I was a bit of an oddity in other ways, too. I watched old films whenever I could access them; I read books – novels, short stories, mental textbooks, true crime, how-to guides and even once, part of a telephone directory on sale in a relics shop where I was a regular customer.

About half a year passed at VR with me assigned to a range of aptitude testing jobs; I performed abysmally at the lot. One of the managers, RL, was convinced I did it deliberately. My motive was never declared, I was just awkward.

The VR world had developed so far that most people thought the algorithms could and would create everything needed for immersive reality. It was only that I came up with a few ideas based on actual living people outside the company, ideas that were original enough to be in demand.

As a last resort, on my final assessment I was sent to the almost forgotten corner of the original VR Universal buildings – from when it was VR National before it became VR Global, much less VR Universal.

It was the Backstory Department and I was pushed in there to see if I could be a writer; to see if I had a future, really.

RL lead me into an office straight out of one of the old historical landscapes we used to sell, where some dysfunctional private detective would be approached by a helpless damsel in distress out of options and he or she would solve the mystery of why her no-good man had wound up in the sewer system.

Piles of old books and papers, magazines that were no longer made and so much dust a sensible person would wear a mask to enter. On my first visit, in the darkest alcove I thought one of the writers had actually died at his desk and simply rotted. But it was a desk used as a coat rack and general dump.

They were a team of three oldies; I was the fourth. When I asked they told me all the women had been promoted out of backstories decades back; I was the first female they'd seen in years, and they were very pleased to see me.

Those oldies remembered that young people used to learn at the desks of older people – they'd do dogsbody research, fetch and carry, make tea and be the butts of numerous jokes and banter.

Therefore, I was welcomed. They all thought I was too young to contribute either experience or a maturity to creating character backstories in the new range of psychological games being developed but I'd make them all feel better about being alive.

RL, short and carrying too much weight to be fully healthy, his lip curled and a pained expression creasing his middle-aged, weathered face, pushed into the suite of two rooms as if entering the seventh circle of hell. Work paused, if work it was.

A very old man playing an early form of Solitaire on an archaic desktop computer looked up; a second paused while making a house of cards with battered old books while the third stopped delving around in the sink and shelf area to find something to eat that wasn't too mouldy.

Having scanned the three men up and down, twice each, RL informed them who I was, with obviously no idea who they were as individuals. He pointed to a desk by the door. That was mine, obviously. The fact that it was heavily laden with somebody else's possessions and work pads was of no concern.

'Who does all this vomit belong to?' RL barked at the room.

'Old Simeon. He sadly passed away last year.'

'More like the year before last, I'd say.'

'Actually, in my diary, it says that old Simeon called it a day five years ago.'

The team, ignoring RL's self-appointed majesty engaged in a lively discussion about when the occupant of the desk had last used it. Then they ignored RL's rising irritation of a red face and flying spittle.

'Clear it, get yourself on the system and start work. Create some backstories we can work with and you have a future with VR Universal. Throw this opportunity away, and you'll be on janitorial robot support services the rest of your days.'

And RL was at the door, visibly relieved to be leaving. 'How long is it since Health, Safety and Enforcement were down here?'

As if in a well-rehearsed comedy routine the trio started a pantomime of old person ignorance and dumb foolery. 'Health?' 'Safety? 'I've heard of that. What is it?'

RL stared back at them, unamused and biting his tongue, while a few drops of patience slowly regrouped in his body.

'Get it tidied up, all of you. I will be back to check.'

They were a friendly bunch, been together for years and years and kept repeating how much they loved having a fairly young person among them.

'It means real backstories may have a future after all!'

'Unless this young lady is an artificial intelligent creation, let's see.' The doddery old man, I later learned was Freddie, clutched the desk and approached me, his eyes bright and mouth open. He grabbed me by the breast nearest to him and squeezed.

166

My yelp made them all laugh and the old man came closer to check my backside was flesh and bone. Such behaviour I'd read about. Not only was it illegal, it had fallen out of fashion, I thought.

The worst offenders were chemically controlled nowadays. Somehow, these old relics had escaped. They were a law unto themselves. As long as they fed in backstories to characters presented on their screens, and they broadly worked but could adapt as stories unfolded, nobody bothered the department.

Indeed, almost nobody in the company had any idea they existed. They were secure for life, forgotten and as nobody could be sacked as in the old days, there they were. And I was now among them.

Soon enough I realised that if I kept beyond the reach of their bony hands, their leering eyes, often filthy jokes and the occasional smell that poured off Freddie and Charley, (or was it Freddie and Leroy?) in need of a shower, I was fine.

In fact I was impressed with their work. On their screens, characters became rounded, credible, sustainable and believable through their backstories.

RL had informed me that 'it would be a walk in the park for me to write backstories and there were presumably some guidance instructions somewhere among the junk in the place.'

It was his idea of a joke as the newest piece of simulation was about a walk in a park that included uneven ground, dark holes, vegetation with a life of its own, buildings, stairs that led nowhere and people who could have staged a horror show before enjoying an hour on a psychiatrist's couch.

A number of frameworks, advice and top tips that had survived from the early days of the Backstory Writers department were indeed hidden among the detritus. Then, the staff had been engaged on writing to order, really. Others would enact the stories before they were all envisioned by graphics programs.

Rags to riches; riches to rags: man in a hole gets out; the Icarus one - a rise before a fall; the Cinderella tale - rise, fall and rise again, or the Oedipus warning of fall, rise and fall again.

If all stories were one of those, which I doubted, I came up with my own version – woman in rags falls in a hole; a small rise and finally a deeper fall in even more rags.

A neat three acts. Beginning, middle and end. Perfect.

Then I found a copy of Freytag's Triangle principle for the writing of stories.

Things going along nicely on the level, some conflict and rising action to a climax, then some falling action into a resolution back on the level it started. That might do me. With just that added twist that the finishing point should be lower in a pit than the starting one.

One of my predecessors had scribbled on one document, 'Am I eternally to be the brushstroke in someone else's painting?'

When I mentioned out loud to my fellow toilers that I liked it as an expression, they remembered that they periodically invented a range of such truths that they employed to keep themselves sane when they realised that backstories would be the story of their lives till they passed on.

It wasn't just Simeon who'd coined a few; Freddie had come up with, 'am I the semi-quaver in someone else's opera?' and Leroy had first minted 'am I a rice grain in someone else's curry?' Charley had never thought of any, but enjoyed the ones that others created.

Over the next few days, one man would suddenly shout out another they'd either dreamed up or recalled. 'Am I a tyre valve in someone else's limousine?' Everyone duly chuckled their appreciation.

RL was true to his word and returned several times, always at a moment when at least two of them were not heads down at their screens. Always at a moment when the interference of a senior functionary was unwelcome.

Ostensibly RL was there to tell me that my writing was poor, I'd confused a couple of older people in a scene in a home with three rocking chairs that swung only when unoccupied and I'd failed to give a backstory to the cousin of the heroine who was adrift in a quagmire.

It was only true in the sense that I hadn't quite completed the necessary backstories. It wasn't that I'd neglected my work. RL became more aggressive and turned much of his ire on the team, who nodded, sighed, shook their heads or tut-tutted in tune with whatever they deemed RL wanted.

'There're going to be changes round here. This area is wasted space. You should all have been converted to a writing program years ago and this will make a fun area for staff recreation.' This was said as he crashed about the restricted space, dislodging piles of paper, setting off a dust cloud that almost obscured us from his view.

It was one of the quirks of the system that despite so much automation and smart this and that's everywhere, it had been decided in a strangely retro policy that some actual presence at work was healthier, a bit of physical activity and social interaction with others would be beneficial.

'This will happen soon.' Ominous, but not too serious yet. The three oldies had been threatened years ago and were still there. 'Am I a stitch in someone else's liver operation?' asked Leroy after RL had left, coughing.

My shoulders tensed; the team looked relaxed. I'd not been there long enough to be ready to be moved on already. I was enjoying the freedom, the anarchy of it along with real inventions and ideas.

A succession of officials took to visiting the department over several days. Some delved around in the ancient material; others simply checked out the temperatures, smells and heights of my three colleagues.

Simeon had also left me advice to draw on actual life, my own if possible - take an existing story, change names, dates, setting, add some relevant fabrication and there would be the ideal backstory.

Freddie had apparently written on the notes about Simeon, 'The Mark of Cain' would be good for him, on account of the huge chip he had on his shoulder.

When Simeon had looked up what a mixed metaphor was he thought that was a good example and that backstory had appeared in a game.

Secondly, I read I should write in the first or third persons; don't mix them up. Write in a steam of consciousness like a monologue but remember the audience/readers. Write quickly without pause; write slowly, taking lots of breaks.

Write only about what you know. Write only about what you don't know. Do/don't write half what you know and half what you don't.

Polish as you go. Revise only when the first draft is done. Don't be distracted. Play some music. Work in silence to hear your heart pounding. Work alone. Sit in a crowded place to stimulate the creative juices. Find a trusted mentor to bounce ideas from. Keep everything secret till its' complete.

Another sheet warned me that some stories – back and front – are circular and that was fine, as many punters liked the idea of starting again in the hope of a different outcome. Or the same if they were particularly sadistic or autistic.

Under yet more junk on my desk, I discovered a laminated A4 sheet of pink paper on which was printed instructions about how to work SMART - be Specific, do Measurable work, give yourself Attainable targets that are Relevant and keep yourself Time-bound.

Right, got it. Now I didn't need to worry about delving for the truth behind my backstories, I simply had to be SMART. I swept it to the floor. For goodness' sake.

It landed upside down beside me. Glancing down I saw that other rules were on the back, so I picked it up with a sigh and gave them some thought.

Being Effective:
1. Be proactive, tell yourself you are in charge.
2. Begin with the end in mind, make a plan.
3. First things first, difference between important and urgent.
4. Think win-win.
5. First understand; then be understood.
6. Synergise – teams achieve bigger goals.
7. Take care of yourself.

Blimey! If I followed all the advice, instructions and rules, I'd a) never start and b) never finish. So I needed to do it my way. As I'd done all my life. And that's why I'm a girl in rags in a hole with no prospect of getting out or of wearing anything except more rags.

Well, if that narrative had not been used recently, it was a good one. Every game needed some down-and-outs, expendable people of low self-esteem.

Contradictory advice? That just confirmed that advice was a variable feast to be taken or left. If anything, it supported my increasing conviction that I was doing my own thing well, and I preferred it to other options.

Our instructions to pack up and move out of the offices came via messaging the next day. Apart from a little discussion about the senses of humours that senior people may or may not be displaying, none of us did a thing to comply.

So they sent down a handful of security bots, each programmed to give out instructions and to move on only when the person being instructed actually, physically moved in obedience.

After twenty minutes of each of us being shouted at by the bots and told what to do repeatedly, I got up to stretch my legs and the bot facing me stopped and moved away, reporting success.

The others cottoned on and soon we were rid of them and got on with our daily work. Freddie wrote in some obedience bots as part of the backstory he had already fashioned on what he imagined JL's private life would look like.

Two days later the bots were back, now upgraded to take hold of us physically. RL appeared in the doorway to reinforce the orders.

We allowed ourselves to be moved, and started packing up – by moving stuff around a bit.

'Two days and you'll be out of here,' RL stated as fact.

Our next move, after discussion and the rhetorical question - 'am I a pubic hair on someone else's privates?' – we dismantled part of the stud wall partition leading to the corridor to give us a new entrance to the suite. We then blocked up our main doorway from within by moving as many desks and files as we could manage.

The argument was that the system recognised the door into our area; not a new unofficial entrance. So we could come and go at will.

And so it proved. Bots were piled up outside the blocked door awaiting heavy removal equipment, while we just came and went through our new gap as normal. Beautiful. Crisis averted.

The work now reached a point where some serious psychological backstories were needed. I had to find a story for a woman named by someone else as Cerisse, who'd raised a child on her own and had been young and fertile during what historically was called the 1960-70s.

I adapted the backstory from a diary I'd read about a real student in that era who during the hot early summer of her final year at university, had enjoyed a weekend of freedom and madness that subsequent generations would've found incredible. I suppose she was a fantasy of my own, if truth be told, although it was probably a very male view of the girl.

She had unprotected sex eight times with five men between one Friday night and Tuesday morning.

In my version, on the Friday, Lawrence, who she'd met at Easter at a fashion exhibition, called. They'd got on well, but she'd not felt inclined to go all the way, though he'd pressed hard. Everybody did it, he argued.

His visit came about because he claimed there was a bloke he needed to see in Canterbury, right where she was and he was coming to sort out unfinished business, so could he take her out to dinner?

No harm in that and it was an agreeable meal. When it came to arriving back at the female accommodation block on campus, Cerisse felt fine inviting him in for coffee. It then seemed natural to let him make the moves and squeeze into her single bed with him.

Afterwards, she put it down to the time of her month and feeling ridiculously randy - she fancied him. And in the morning, when they stirred for a repeat performance, even with the cramped legs and bad breath of a squashed night she neither objected nor raised the question of contraception with him.

By early afternoon Lawrence was gone to sort out things promising to catch up with her again in a few weeks. Within the hour, Kevin arrived, as planned, but a couple of hours early. No matter, she was pleased to see him – lovers since her time in the school sixth form, when he was the engineer who fixed her parents' central heating, they'd grown apart recently.

He usually took precautions but this time it slipped his mind. Very soon after that, Kevin was taking his leave as he had to get back to Chelmsford for a works do that evening.

For Cerisse Saturday was disco night on campus. Students from all years, all types and of all sorts. She enjoyed herself, dancing almost continuously, drinking just enough to feel good and flirting with loads of boys.

The one who took her to bed, Tosh, she'd entertained before and he was normally careful. This time, on his narrow bed in the male accommodation block, he wasn't, especially after she whispered in his ear that he was her third that day. Nor was he careful in the quick session on Sunday morning before he went to church.

Sunday evening she joined a party of students on the bus to see a film in the city centre. She never was sure which film it was, as an assertive girl in the group had reassured them it was a great film

It was rubbish, so when they met up later with a couple of older men – Paul was a tutor at the college – she was happy to have a drink with everyone, then another just with him as his friend and most students went their own ways.

Paul drove her back to the uni halls, stopping in a wooded area that was not exactly on his route, but afforded him the chance to tell her how his wife didn't understand him and he'd always liked Cerisse.

Partly because he was older and held responsibility for welfare and equally because she wanted to show Kevin she was fully out of his influence now, Cerisse allowed Paul to have his relief and good girl that she was, never dampened his passion with mention of birth control.

Monday she spent studying and hoping that she hadn't been too silly over the past few hours. Mid evening, Wesley arrived to take her out for a dinner. He was a lad a year below her in the uni who'd often tried to chat her up and had always seemed shy and uncomplicated.

Once back in the student house his parents had bought for him to rent to mates and naked on his bed, she found out that Wesley was uncomplicated if not shy. What he wanted was simple enough.

And so it was again in the early hours of the morning. Her eighth time since Friday.

When term ended in June and Cerisse was home with her parents, she found herself crying a lot and wondering. She guessed that Lawrence was the father of the baby as he'd got to her first.

It was a good backstory – well, just a weekend in this character's life - and I enjoyed writing it up and suggesting scenes to illustrate it. I was definitely a little bit jealous, if I'm honest. Such things just wouldn't happen now.

If a girl wanted to meet a boy or man, she had to apply for one from the approved and vetted list. It was a good addition to the game they were making. Certainly my teammates raised eyebrows and made lewd comments when they read it.

'That will trigger a real life perfect shitstorm, that will,' opined Leroy.

The response from the higher levels of the authority in the company was swift and heavy-handed.

We were all called upstairs at the same time but into separate interview rooms. In mine I was ordered by the accompanying bot to sit at the single chair, very low to the floor, facing a large screen.

RL appeared after a few moments of waiting to make me feel uncomfortable. I had to crane up to see him from my ridiculous chair.

'Tell me about your backstory for the Cerisse character.'

'Well I haven't finished yet and I – '

'Tell us about the weekend you have written about. It's not a backstory, it's a piece of sensationalised fiction which takes on more significance than anything the character is doing in the present which the users are trying to work out.'

'I thought that particular moment in her backstory revealed so much about her state of mind when she was 20-years old, that –'

'Psychobabble is it? You're bringing psychobabble back?'

'Not exactly but many old ideas re-circle from time to time, as you know.'

'You're not responsible for what I know.'

During a prolonged pause I thought we were done. Besides, my stomach felt cramped from being so low down as well as the gathering pain in my neck.

'I told you that this was your last chance. You have offered us historically offensive sexual titillation which is out of keeping with the times and offers no real insights into the character. You have a little talent, of course, but you have destroyed all chances to use it to the company's development.'

I didn't know if I was supposed to respond to that. He continued, 'a good backstory writer does not make it all about himself! Or herself,' he added hastily.

'I haven't!'

'And we no longer torture people, though it's still an option. It's just that there has to be some learning done through each of life's levels however hard the codes and clues are.'

Leaving me without any hint of what RL was talking about, the screen blanked and the doors swung open admitting about twenty of the security bots, half my height when I'm standing and by themselves harmless, comical looking toys. Collectively and using their vicious pincers, they ensured no human being could resist their instructions.

I was dragged to upright and led into the reception area of the office building where I'd only ever been previously on my first day at work. There were Freddie, Leroy and Charlie, each being manipulated by his own phalanx of bots.

'What happened to you?' I shouted as I was pushed through reception.

Freddie shouted back, 'we're being retired, all of us.'

'You're going to the sewers, they told me that,' shouted Leroy, disappearing through the exit.

Charley shouted as he reached the door, 'I loved working with you. They just wanted an excuse to get rid of us.'

They were gone; I was in a corridor that led to a maze of further passageways, down a lift to the basement, even lower than our department had been. I could smell the sewers already.

Once I'd been forcibly undressed and kitted out in a janitorial uniform, RL stood in the doorway. 'There's a lot more torture in the interrogation scene, but no appetite for it today. Really, that physical deprivation and pain is old hat. Kids want something more of the mind these days.'

Walking near me, safely out of my arm's reach, RL spoke loudly, pompously, 'It'll be possible for a clever player who's worked out your mental state and collected the tokens en route through the woods to save you, to reset and start again.'

RL managed a lopsided grin. 'But really, don't you think Cerisse's short story from the 1970s is making a great backstory, about raising a daughter who becomes a backstory writer?'

I was dressed ready, but still pinioned by the bots. A door opened in front of me. Waves of putrid stench hit me like a hammer blow, my gorge rose.

'This is hell.'

About a dozen people were standing waist deep in excrement and squalor, all filthy, slime dripping from their upper bodies. Sounds of vomiting rolled from the echoing distances. My three colleagues were being ushered into the mulch from the far side, their ankles shackled by metal cuffs. They were positioned, scattered among the filthy people.

Suddenly, with no warning, a mechanism hoisted every man and woman and some of less obvious gender into the air by their ankle chains. They were hung over the pit for a moment before being dropped down till their heads were submerged.

Then they were wrenched up, paused and lowered again. Each person went in at different speeds, was held under for a few seconds or almost a minute; some were given longer than others to breathe and spit before going in again.

'It varies, you see. Players can alter this to put them in for however long they want. The only rule is that nobody can die in here,' RL informed me.

I would have given almost anything to get away. Freddie was not coping well with his dunking and Leroy was mouthing obscenities from the past after he'd cleared his mouth and nose before going down again.

'Now, in there somewhere are the five men who fathered you. Well, one of them did. Each has his own backstory. One in particular has his avatar in here while he's enjoying a very good life running VR Universal. Now for your choice.'

I was dragged to a pair of buttons. The red one on the left was labelled, 'More Hell' and its sister, green, was labelled. 'Reset.'

RL nodded approvingly. 'You can go on with more hell for them. Oh I forgot. Cerisse is in there too. More hell will give you more tokens and points which will lead to a big cash prize. Or you can press reset, lose all your points and start again.'

'What happens to everybody in there?'

'The end result is the same. But Reset gives them a longer break before being dunked in the cesspit.'

'And me?'

'Oh you bear the responsibility for the decision, either way.'

There really was no thought needed. As I reached to press Reset, knowing that it would immediately be my first day starting at VR Universal again, the world shattered.

There was an explosion, filth erupted like a volcano. I was drenched and bleeding. Bots were scattered in thousands of bits.

It took ages for the noise and dirt to subside and my ears to ease up on the ringing. I looked down. I had no arms. RL was

180

now half a head atop a twisted torso with a malfunctioning voice. The chains were dangling in the shit room. Only three people remained upright; all others were lost beneath the surface.

And I was being wheeled to the entrance of the offices. It was starting again, but I was incomplete.

It wasn't till much later that RL2 informed me that the game had been hijacked by a 10-year old snotty kid in Leicester who'd paid extra for a new set of backstories that wrote him as a future world dictator.

I wasn't aware that immersive VR had got that far. But I was now as RL led me into the Backstory Department to see if I had any future.

'Am I a rivet in someone else's battleship? Yes, I am.'

# Plain But Adequate

Plain but adequate. Basic but satisfactory. Unconventional, occasionally original. Unorthodox disciplinary approach.

Old school report descriptors flooded back as she looked over the class photo. Black and white, curled at one edge and with a tear across the left centre. But the shiny faces of the 11-12 year olds were still clear.

What was only clear in retrospect was what they would become.

She knew from her own teacher training many years later, that a teacher really only knew two things. A child is not a tiny adult and you never know who is sitting in front of you. What he or she might turn out to be in life.

There was a discussion about if the midwife who helped his mother deliver Adolf Hitler had known what he would become, would she have strangled the infant?

Teachers have never known and with all the testing and psychometrics of today, they still don't know what sort of adult any child might grow into.

The stuttering, shy, socially awkward primary child could develop into a fine actor. The out-going, outspoken class rebel might become an office organiser, a business entrepreneur-disrupter or sell his/her body for money.

The placid, unquestioning conformist may grow into the placid, unquestioning conformist with three junior placid, unquestioning conformists to carry on the good work.

That troubled, restless, dark minded youngster easily could give way to a criminal, a medical pioneer or a politician.

No, teachers just never know.

Of course, these days, teachers bend over backwards to stress the positives. Tries hard. Makes real effort. Give the child a certificate for the best coloured writing book cover. And three words – or, worse, just two - 'lacks imagination' - have been replaced with copious, lengthy, detailed notes and lashings of photos of the kid exploring, discovering, discussing, concluding and evaluating.

Plain but adequate. That was the killer, dismissive comment, typical of the period all those years ago on a piece of creative writing in which she'd invested hours and which her doting parents thought was Nobel prize winning at least, though her older brother condemned it as drivel.

Children didn't have feelings. They were there to be taught, told what to do and get on with it. At least that's what Joy remembered. She picked up the old photo again. Class 1F were on the lawn outside the first years' block at the Grammar School. A sunny day, early summer as she recalled. Two of her classmates were squinting in the sunlight.

There she sat, her chair on the end of the neat row of wooden school chairs, dumpy, dark tight curly hair forced back in a bun and her hand trying to cover the juice stain on her summer uniform dress. All their clothes could only be washed once a week, whether they needed it or not.

Would any teacher then have looked at Joy and thought she'd become a teacher? No, later on school careers advised her to apply for office work in the seasonal foods industry. What on earth else could Joy Ballantine possibly do?

She had no close mates, neither in school nor out. Guides and sports clubs were hardly welcoming. They just took one look, she felt. She was always the outsider. Always the one who couldn't do what the others seemed to find second nature.

Did anyone realise then that Michael Henderson would go into politics? Hardly, he was lacklustre at 11 and after. Or that Carl Dorling would become a policeman? Jane Oakley would nurse before becoming a matron? Or Kenneth Long, Michael Thompson and Simon Fisher would join the army, with Kenneth never coming home?

Or that Keith Bradley would become a tax official; Susan Carmichael would marry an American and move to California? James Toddy would run a corner shop? Pamela Brown would marry five times and have one child who went to prison. Or that Christopher Smith would die coming off his motorbike just five years after that photo?

Did anyone have the faintest inkling that the father of Gerald Carter would be found hanging from his banisters while Gerald was sitting his A-levels in the 6th Form? Or that the childhood sweethearts Mary Price and Alan Rogers would stay together for the best part of forty years before cancer parted them?

Joy knew what had happened to almost all of the class because over the years of growing up in the town, going away for teacher training, returning to the town and spending most of her career in that very same school, no longer a grammar, because she kept track of them.

She filed press cuttings, jotted down news and gossip she picked up. Once social media arrived, she used it to follow their lives even more closely. Gradually the hope of having someone to love rotted away. She had her teaching, instead.

And Miss Newton, their form teacher, grinning fixedly in the centre of the class photo… what happened to her? Well, Joy later realised that Miss Newton was actually Mrs Newton married to Mr Newton who was the Head of the boys' secondary modern across town where those who failed their 11-plus exam went.

And the Newtons later still became famous for being lost at sea when a passenger ship went down one summer in the South China Sea. Not only did teachers never know who was sitting in front of them, they never knew what was in store for themselves.

Joy finished the reports on this year's crop of future geniuses, fools and those in between, stopped cutting and pasting their reports. Only on the granddaughter of Anne Tullett (who became a doctor) was she tempted to write 'plain but adequate'.

But the computer checking program would find and remove it. In any case the kid was very clever, like her grandmother had been. She was just as arrogant, too. But Joy let it go with a sigh, pushing her straggly grey hair back behind her ear and copying in the phrase, 'very creative, inventive and original observer of life and writer of some effective and perceptive work.'

How she would have loved that praise herself back in 1959. Plain but adequate. Was that harridan actually jealous of the juvenile Joy? Or did she just not recognise quality; could not understand how a youngster could command wide vocabulary and subtle meanings?

This summer's holidays were approaching. Time to put away the past, so the photo of class 1F went back into its box. She had six weeks to look forward to.

Six weeks of near daily visits to her old dad in his little room in the home he had reluctantly moved into, fighting her every inch of the way. Who would have thought looking at him now, that William Cowan had once served Her Majesty's judiciary with distinction, sitting in judgement on some of the most complex financial cases of his day?

Joy took little from him, instead being more like her long departed mother who hardly ever seemed to leave the house, supporting the Judge from home and keeping everything to his exact liking.

The one feature that made her petite mother special for Joy was her observations of people around them, often with a cruel and/or hysterical perspective written into little thumbnail sketches that Joy had plundered to people her novels.

Joy would definitely get back to the current one this summer and finish it before September. Self-publishing meant that publishers' rejection slips were history. Now she could hide behind her alias, Melanie Tempest, and get another story of mangled limbs, kidnap terrors, hideous vengeful tortures out of her system.

Who'd have thought it? Who would have guessed? Who knew what she was capable of? Who cared in those distant days? She was plain but adequate then.

A young, wheel-chair bound mixed race girl in a white community back then would surely end up in some crime-infested ghetto? Not becoming Head of English in the very school she had been a pupil in and a moderately successful self-published novelist?

# Ghost of Christmas Shopping

You've asked me about Scrooge and The Grinch. These were fictional characters. I modelled myself on neither – they were both redeemed by 'seeing the light' in the end. My redemption was not like theirs at all, but Christmas did wind me up.

Well, the shopping part of it. So, I'll confine myself to Christmas shopping, not the real meaning of Christmas.

Yes, centuries ago, people appreciated that Christmas was actually a celebration of the birth of Jesus Christ and the faith that believers have in him. Then it became a period of forced jollity, guilt trips if you didn't wallow in sanctimonious pity and generosity and spend all your money.

Here goes. You're not old enough to remember when supermarkets were major players in the nation's economics, when their loss of growth in market share was front page news.

Of course, you probably don't know what I mean by 'front page' news anyway.

The fact is that most of us bought our supplies from super and hypermarkets. This lifestyle reached its peak in the dawn of the early days of the digital world we're now obliged to live in, where everything is done for us by algorithms.

You know what they are! Of course you do. You're probably one.

I ought to explain my aversion to shopping. I was born and raised above my father's shop; we were a retail family and I'm proud of his success through hard work which helped to make me what I am today! Or what I was.

One (of three) of my friends pointed out that with my background my loathing of shopping was a bit of a mystery.

What's a mystery? Help! Everything is now so perfectly planned and ordered that you don't know that a mystery is an unknown, an uncertain element? Christmas in its original form was a mystery, the mystery of the virgin birth of a baby that was the son of God.

Not now. We don't have enough time. Don't they teach you any history these days? They should, you know.

Well, what I disliked was not so much retail itself (essential part of our economy, enjoyed by millions, provided vital employment in difficult circumstances to millions and all that), but that it evolved into a lifestyle, religion, cult in its own right; everybody was expected to worship at its shrine.

Anyway, in the spirit of open-mindedness at one point, I thought an ideal part-time little earner for me would be to become a mystery shopper! There we are - mystery again!

There were several packages you could sign up to (buy) on the internet and receive training! What, training to be a shopper? Well, it was an art, apparently, going into a given shop, restaurant or other outlet at the request of their head office and buying things from a list. All anonymously. They needed all ages, all shapes and sizes, even grumpies.

It was how companies spied on their staff to ensure quality control. If one organisation did it, the sheep followed.

You could never reveal you were a mystery shopper; only make notes when out of sight of the shop, remember names and details of who served you and rate their performance afterwards. Sounded easy. And you got to keep what you bought or ate! You might even be paid a fee.

You had to bid for each separate job, and these agencies existed to make it easy. I looked into it. A small fee...? OK, guaranteed money back if not happy. OK... then there was tax to take off your earnings. Did they forget to say that? Of course. Do it through PayPal, should be safe.

Never heard of PayPal? Oh my word!

Mystery Shopping, it was clear at once, was never going to be a great learning-about-life opportunity. You needed to live in a city with sufficient outlets that subscribed to this way of raising staff performance. We didn't.

Perhaps you don't know that in those days people by and large chose where they wanted to live and could move around without official approval!

Mystery shopping needed a dedicated email address to handle all the endless messaging.

Now I'm going to assume that you've heard what emails were, how popular they started out and how they morphed into a nightmare of scammers, fake news and tidal nuisances before Sharing Three was invented.

Stamina galore was a prerequisite; patience in industrial strength and a deep love of shopping was another of the unexplained mysteries of life. And it was not supposed to be a revenge-opportunity on certain shops or particular staff.

OK, just ask for your fee back from the mystery shopping agency? Easy, you'd think. Fill in a detailed form asking more information about you than you had to give to sign up in the first place. And post it to arrive at an address in Canada before a certain date. Easier not to bother, which was, naturally, how they made lots of money.

Post? Oh we used to pay to send letters and packages and goods to people's home addresses and offices almost anywhere in the world. Then it became easier to just do everything on a screen.

You don't know what offices are? For goodness' sake.

It gave me an idea to establish The Revenge Shopping Agency – get your own back. Become a Mystery Shopper with my competitively priced ten week intensive training programme; shop till you drop and rate everybody and everything; then complain, take it all back and pocket large refunds, grumble about stomach aches in restaurants, report all bad service, however good it really was.

And if you didn't think it was for you, you'd discover the mystery of my money-back scheme into the bargain. Spoil yourself! No, that was what used to be called sarcasm.

Nobody signed up but I felt better for writing it all down.

Writing? You're kidding me! We used to learn how to read and write and use our brains to communicate.

Sorry going on about shopping in general and supermarkets in particular but as you've no reference points these days, if I'm to be heard I must speak out.

The best thing about a trip to a supermarket was getting back home again having survived it. Pack away all the stuff and breathe a sigh of relief. Let the heart rate calm down to normal again.

Throw out all the old junk, past its sell-by date food, and replace it with the new. Chucking that out would be next week's job, but for now a brief, virtuous feeling of satisfaction pervaded. One New Year we would resolve to buy more appropriately to our needs and decide every meal, every cup of coffee, every snack a week in advance.

Oh yes, sorry. New Year – some people made resolutions as if the turning of the calendar to the next year made a determination to do better that much easier. And, as you've guessed, those were the days of excess and surplus.

Obviously supermarkets gave us what we wanted, which is why they succeeded. I loved the loyalty points, the bulk convenience, the special offers and the chance to recycle something in the car park.

But the actual torture of getting stocked up in a supermarket... oh dear.

We had Morrisons up the road, Asda, Aldi and Lidl on the way to Tescos. Sainsburys was miles away, but they all shared certain common features.

No, it doesn't matter. Trust me; they were the names of the big supermarket chains.

First impossibility was finding a trolley that didn't inflict a hernia on the pusher. Was it really beyond the wit of engineering to make a trolley that actually steered? Yes, it was.

The second challenge to patience was the endless assault of repeated announcements.

Attention please, staff call for Kirsty, please pick up extension 356, that's Kirsty, please pick up extension 356, thank you...

Why in the name of sanity did they say it twice? Was Kirsty so thick or lost in conversation with some customer that she was unaware of a message?

Why couldn't she have a little bleeper thing, so the entire shop didn't have to hear the instructions?

But the most annoying thing was why they said thank you at the end? They all did it. Being forced to listen to interminable announcements was a cruel and unusual punishment.

Their worst announcement was – all till trained staff to checkouts, all till trained staff to check outs, thank you ... why couldn't they just send an electronic signal to all such staff to get to the tills and let sensible customers part with their money, collect their loyalty points and get the hell out?

Who was being thanked? That's the Big One. Kirsty for being a moron? Or me for being forced to listen to it? Nobody else seemed to be aware. My wife, Sarah, just didn't hear those messages. Neither, it seemed, did the staff they were intended for.

Pardon? Oh yes, hell was a place where bad people went after death but was popularly understood to be other people on earth. My wife? The lifetime partner I was blessed with. We chose each other, no approval needed.

Every time I faced shopping, I was forced to wonder why so many people went to a supermarket to exercise their social lives. Was that really fun? Did they have no other lives?

But there people stood, blocking aisles while they droned on about house prices, wages and trivial nothings to people they saw frequently.

Oh excuse me, while I just reach across your ludicrously piled trolley and your gassing mouths to grab a box of eggs.

Then pardon me while I put my own body and veering trolley into a slalom down the aisle that you are declaring a no-go zone for sensible shoppers.

No please don't let me stop you telling your entire life story/job description/annual holiday/medical details that should be private between you and your GP or your psychotherapist.

Even worse were these people talking to me! Either they knew me or thought they did. I came to shop and exit clutching a fragment of sanity. I didn't come to tell anybody my entire life story/job description/annual holiday/medical details or to listen to theirs. Or, worse still, to hear again the entire life story/job description/annual holiday/medical details of the person I was just talking to!

But there was even worse than that. Get me out of here, I'm an old celebrity, but I couldn't get out without the absurdity of the checkout. Until robotic checkouts became mandatory, supermarkets who wanted you to buy so much you filled a car, offered a jokey, pokey area after the till to get all your stuff sorted and bagged badly while fumbling for credit cards, loyalty cards and the bags you brought with you.

The biggest horror of the checkout, apart from the queue, was finding the people in front were the same ones who blocked your progress and were now telling the checkout operative the entire life story/job description/annual holiday/medical details of themselves, everybody they met and you as well...

The only announcement I actually longed to hear in a supermarket was: Execution Squad to Aisle 3, selfish people blocking the passage of shoppers on time-sensitive budgets, that's Execution Squad to Aisle 3, selfish people blocking the passage of shoppers on time-sensitive budgets. Thank you.

I once suggested they imposed higher charges on shoppers who were in the store to talk, and lowered them for those there to buy.

Shopping was a plague to be avoided, so I was delighted when online shopping took off. Up to a point. It was the seventh circle of hell, (yes, I've just explained hell) made worse by the fact that I was in the minority, quite clearly. For so many customers and retail workers, shopping was a vocation.

Once in Norwich I finally admitted I needed a shirt for an upcoming family holiday, a pair of trousers and a jacket to see me through the next decade.

Bad enough that this necessitated sweating in a cubicle and trying on four – yes four - pairs of trousers. By the time I'd chosen what I wanted and got two identical pairs, I was exhausted.

They didn't have any jackets for my age and – I hesitate to say it – style. So I settled for that. My old jackets would do. Very cleverly my wife had got my task out of the way at the beginning, so I was allowed to sit on a bench and read and/or people-watch while she ticked the remaining 98% of the items off our list.

As I sat, I'd calmly analyse what was so bad about the experience. Thirty minutes of my life that I could never have back. When one of the banks opened a Money Lounge for often elderly, mainly male, customers to sit and read papers and drink free coffee, I almost wanted to go shopping.

After the second time, even that palled.

But I've strayed from the supermarket to general shopping. Let me return by telling you about a news story I saw which said that the chief executive of Tesco was walking around one of the supermarket group's stores in Essex with his UK management team.

And that summed up what was wrong. CEO walking round the store was brilliant; with his management team, pointless.

I offered to walk him round. Yes, I wrote to the man and offered to walk round my local store with him, unannounced. I did this more in sorrow than anger, as I had a soft spot for that retailing giant's loyalty points and rewards. Have I mentioned that already?

A reply from someone low down the Tesco food chain regurgitated a pile of waffle about offers, price variants and retail-speak. But the chief executive couldn't actually go and look at it on the ground, neither in a suit nor disguised as a real shopper.

Had the boss come with me, I'd have started from outside by trying to enter the same door that people were exiting through. Great 'fun' and no choice. They provided only one door.

Then I'd have pointed to what was whimsically called *Customer Services* with a semi-permanent queue that often blocked other aisles. This was because it dealt with everything from returns, to checkout problems to lottery tickets to payments to their bank. And it didn't open till 8am. Did nobody need service before then?

We'd then have wandered the aisles, me doing a shop and trying to work out the alleged offers and disguised cons that the BBC TV's *Watchdog* programme once featured under the heading, 'sharp practices'.

BBC? Oh, it used to be the premier broadcasting organisation in the world; people trusted it. Then it became a political mouthpiece of the Left Wing. Nowadays you might find a few traces in the Government Information System.

It was unlikely the fruit and vegetable area would be full and inviting. In fact on one Friday evening visit, no fresh fruit at all was displayed. I'd point out, an avid spokesman for capitalism, how their rivals presented fruit, vegetables, salads in an appealing, never-empty way.

Capitalism? Enterprise? Free markets? Another day, perhaps.

Chances of the aisles being jammed with trolleys were high. I'd point out the blocked aisles and empty fruit shelves to the CEO only to be told products just flew off those shelves into trolleys so quickly because they were so popular.

On the way round we'd be assaulted by those endless staff announcements about getting on a checkout or wet-spill somewhere. To make sure the CEO got my point, I'd stop to listen avidly to every announcement and raise an eyebrow at him.

After the fifth message, I'd have wailed why couldn't individual staff be bleeped and directed somewhere rather than intrude on customers' thoughts and patience? He would have taken his head from the bag he'd put over to suffocate himself and agreed with me.

And at the end of the walkabout, the chief executive would've shaken me warmly by the hand, his eyes glowing with revelation, his face lit with a messianic fervour to transform the shopping experience to minimal hassle for the customer before pressing money-off vouchers into my hands by way of thanks.

You see, the world assumed shopping was universally enjoyed. Many sports enthusiasts took the same blinkered view about their hobby. Yes, we had to eat, drink, be clothed and buy household and cleaning products, entertainment and medication, and we had to make choices. But it was a chore, never a joyful experience.

You will scarcely credit this but a line of shelves groaning under over thirty types of breakfast cereal was not uncommon. What? Oh it was a food that people swallowed with milk as the first meal of the day.

In passing, I mentioned queuing. It was a uniquely British habit of standing in line to be served. Even when self-service checkouts arrived, you had to queue to use them and when they failed to recognise something from your basket, you queued for a staffer to rescue you.

With additional tempting offers piled around the checkout, such as magazines, leaflets about pet insurance, batteries or some teeth-battering confectionary, there was no sense of urgency in most till operators.

Of course, they had to chat appropriately, especially to people they knew. While most of them were pleasant, polite, helpful and courteous human beings trying to hold down a job on basic pay, a few milked the talking sociability with friends; there should have been an instruction to keep things moving. Anything else was sloppy management.

And the actual checkout! Nobody from Tesco high command had been to an Aldi check-out and seen how swiftly they did it. Goods were practically hurled through the tills; bagging on shelves away from the tills and staff who shifted quickly were joys for customers who had other things to do with their day.

All the ads, price gimmicks and reduced-product-sizes-for-the-same-price in the world never achieved what they advertised as the holy grail of 'a great shopping experience.'

They started to call shops 'destinations' to encourage people to make a day of it!

Let me broaden your learning a little. Yes, yes, I'm getting to Christmas shopping and the festival of commercially-hyped indulgence.

You've heard of centres of excellence, of learning, of entertainment, of towns and villages, of people's hearts and well-being. Centres were good. Shopping Centres were not. The bunching of outlets under one roof or in the open air theoretically made it easier to spend money.

Don't get me wrong. I'm not knocking wage slaves who toiled in retail therapy. Many enjoyed it, I'm told. Good luck to them and all the jobs that went with them, I used to say, in a half-hearted moment of generous concern for the welfare of others.

No, my complaint was with the urban blandness of centres and shopping. Why did they all have to be identikit, only minor variations on geography, heights, size and number of attached car parks? Shop interiors were the same in every shopping complex.

The argument was that a travelling shopper should feel at home and know where to buy his or her 'favourites' whether the centre was in Croydon, Cardiff or Carlisle.

All the major stores had to be there, often on several levels with entrances from different directions, all selling the same products as not only their own branches, but also as branches of their rivals at home and abroad. Their market research told them it was essential to have a presence in a mall if another company did. So there we have it, my Vicious Circle of Centralised Shopping Theory.

Of course, I speak of the time before retail began to eat itself and major players started to die off, mortally wounded by failures to keep nimble in the face of changing tastes and the internet.

Later there seemed to be a way back from where we were then. Small, independent retailers with unique, local and sometimes quirky offers began to be re-established. Often they rubbed shoulders with cafes, betting shops, cafes, tattoo parlours and cafes in the high streets.

And car parking in those days?

Yes, you had to drive and park your own car! Unbelievable, I know.

Car parks were usually far from shops, identical design again, soulless concrete deserts, monitored by big brother cameras, charging by the minute. They were essential and unavoidable, public transport never being able to render cars obsolete in such places. But they exploited captive shoppers ruthlessly, it being impossible to visit without parking.

And you needed to be fit! Their definition of disability was anyone in a wheelchair; but disability took many forms.

Yes, nowadays everyone is labelled on the Able-Scale, I know. But not then.

Seat to sit down? Fat chance. However old, decrepit or weary people were, seats were not provided in anything like sufficient numbers. Not all partially disabled people were in wheelchairs. Not all families with toddlers and children could keep moving all the time. Even in stores, the seats for partners to sit on while clothes were tried on, were rarities.

The problem was that much of the working, daily world was made for and by fully mobile people brainwashed into parting with money in whatever city they found themselves, reassured by its blandness.

I know, but virtual augmentation for trying on clothes wasn't invented. Can you contemplate that? For example, my grandmother lived to her late 90s and never once left this country, never travelled on a plane and never had her own telephone receiver? What? Oh, never mind.

If only planners had spared a thought for that handful, that brave minority who were reluctant shoppers, and provided plenty of free, guaranteed available parking and seats everywhere to let us sit and moan and whinge and whine and rest our poor feet.

That way we might have felt more like buying a shirt, a jacket, clothes for all the women in our lives of all ages, a meal, another mobile phone, a round of coffees, shoes, the latest TV screen, snacks, CDs and a holiday.

Then we might have the energy to face either coming back again or going to another replica centre to buy a shirt, a jacket, clothes for all the women in our lives of all ages, a meal, another mobile phone, a round of coffees, shoes, the latest TV screen, snacks, CDs and a holiday tomorrow. And for ever and ever. Amen.

Alright, alright. Christmas is here. Yes.

From October to December, if I heard one more refrain of the all time Christmas classic 'favourites' in a shop, I vowed to rip somebody's head off...

As The Day came within touching distance, I sighed relief that the first phase of the nightmare was done. Christmas greetings cards I didn't want received; a handful sent to people I didn't want to greet, especially if they lived across the road.

Clearing up, sorting out, storing good-idea gifts, credit card bills and all that formed the post-Christmas nightmare, so I could worry about that later.

A funny poster I saw cheered me up one year. Don't forget to buy 27 days' worth of food because the shops will be closed for 12 hours!

Gradually, we shopped more online, my argument being that my long-suffering wife having shopped for decades in the traditional, tortuous, frustrating and stroke-inducing ways, needed a break. So did our wallet.

Wallet? Surely you know it was a little holder containing our cards and cash? Alright, cash, you've at least heard of that?

It was theoretically simple online. Comfort of your own room, laughably slow broadband speeds. Choose your stuff, your bargains, your three-for-ones, your suggested (by your kids) pressies for the grandchildren. A few clicks, credit card details and wait for the deliveries.

It never was that easy. Cards and numbers sometimes didn't match up. Security questions and passwords forgotten or not recognised. Why you needed a password and registration with a company that either you would never do business with again, or would be bankrupt by next year, was never explained.

Two capitals, two lower case, two numbers, three symbols – yes, they got all that. But still their dumb system wouldn't accept it. And if you had to ring up anywhere... just taking you through a few questions for security. We got screamingly sick of confirming the first line of our address, our mother's maiden name, our favourite holiday destination and what we had for breakfast three months ago!

Mother's maiden name? Is that maiden name or mother you don't understand?

Don't get me started on deliveries. You could never go out from early morning till late at night in case you missed your parcels from what used to be the Post Office or other carrier. If you did go out, they thought you were out or pretended that they thought you were out even if they could see you through your window, it'd be left across the road with people you might or might not trust.

And then you had to make fatuous seasonal conversation with them when you went to fetch it – yes, it's very cold/mild for the time of year, yes the family are coming home, yes I love Christmas too, they should have it every year!

Or you had to queue longer than a Tesco checkout at this time of year at what was whimsically referred to as a sorting office. You made the same mindless, self evident comments to fellow queue sufferers (and if they knew you at the desk when you finally reached it, to them as well) – yes, it's very cold/mild for the time of year, yes the family are coming home, yes I love Christmas too, they should have it every year!

But hey, it was Christmas. The reason for the season, wasn't it? It's what made the economic wheel go round. So pass me a scrap of wrapping paper – I'll start a new shopping list for that gap between Christmas and the New Year.

Christmas was supposed to wring the heartstrings of soft people opening up their wallets to support retail but also doing their bits for charity. That was a noble cause, no doubt.

But attached to it there hung the ball and chain of emotional blackmail. One bunch of local citizens, members of a social charity club, hired a musical carousel about a tenth real size and lugged it about the area on a low-loader. Illuminated with flashing lights, stuffed reindeer and fat Father Christmases, it excited toddlers the first couple of times they saw it.

The contraption, parked by supermarket entrances, blasted out a permanent loop of Christmas tunes, distorted carols and a comical vocal sketch that was mildly amusing a decade ago. A handful of the men – they were mainly men – shook collection tins at customers going in and out of the same doors.

It was laudable, honestly, raising thousands for local good causes annually. It was moved randomly after an hour or two, so all supermarkets had a battering; they even drove it though the outlying villages and suburbs in the evenings to raise still more.

Jimmy used to work in insurance and I'd known him for years. When I first encountered him on the carousel circuit, we chatted - yes, it's very cold/mild for the time of year, yes the family are coming home, yes I love Christmas too, they should have it every year!

Strangely I felt obliged to drop a coin in his tin. When I came out after some shopping, they were still there, waving tins. Another coin went in.

After several experiences of this I tried to work out their routine to avoid them. One day I drove up to Tescos, saw them in full flow outside, so decided I couldn't face Jimmy again, seasonal goodwill or not.

We needed just a couple of items, so I drove back to Asda. There, like a recurring nightmare was a team with collecting tins around a carousel. They'd invested in three more identical monstrosities, so no shoppers would lose an opportunity to give.

Jimmy smiled. Yep, we've even got one in the main shopping area now. People love giving.

Don't they just!

For the Christmas shop itself, we took a trolley each. Sarah worked through the list (two sheets of closely written A4 paper) while I took up a central position, guarding the two trolleys as she filled them, trying to maintain my cheerful seasonal face which was a blessing to fellow sufferers...

One time a woman employee approached to ask if I needed help as I was looking about wildly. No, no thanks, just waiting – ah there she is!

As Sarah hove into view through the crowds, the employee said, Oh that's OK, you're with a woman. She wandered off to rescue some other poor sod adrift in the chaos.

OK, yes, you've waited to hear. My little spot of trouble.

Well, it was very near Christmas and we had to queue to get into the car park – never a good sign – when we encountered a jumped up, dictator in training driving a big, high, absurdity. No sorry, I neither know nor care about cars. I think this was an SUV, or SUT or SUG or something. Size mattered to him.

Cruising up and down full rows of cars, I was only mildly annoyed, trapped behind him. He passed an empty disabled bay, stopped just past it while his reversing lights told me he was going to back into the bay.

I got there ahead of him! Forwards! I was delighted!

Exiting his ludicrous car, the door swinging alarmingly, he shouted off a stream of unpleasant invective and comments about the legitimacy of my birth. Politely, I pointed out that it was a bay for disabled drivers and here was my blue badge to prove it.

If he possessed such a badge, I'd have gladly given him the space. But he hadn't; he was simply going to abuse it and let a genuinely disabled person suffer. Further shouting and gesticulating made quite a spectacle of us in the car park where we competed with piped musak from the charity roundabout.

The woman with him – poor thing – kept tugging at his sleeve, afraid, perhaps that he was about to assault me.

You don't look disabled, he shrieked as a final stab at me.

Well, you don't look stupid, but there we are!

It was a perfectly reasonable comment in view of his provocation, I thought. Sarah was alarmed as he strode towards me, fists clenched, frothing at the mouth.

Only when he took in that several onlookers were filming the encounter on their phones and Jimmy was rattling a collecting tin at me, did he stop and climb back into his car.

Sarah was in no mood to speak for a time, but at least we had a parking space. Her head was filled with the sudden notion of looking in the department store next door, before we entered the hellish superstore.

Somebody had asked for cushions, so she had to check out prices. She could have done it online, of course, but no, she wanted to see them, squeeze them and hold up a fabric fragment to them for matching. As if it mattered.

It would've been better to have left me in the car. But in we went, like lambs. I needed a pee. Finally, we found the toilets on Mezzanine 4B up three escalators and down four steps, discretely hidden behind the menswear section. Already weary, trying to close my ears to *God Rest Ye Merry Gentlemen* on a loop, I pushed into the gents.

And you know what? There he was, the man who'd tried to steal a car space from someone who needed it was sporting a Father Christmas costume and standing at the urinal!

He was the store's Father Christmas, for goodness' sake. You've been indoctrinated to refer to him as Santa Claus, no doubt?

Talk about season of goodwill.

Seamlessly, noticing me from his peripheral vision, still peeing, he turned to accuse me of every debauchery yet known to mankind. Ignoring him I relieved myself, wondering if he'd appreciate being told his shoes were lapped in piss, but sensibly abandoned the thought.

Instead, I muttered about pitying any children who sat on his lap that day and had he ever thought about cleaning his teeth to overcome his halitosis?

As soon as I was done, before we got into a willy size comparison stand off, I removed myself, disappointed he didn't say something about didn't my mother ever teach me to wash my hands? To this I'd have replied that no, she taught me not to pee on my hands.

As it was, our interactions had been noted by joyful shoppers and relentless CCTV cameras all over.

In my interviews at the police station and in cross-examination in court, I maintained I didn't see the gang of young undesirables close up so couldn't identify them. But I noted them from a distance.

Definitely on something. Certainly up to no good. Probably criminals. Absolutely a menace. No, I was not biased against young people; not for a moment. Tomorrow belongs to them, and all that.

When those two children with their hapless parent discovered that old Father Christmas had gone to that Lapland in the sky, his throat cut and blood all down his elasticated beard and already red coat, their screams triggered alarms everywhere. Panic, like an epidemic swept though the store, though I noticed a few hardy folk shopped on.

Sarah and I were leaving the store, clutching three overpriced cushions, when the security gates clanged shut and all trapped customers were barked at though a loudhailer to stay where we were and await further instructions.

The only benefit I derived from our three hours of captivity was that we abandoned the food shopping and I wouldn't have any more fights with Father Christmas.

Questions, personal details, more questions. The police said we'd be tracked on CCTV and spoken to again, if needed. Had we seen either the group of young people or Father Christmas?

Sarah felt the need to report our encounter in the carpark; I forgot about the second one in the toilet. I suppose it was that which led them to believe that I was the culprit.

That and the fact that the reported gang had vanished, having got out after their laugh, well before the body was discovered and the place was locked down. My guess is that they didn't realise they were killing a real person; they thought it was one of those immersive games you play.

For the forces of law and order it was a quick result, just before Christmas and would help their crime solution figures nicely. I was bang to rights with more witnesses than they needed to the car park event and enough phone footage – most already on social media – to put me away for the rest of my natural.

Only at the trial did I realise they had cameras in the toilet, too. I assumed that was illegal, but apparently not. More crimes were solved through toilet footage than any other method.

Why did I think that? Because in my day people still maintained a few rights to privacy and the assumption of presumed innocence until proven guilty. How naive, I know.

So, I blame shopping, Christmas shopping and a world in which standing out from the crowd was a dangerous place to be. Look at Father Christmas then. Look at me now.

By the way, thanks for your patience in listening. It's always a joy to help you young people understand how it used to be. And so good to see your faces, sometimes hardly able to believe how we lived, often amused by the games we played.

I observed how shocked you were at some of my views. Not just old-fashioned, but beyond your understanding. You have sympathy with the children deprived of a Christmas experience, however meaningless, and with the dead man who'd never shop again.

This time has gladdened my heart. Even if you're only visible to me on a screen and I'm so long gone from the flesh that without all this artificial intelligence stuff you've transformed into a real world, I'd be forgotten and all my ghosts with me.

# Cages for Laughter

I composed my first, and possibly only, Happening to be performed in Lowestoft in the great Hippie Era, 1967 – 72.

A Happening was an event that was a bit of theatrical performance crossed with several aspects of a living art installation. In the eyes of many, it was a pretentious title spouted by bunches of young people with too much free time taking the piss and wrapping their often drunken/doped thoughts up with pseudo-artistic credibility.

Lowestoft is a town on the east coast with a population in those days of about 50,000. Only 120 miles from London where it *was* all happening in terms of young people and hippie activity, it was slow to catch up. A few pioneers broke new ground and my piece *Cages for Laughter* did that, although looking back it was more pure drama than Happening. It was a sort of poetry.

My friends were mainly students with a few late teen/early twenties locals who hadn't moved away and at Christmas, Easter and in the summer we worked on something or other of an artistic, creative experiment.

We called the ensemble The Pervarsity Society, which was as good as any. For this particular show, I had an idea of a circular, universal play with characters simply defined in an abstract way, a plot that was not the main point but was in 'mind dimensions' and with a rising sense of hunger throughout.

I knew that some people watching it would experience rising senses of bewilderment, irritation and discomfort, which was part of the attraction. I should say we had one older guy – Phil - who took the part of honorary grandfather to the team, who'd worked for the Fisheries Laboratory in research, but had become ill over decades and got into the esoteric, fantastical and bizarre before gravitating towards us.

In my memory, I can't remember any advice he gave that was taken, beyond inspiring the Voice from the Past.

He did encourage me to revel in the fact that some people couldn't decide if I was a madman or a genius and he himself coined the phrase, 'a cross between Lewis Carroll and the Marquis de Sade!' which he repeated to anybody who'd listen.

We staged the first showing in a garden in Corton Road in the summer of 1969, as part of the Pervarsity *Sick Poet's Conference*, but the main performances were earlier in the January. We hired the Labour Hall on St Peters Street because it was the only space available and drew a crowd of 35; three days later a performance at the Theatre Centre, a Victorian school in Morton Road that later became The Seagull Theatre pulled in 25.

My *Cages for Laughter* opened on a set described as something approximating to a churchyard with 'vague things floating in the background' and I asked them to play it 'midway between the ridiculous and the morbid.' That immediately offers a flavour of the entire thing.

Voice from the Madhouse said, 'It must be getting near midday now. Not that it matters, we don't eat till five past and no one is in the slightest off way, hungry.' Voice from the Madhouse (V/M) discovered a tomb. 'So this is where I've been all this time! The Voice shall rise again. But if the records are correct, I've been here a hundred years. Over there is a building with stained glass and splintered benches.'

He/she – I deliberately wanted the abstract figures to be sexless – became agitated as Voice from the Past (V/P) appeared and said after a long pause, 'The bells have not yet

210

chimed the day when all these rotten metal number plates will rise up and take vengeance for being unnamed.'

V/M asked, 'Just us?'

V/P replied, 'Just me. No, it's not the same thing. It dates from when this was the County Asylum and people were certified into it.'

V/M; 'I was?'

'Oh yes, you came to the Ladies of Mercy with their rush lamps. You were here.' The Voices sat by the tomb and pondered before V/M demanded, 'Who am I then?'

The reply was. 'You are old enough and sick enough to know that in this place I am the last one to presume to know who I am.'

'But it doesn't hurt to ask, does it?'

'If you like being hurt.'

'You don't change much, though you should.'

V/P smiled. 'Did you know you were hanged once?'

V/M displayed little interest, 'No.'

'In the Eighteenth Century, for theft, stealing from a church.'

V/M was more interested. 'What did I steal?'

'A priest.' This got a laugh, the first time the audience began to wonder whether they were supposed to laugh or scream at this. On the second show two people left the audience at this point.

V/M asked like a doctor, 'Do you often or have you heard voices?'

'I am a voice, complete voice.'

'Does you mind go blank at times?'

'I am my own mind.' After a pause of mindless pacing, 'Why was I here?'

With a laugh, V/P said, 'You know why. You are quite, quite mad.'

'I am no more unbalanced than the mixed up bricks in there with their white coats on.'

With an angry walk, pushing V/M back, V/P driving the point home with finger jabs, cried out 'You are paranoiac, obsessional, disturbed, suicidal, homicidal and prone to schizoid interludes with lashings of delusions of grandeur. Last time round, you murdered yourself.'

This shocked V/M. 'I thought that would change the face of your moon!' cried V/P triumphantly. 'Last time in this place you did away with yourself. No, don't ask, I cannot tell you. Perhaps it has to happen again.'

'But suicides are not buried in sacred ground!'

'A madhouse is sacred ground. Sacred ground is a madhouse.'

The sudden entrance of the Original-Original started them both. 'Who the hell are you?'

The Original-Original (O/O) replied in a sing-song chant, 'I am the Original-Original. I know who you are.'

I should just explain at this point that the idea of an original Original was all my own and any resemblance to later ideas that emerged in advertising in the 1970s flattered but did not recompense me.

V/M claimed to remember him/her. V/P echoed it. 'How can you remember the complete Original-Original?'

V/P said, 'Oh you have modified your elements, probably just as well.'

The O/O moved away from them, 'Originality is the key in this place and time, my friends. No conformity here.'

After a pregnant pause, V/P pointed at the O/O. 'You have lived before and will live again. You will make the same mistakes over and over. And for you, Voice from the Madhouse, there is no escape.

V/M shouted back, 'Why should I want to escape? The Original-Original is my friend.'

The O/O smiled at V/M as he/she knocked the Voice down with a fist. V/P responded with an instinctive knock down of the O/O which produced, 'how dare you hit me, don't you know I am sick. And I can have no friends.' The sudden violence was meant to be shocking. But for most it was merely puzzling.

The V/M changed the subject. 'Why have the fingers of the bells stopped playing?'

The O/O answered, 'because the sycamore trees are in love with the pine stacks and have given way under the concrete bridges.'

V/P contributed, 'But surely the flower salesmen and imagined translations did not forget about the lawn party tea?'

'Oh no,' chimed O/O, 'but the platinum gear boxes were not sent the lyrical underground invitations in time to grow new wings.'

And V/P finished the section, with 'which explains the presence of the blonde-eyed prostitutes.'

Now I should explain that this was an attempt to blend poetry with surrealism and introduce Violin who, dragged in by a long rope, prompted the three on stage to try to win it over to themselves.

V/P smarmed, 'Ah Violin, you have changed for the better since we last met on the field of carnage and love.'

The O/O asked, 'Good brother or sister Violin are you ordained yet?'

V/M's effort was, 'Good Violin, I have seen you on an elephant dressed in blue armour holding a harp speaking in Latin, I have called you friend, Violin, friend.'

Violin's response was neurotic, 'I am the fantasy known as the Great Violin. I am quite sound. I am going out of the window. I shall count the tiles and shall never come back here or anywhere. I cannot at the present visualise coming back here. I am neurotic.' The rope is used as a threatening weapon.

It went on, getting louder, 'I must have my vengeance. The revenge of the violin shall be infinitely grater than the flagship, Voice from the Past, Voice from the Madhouse and I shall stop only when all are annihilated!'

Again changing the subject, V/P asked why there are no carnations as there always used to be. 'They have been destroyed.'

214

The O/O had an overlong monologue, a Lament, about all flowers being crushed and rotting. 'Let the dawn of a thousand suns set in the merciless, timeless horizons, let the forest drip away in streams of purity, let a lonely, innocent long-haired woman hide in the humid mantel of paved cities, let poets weep, let warriors rain their blood into the gardens of oblivion.'

As this mumbo-jumbo neared its end, the other characters started a mumble that became a chant that became a shriek, 'All freedom is gone, stained glass is gone, casements and crystal eyes have gone, back to the nothing, back to the nothing...' They mimed some action to accompany the words; they adopted still-images with deliberate physicality using the semiotics of lunatics.

All good drama school stuff. However, it wasn't entertaining – I can see that now – so it did challenge the patience of most of the audience and as I realised later, at least one of the cast.

During rehearsals there was discussion about slimming it down at this point as it rambled on with lamentation, chanting and poetic gibberish spouted at high volume. I was reluctant to give it up, especially with such stage directions as 'Violin speaks out harshly like a bush.' Ellie and Sy supported me, wanting this scene to run a long time, for some reason.

I should say a word about the cast. The girls who played the Voices with false male depth were sisters who were still at school, the elder one going to drama school in the autumn and the younger hoping to make it as a singer. I liked them both and had made a pass, but they seemed more interested in someone else. The Original-Original was my sister's boyfriend, one of the Pervarsity Kingpins who also doubled as Legend, as the first guy chickened out when the show dates approached.

Violin was taken by Jim who went on to be a successful jobbing actor, but at the time was glad to be part of anything

215

he could get into. I suspected him of secret desire for all the girls but never saw any evidence.

The Voice of Beauty was my sister, Elaine, who seemed quite taken with a couple of the blokes beside her boyfriend. All the Minions were played simultaneously by Phil who was a willing volunteer for anything and was a mean guitarist too, as it happened.

Sy (Simon) played Him and Ellie played Carole. They were the only human beings in it, and I noticed they soon hit it off, which didn't suit me as I'd taken a shine to her, having noticed her in a poetry event at The Ship pub in Pakefield.

We talked a lot, hours of ideas, some banter and a shared enthusiasm for experimental theatre, shocking the norm and shaking things up a bit. It didn't matter what we shook up or what replaced it – shaking up and shocking were justification enough.

I was building up to asking Ellie for a meal, just us, after the show was finished so I could share my next idea which was for a play about a madman who wants to draw a map of the shifting beach sands.

I thought it was going well, and like a fool never dreamed that Sy had actually already staked a claim to her. Sy was one of those long haired, cool young men who swallowed the hippie doctrine in full, which of course included free love, so she was going to be just another notch on his bedpost.

Sy, really, was the sort of bloke I disliked. He'd run through the girls like they were simple objects to be used and discarded. Why and how they fell for his easy charm, slightly arrogant certainty, drove me crazy. But I needed him in this show. I liked to think I was more caring and sensitive. Fat lot of good it did me, though, even in those free days.

It was during the second show that we realised why Sy wanted the first scene to run as long as possible.

A table was dragged on by the Minions (just Phil on his own, of course) and a drink and glasses placed. The Minions left. Him was supposed to come on carrying a pile of random papers which he worked at. Legend entered and watched him for a moment. On this occasion the Minions set the table and Legend entered. Him didn't.

There was silence. Legend waited, flicking dust off the table. Gradually in the silence from the back came some obvious sounds of people having sex. I wouldn't rate it any higher than that. They were sexing. I knew it could only be Him and Carole. The audience, of course, thought it was part of the show and one or two giggled.

Him rushed on, gathering his clothes. I was never sure if Sy did it on purpose for a laugh, came on late because he was screwing the female or because he was so incredibly driven by his cock that he didn't care about anything else.

Legend barked at him, 'Who the hell are you?' which was the line, but by which he meant, 'where the hell have you been?'

'I am Him. A poet. A worshipper of beauty. And a good lay too,' he added to get an unscheduled laugh from the audience.

'I write poetry, too,' said Legend.

'I said I am a poet. I didn't say I write poetry.' Sy was back on track and picked up what became a torrent of scripted abuse towards Legend about how Him was selected to wait for beauty, to recognise her and then serve her (another small laugh on that).

Legend explained that he/she was 'Legend, legend of a mistake. I was meant to be in at the end, but Violin my mortal enemy beat me to it and I was merely assigned the end.'

I have to confess the audience were thoroughly confused by now. Was it a piss-take with the cast mocking themselves? Phil always maintained that it was deeply philosophical and a metaphor for the theory of reincarnation and despite being present at every rehearsal never seemed to realise that the sex sounds off were a late addition.

Legend and Him agreed to maintain a vigil for Beauty, but wrapped up with copious proclamation, declamation and what passed for blank verse. I wrote that a 'troop of Minions file on carrying articles of rubbish to clutter the set for the rest of the play.' It was meant to be a statement about the pointless of everything until Beauty arrived and explained all the fragments of life.

The fact that we had only one Minion was faintly amusing – making a virtue out of what had appeared a disaster when the other five Minions found something else to do instead of turning up. The rubbish gathered and I got Legend and Him to fight each other – again, drama techniques to change the tempo.

Carole dressed as a schoolgirl entered, smiled at them, cracked a whip and they stopped instantly. Legend mistook her for Beauty, but Him explained that 'she is Carole with all the trimmings', a schoolgirl, beautiful enough. Him introduced Legend to her and she snapped back, 'I am Beauty, now get back into your cages which I will hang from a cliff edge!'

I know, yes. It had become very sadomasochistic, but at the time it wasn't designed that way.

She found a hand gun in the rubbish and demanded that they play Russian roulette. Him argued that he must just wait, so Carole held the gun to Legend's head. Click. He was alive. She

218

was thrilled so had one stood on each side of the stage and alternated firing at them.

Of course, nowadays we'd have to jump through endless hops to fire a toy gun on stage, but in those days, it was fine.

Him still argued for time to wait as he'd been instructed so she fired twice at him in anger. He lived. The next shot took Legend out, stone dead. Carole was delighted. 'Who *was* that?'

'Only Legend, a thing created by the Original-Original for amusement on a boring night.' Him knelt beside Legend and performed the Funeral Ovation, flowery, rambling images and expressions. Carole mocked clapped it, 'Very moving. Almost brought tears to my elbows. A shame nobody will be around to witness the laughter when YOU go back in your cage.'

Him was depressed at both his continuing wait and Carole herself, but she reassured him that he too came from this place. He'd been here before. She ordered the Minions to remove Legend's body and bring it back as dust for her 'glass case of specimens.' She assured Him that there was a glass case for him as the Voices returned, carrying flowers for her.

'Is there anything you need, Carole?'

'Yes,' she smiled sweetly, 'your exit.'

To transition into the final section I'd written the Voice of Beauty for a long time girlfriend who'd shipped out when this piece was being finalised on the grounds that I was 'just too much, sometimes.' So she was a taped voice, 'Sunshine, endless music...' on a loop, over and over.

All the cast (except Him) clambered onstage wading through the rubbish dressed brightly, even the Minion(s). Carole announced the Inauguration and all were delighted, a party-like mood descended. Him staggered on dressed like a tramp, his eyes wildly deranged and challenged Carole for starting without him.

The Voice of beauty on tape recited, 'The trees are happy and sunshine is kind; rains are near, Zoo keeper doesn't mind, as long as the animals remain calm, cages are ready on the music farm...' We had recorded an echoing laugh sequence with the help of someone we found attached to us who was partially deaf and short sighted but worked in sound and music.

The final sweep was meant to be deliberately confusing. Well, even more confusing. The gist of the story was that Him had waited too long and failed to recognise Beauty which was in any case not confined to an idealistic woman and that he had to go back to his cage. Him went through a range of emotions in two minutes from anger to amusement, from rage to disbelief and finally to grovelling for a second chance.

Yes, alright. An explanatory note for the audience would have helped.

There followed a mime sequence with copious chain sound effects of putting Him in a cage and burying it. Carole ordered the Minions to kill Violin and the Original-Original as she was weary with their failing to learn after many lifetimes. Him was handed a rusty chopping axe which he played with meaninglessly and unthreateningly.

The Voice of beauty told everyone she was disappointed the cages had been allowed to grow rusty and people had enjoyed destruction too much. The laughter on the taping machines was stuck in a rut. History repeats itself.

The show then started again, the only difference being that the set was full of the rubbish. It ran a minute, just so everyone got the point about a circular story.

As the light faded, The Voice of Beauty on tape spoke like a doctor, 'Come on Him, this is treatment day. This doesn't knock you out, just lets you see things more clearly. Now what's all this about you waiting a long time in some rusty layers of cages somewhere amidst the laughter?'

My final stage direction for them was, 'the event would appear to be at an end.' I wrote that because I imagined keeping the mystery going in strange sounds and words as the audience left. That never happened. Most were just too ready to talk all at once, especially as the cast dispersed among them.

I had to wait several hours before I got Ellie alone to ask her what the hell had gone on with Sy? She shrugged her shoulders, flicked her long blonde hair off her face and said, after a moment's pause, 'whatever you want it to be. You're the man with the imagination and the ideas, so whatever you want.'

'Jealousy?' I demanded.

'If that's what you want, yes. Free love? It was nothing. Makes you jealous? OK, go with it'

And that's all I got from it. 'You're not acting now, Ellie.'

'Aren't I?'

I sometimes wonder what happened to them all. But then, I don't.

# The Blue-Arsed Fly

Even as a boy, he rushed about madly doing this and that, arranging and sorting, fixing and improving.

Of course, lots of toddlers do it. When they're a bit older they might slow a little. Roger never did. He just moved more quickly with ever increasing eagerness to get things done.

By the time he was nearing the end of primary school his manic approach to almost everything was the subject of much humour, a little alarm and a report to the school psychologist.

He was perfectly normal, though - the apple of his fruit and vegetable shop-keeping parents' eyes; the class superstar who had a dose of gunpowder down his pants, that's all.

At 11 two things happened. He began secondary school and started in the local Scout troop - best in town - the 19th.

At both he met Claude, a boy twice his size and a few inches less in height; a young man training to become a fully-fledged member of the fat cat class, developing a permanent air of weary entitlement. Claude looked at the world through small, dark eyes already struggling to keep from being swallowed up by spreading face flesh.

Claude, first son of a wealthy haulage, coal and commodity company didn't disdain Roger, neither did he despise him. He saw his peer, at first, as a total irrelevance in his life and future, but soon instinctively realised that this energetic boy would provide much fun and amusement which he could use to impress others.

Roger joined the Scouts without the benefit of the Cubs first, so arrived in a situation where he was very much the outsider. Claude had been in it from the beginning, so knew everything and everybody.

They were put in separate patrols and on the horseshoe semi-circle parade that started and concluded each evening with a breaking of the Union Flag and a hauling it down, Claude had opportunities galore to survey the agonies that Roger went through trying to stand still, at attention.

In the games – British Bulldog particularly – Roger was nimble and escaped capture. After a time Claude suggested to some of his new mates that they work together to bring him down. Roger needed stitches in his cut eyebrow the night this plan worked brilliantly.

In any scouting activity – from knots to stave fighting, cooking to a wide game played attacking a base on the sand dunes avoiding capture amid the regular sweeps of the lighthouse beam, Roger's darting about was a handicap.

At the first scout camp experienced by the new boys, their trial of initiation had to be endured. This was invariably laid on late at night after lights out and the scout leaders had adjourned to their own tent a few paces away from the semi-circle of boys' tents and roped kitchen areas.

Claude avoided any strenuous initiation. It was common knowledge he treated the older boys to a bag of sweets apiece. Roger had access to no such bribery. His parents could barely afford the scout and school uniforms.

So Roger ended up staked out over an anthill, his wrists and ankles tied to tent pegs. It wasn't his crying or protesting that alerted the leaders, it was the other boys laughing at his frenetic attempts to tug free of his ropes.

Claude first called Roger 'Blue-Arsed' after the idea that a blue-arsed fly can't stay still to be caught, in a spate of nicknaming giving.

They were supposedly clearing up after a camping training session, taking their empty cans of beans – 'burn, bash and bury' was the instruction before the fun ritual of pissing on the campfire to extinguish it.

Roger was gleefully pratting about, getting the task done quickly and Claude snapped, 'Sit down, you blue-arsed fly, before someone swats you.' 'Blue-Arsed' was so apt and funny that other lads soon cottoned on.

Roger looked at Claude, particularly the eyes and said, 'you're Mr Pig.'

'Mr Big, Blue-Arsed, very appropriate!' Claude swept aside Roger's half-hearted protest and rejoiced in that label for ever more.

Only when a leader heard 'Blue-Arsed' and lectured them that a) language of that kind was unacceptable, b) Roger would be upset and c) his high physical activity showed how committed Roger was to getting on with things, did Claude drop the 'arsed' and just called him 'Blue'.

Everyone knew what he meant.

And the funny thing was that Roger never held a grudge. He always lent things and offered to help in any way required. Some accepted and then abused his kindness; most ignored him.

And at school where they'd been put in the same class, Claude used the term freely, daily and invariably led the laughter that accompanied Roger's hyperactivity.

His parents never got wind of it, so he stayed Roger at home, but everywhere else he became Blue.

Claude carried a plastic fly swat in his school bag and up his scout uniform sleeve whenever he could to reinforce the nickname, the joke about Roger and Claude's power over every situation.

Roger would often be flicked, swatted or stung very hard with the thing, usually when he didn't see it coming and couldn't dart away to safety. Or from behind.

'The common fly jumps backwards when it takes off, so the best way to swat it is from behind and above,' Claude informed everyone, amidst the laughter.

People thought Roger would be good at sports – or physical education as it was then - but he was too uncoordinated and got on the teacher's nerves, so was given a torrid time. Claude's father was a drinking buddy with the PE teacher, so Claude got away with being over-weight, uninterested and a pain in the neck.

In other subjects, neither boy shone, but generally Roger did his best and rubbed almost everyone up the wrong way, while Claude got by, doing the minimum and stirring trouble without ever getting caught. And he was a master at turning the spotlight on Roger, who couldn't resist making a fool of himself.

As they climbed the secondary ladder, Claude became adept at getting out of things he didn't want to do and getting things he wanted to happen or own, spending money carefully to secure what he needed. He showed some entrepreneurial spirit when he dreamed up an insurance scheme in which his peers could cover themselves against corporal punishment.

Cover against a single thrashing of six strokes of the cane cost a penny a week and paid out two shillings. Repeat offenders were not covered within a term. One Saturday morning detention paid out a shilling for a penny a fortnight, and again, it was valid only once a term.

When the Head heard of it and called Claude in to his office, the scheme was crushed. Both Claude and his parents were outraged. He'd shown commendable enterprise and had contributed to good behaviour in the school.

Roger escaped both detentions and the cane, but got his knuckles rapped with a ruler, his legs slapped and a board rubber tapped on his head as an aide to his memory that he needed to stay still.

Once the boys in their year group started to discover that girls were different, Claude found himself popular. He hadn't grown very tall, was pretty wide and still had his dark, unsettling eyes, but he was the first boy who needed to shave, who had pubic hair (witnessed by other boys in the communal sports showers) and the first to get a moped.

As soon as his test was passed, he moved up to a small motorbike and made himself available to give girls lifts home after school.

Roger didn't need a shave till he started university, was hardly in the shower long enough for anyone to note how thin his pubic hair was and could afford no wheels to take anyone home, even himself on a pushbike.

Having passed sufficient O-Levels, the boys were among those offered places in the 6th Form. Two more years of banter, jokes and lewd suggestions at Roger's expense.

There was an incident that pushed Claude's loathing of Roger up a notch. An hour after school, Claude had taken a

226

girl home on his motorbike and was hurtling to his house, ignoring the speed limit. He hit a pothole and came off, rolling several times before coming to rest against the kerb.

Roger happened to be walking home following an after-school German class and ran on to see if he could help. He knew it was Claude as he knelt beside him, assisting him to turn and sit, shaking off concerns that he might be injured. His trousers were split and he was bleeding from one knee.

As the bike was still running on its side, Roger picked it up and stopped the engine, hauling it onto its stand which he'd seen others do a thousand times. It was heavier than he expected.

He helped Claude stand upright. Claude, lucky to have escaped serious injury, was determined to get away before anyone else saw his misfortune. No, there was no pain, no problem.

Without a word to Roger, he limped to his bike and walked with it along the road. Roger watched him go, amazed that Claude couldn't say thank you or even look him in the eye. But then, the eyes were too deep in his head.

The next morning when Claude limped into the 6<sup>th</sup> Form Common Room sporting a bruised forehead, raw knuckles and a sore back, he at once made a joke that he'd been bothered on his bike by a pesky fly and had tried to swat it away and came off as a result.

The idea settled that Roger was involved so if later a witness reported seeing the pair and the bike, then obviously Roger had caused it, somehow.

Once scouts gave way to the Seniors both Big Claude and Blue Roger earned their Queen's Scout Awards, though Roger confided in his only two friends that Claude must have paid someone to take the physical endurance badges for him.

It was only when Roger got close to Joanne that Claude turned really nasty.

Joanne and Roger went out occasionally – a few 6<sup>th</sup> form parties, an occasional drink at The Crown or the Foxborough and once or twice a meal at each other's houses. They got on well; she was easy going and was decidedly not looking for a husband at that stage.

He had a life plan which meant university, a few part time jobs to make ends meet, and a career in business management that would pay well and allow his hyper-energies to be used to great effect.

One afternoon, as the Common Room emptied out, Big Claude indicated Blue should listen to him. Roger was keen to get off to complete his homework; get to the public library to read the free financial pages to invest some birthday cash from his aunt and do more to a shed he was making at home for his mother.

Claude blocking the doorway was unwelcome; he wasn't budging an inch. His eyes stared at Roger, unblinking, revealing nothing. Roger noticed that Brian Smith and Malcolm Jarvis were stood either side of Claude and moving towards Roger. It was the first time he realised that Claude had, in effect, a pair of bodyguards.

'You're crowding me, Blue.' Claude muttered, unsmiling.

It was ludicrous. Roger was a good foot taller, lean and gangly; Claude's stocky, podgy look, like a blob of white lard in a jacket, wouldn't catch Roger. In a fight, Roger could strike a blow and dart away. But he was trapped in the room, the lard wasn't moving and the henchmen were getting closer.

'What do you mean – I'm crowding you, Claude?'

'So you admit it! You're crowding me because you're getting close to me, too close and taking what's mine.' The sidekicks stopped, staring at Roger as if he was a specimen.

'What's yours?'

'Joanne is mine, Blue.'

'What?'

Roger was taken aback. 'Joanne is my - ."'

'No, Blue, Joanne's not your anything. She is mine, now. She gave herself to me last night, while you were blue-arsed flying about achieving nothing. She asked me to dispose of you, so this is what we're doing.'

The two assistants advanced and Claude opened his mouth to grin broadly. They held Roger down across a long table.

'Shame we haven't got time to find an anthill or tent pegs, Blue. But if you've got the message, then we won't need to. Leave Joanne to me, clear off, go and dance around with someone younger and leave those who are man enough to enjoy themselves....'

It was a lesson in how someone can be threatened; the innocent intimidated and the seeds of jealous destruction easily be sown.

That evening, as it was getting dark, Roger made his way to Joanne's house to tell her about it, to ask her and to reassure himself that it wasn't true. When he was still some distance off, he saw Claude climb out of an almost new maroon Ford Classic Consul 315 and call for Joanne.

Of course, Claude had been the first 6$^{th}$ former to pass his car test and own a vehicle. Roger watched from the darkness between two lampposts. She came straight out, dressed up and seemed to climb willingly into his car.

It was somebody's party, Roger remembered. He hadn't been invited and hadn't discussed it with Joanne. In any case they weren't romantically entwined. But he couldn't believe she was going anywhere with Claude. It made no sense.

In fact, Roger learned later, Claude had offered her a lift, pretending she was one of three girls he was taking along out of the goodness of his heart. When she found out Claude had tricked her, she had no more to do with him.

He let that go because the doubts had been planted in Blue's mind. Now he'd never know for sure that he could trust Joanne. It was a good evening all round for Claude because Janice Travis accepted a lift home and she was far less scrupulous than Joanne.

University arrived with something of a relief to Roger. He went off to Bristol to study economics. Claude didn't do very well in his A-Levels - a five pound note pinned to his answer papers was obviously insufficient. So after a hasty rethink the family put him to work in studying economics at the sharp end of his father's business.

It wasn't what Claude had wanted – he thought three years away as a student would have suited him perfectly. However, his father made sure Claude wasn't overly taxed, and he soon began to learn for real as he understood how business works, employs people and makes some lots and lots of money.

Roger's studies went along in a mundane manner, with few surprises. He learned better to control his fidgeting, his darting about and his anxious rush to get on with everything in hand simply to do more.

And he particularly enjoyed not being called Blue. Instead he endured jokes about being Jolly Roger and rogering a lot of girls, but it was not in the same league of maliciousness that Claude had favoured.

Even in university vacations, the pair's paths did not cross. A big charity fun run along the seaside prom and through some of the town inspired Roger to sign up willingly. He hadn't gained control of his coordination suddenly, but the only girl he came near to jolly rogering at university was one very taken with charitable endeavours, to putting back into the community.

Roger was caught in a photo that appeared in the local Friday rag in a story reporting the fun run. It quite spoilt Claude's Friday, he having managed to virtually forget the Blue-Arsed Fly.

His family business was growing rapidly. Claude had persuaded his father to enjoy more time on the golf course, preferably one in a nice hot country, so Claude was able to diversify into food production, staffing provision, gas and oil supply on and offshore and derelict property development.

Claude put one of his gofers on the case of the troublesome fly. Within days a report landed on his desk stating all there was to know about university life in Bristol and how his parents were struggling still running their little greengrocers' shop.

Recent shopping developments, some of which included Claude's family, had sidelined their premises. It was rented from an ancient, local family trust with which Claude's father had dealt years back. Claude bought the little row of shops – greengrocers, shoe repairers, a barber and a locksmith.

He gave all tenants notice, buying out leases as needed and demolished the row, pending further development of a carpark he had in mind. Once signed and sealed and a report came in that Blue's parents had retired on a pittance, it made Claude's day.

He then got on with running his businesses, troubling his mind with no further thoughts of the fly. Until university was over and Roger, fresh from marrying Vanessa, his girlfriend of his student days, moved back to town and got a placement at a small accountancy practice to learn the ropes and put his economics degree to good use.

Claude grasped that if allowed to progress, Blue had the potential to make a great deal of money in the decades ahead. And to be a disease to him all their lives. He'd swatted many flies since his schooldays, exterminated several kinds of vermin and cleansed whole areas of the town. Blue was next.

Roger worked hard; still keeping most of his energy focused, but threw himself into the charity scene, regularly a sucker for any and every cause that moved either he or his wife or both of them.

At one of those posh charity dos where raising money for good causes was secondary to networking and being seen networking, Big Claude bumped into Blue Roger, quite literally, causing Roger to share a full glass of white with his jacket and trousers.

'Hello Blue!!'

'Good evening, Big Claude.'

'Well, that's what all the ladies say!'

'This is my wife, Vanessa. And Vanessa, this is Big Claude, we've known each other since we were about eleven...'

Claude was instant charm, slobbering over her hand and openly taking her in from top to toe, particularly her bump.

'Ahh, breeding like flies, are we?'

At that point one of his sidekicks 'rescued' Claude with a request for him to talk to the chairman of some pension company.

'Sorry, business calls. Vanessa, did he ever tell you how he got the nickname, Blue?' as Big Claude wallowed away, his shoulders heaving up and down with laughter.

'So that's Pig Claude?' said Vanessa, clearly unimpressed. His eyes give me the creeps.

'Me too, my love, me too.'

That was all it was, but it unsettled Roger and fed the inexplicable resentment slowly eating Claude away inside.

Roger and Vanessa's baby's birth was reported in a paid announcement in the paper; other information on their lives was routinely part of the intelligence on people, places and events that Claude financed.

Unaware that it would enrage Claude, Roger got himself selected as the Conservative candidate for his local ward in the tri-annual elections to the District Council. His grinning face was among the other hopefuls featured in the paper, with a few words from each.

Roger wrote that he was locally born and bred, energetic, full of ideas, had a passion for helping others, wanted to put back into his community his skills, his economic knowledge and was proud to be a Conservative.

Claude held no political affiliation – indeed his only loyalty was to himself so he worked freely with all sides of every issue. He would have traded with opposing sides in a war if he thought it worthwhile.

So, in the interests of balance, Claude paid people unofficially to canvass door to door spreading half truths and misrepresentation about Roger. Not entirely due to that, Roger wasn't elected. Didn't even come close.

But Roger had felt right to try it. Claude reckoned Blue'd have another go, so had his people do some research and found a sitting Labour councillor in another ward who was experiencing some financial difficulties and had a few past errors to atone for (cover up).

So Claude, in a blaze of publicity, joined the Labour party and when the sitting councillor suddenly stood down through ill health, Claude was a shoo-in as Labour choice to fight the by-election.

In a few weeks, Councillor Claude Barnes took his seat in the Council chamber, enjoying the glory, appreciating the increased business he could do now and particularly that when Blue finally got elected, Claude would be ahead of him. Again.

In fact, Roger and Vanessa decided it was time to move on to fresh challenges. He became a partner in the accountancy firm and they mixed in circles that could make a difference to good causes. He set up a matching pound scheme, whereby for every pound a local business gave, he'd match it, pound for pound.

Claude didn't regret being a Councillor, but was annoyed when Blue didn't stand again. So Claude engineered a merger with Roger's accountancy and a bigger firm he had links with.

Roger was surplus to requirements at the new set up. It had been a condition of the merger. So their charitable efforts had to be toned down for a time while Roger set himself up as a single practitioner.

A number of years passed with occasional encounters between the pair. Claude invariably said something unpleasant; Roger always took it on the chin. However Claude goaded Roger with fly spray jokes, political rivalries or comments about having too much energy, he never rose to it.

The revival of the Scores Race brought a further escalation of Claude's hostility.

The Scores are ancient narrow paths running from the old, former beach village where the town had started to the top of the sand cliffs where a now much neglected area of the town, steeped in history and houses in multiple occupation perched.

The race was apparently run many decades ago, but fell into disuse after the Second World War. It was a big charitable enterprise; Roger was on the organising committee and entered as a runner.

There were professional entries, good amateurs, novice runners and youngsters 12-16. With masses of advance publicity, Roger was well known as a leader in it and wasn't expected to put in a shabby running performance, either.

Claude, by now rated clinically obese, if anyone had dare style him that, was unable to run but got himself invited to start the race, as a representative of the Council who funded much of the event costs. His party was now in control, so it was an easy thing to achieve.

A little harder to engineer because of the need of arms' length, was the visit a couple of youths paid to Roger and Vanessa's house while the race was on in order to relieve them of their TV, spare car and some cash that was secreted indoors.

To throw police off the trail, they hit a number of houses across town belonging to other runners who'd been advance named.

Claude had wondered about spraying a magnificent new wooden fence that had been installed between Roger's garden and the street with fly jokes – fly-posting, really.

But he thought better of it.

Instead he confined himself to glaring at Roger through his little piggy eyes as the runners streamed past him. It was a hefty exertion, up and down alternating scores, about twenty minutes of hard graft from the runners, giving Claude plenty of time to waddle along from the start to the finish point to present the prizes.

Claude could barely contain his fury at having to give second prize in the overall category to a sweat-lathered Roger, and crushed his hand, drew him close and muttered, 'well done, Blue, run while you can. Fly while you can.'

Nobody heard it in the melee; even Roger wasn't sure he'd heard Claude right. What was wrong with the man? Surely they were all grown up now? What did the 'big' man want from Roger, after these years?

It clearly wasn't his little firm, his reputation for good works, nor his wife. And even if Claude had been forced to answer, he himself wouldn't have known. He just couldn't bear to see the Blue-Arsed Fly of his youth doing anything well or successfully.

There were no further clashes, mishaps, events to set Claude off on any spiteful acts. Until the Referendum was called in 2016.

Claude, as a self-proclaimed Labour man loathed and never lost a moment to run down the Conservative government, nonetheless, when the Prime Minister David Cameron called the EU Referendum, Claude came straight out in support.

Should Britain leave the European Union or remain in it? It was a deceptively simple question that took no account of the complexities of untangling four decades of membership, of what life after leaving might look like or what, if any, parts of the EU did Britain still want.

Claude would share no platform with any Conservative Remainer, but spoke at meetings, lambasted people he knew and poured money into the campaign. It was, besides hurting Roger, the most sincere passion of his life, an economic and emotional issue.

Roger took no part in campaigning but felt as passionately about leaving, regaining British sovereignty, making British laws, trading across the globe freely. It was an economic and emotional issue, for him, for the opposite side.

The leaving idea was nicknamed Brexit. People were either Remainers or Leavers, but Brexiteers was the more cavalier term favoured by those passionate to quit.

The nation was divided, towns and cities took opposite views; many families couldn't agree among themselves. While most people and observers and the media expected Remain to comfortably win, there was an air in many places that people had had enough of being told what to do, paying so much into the EU Budget and seeing too many EU citizens take jobs, hospital beds and school places.

Remainers argued that it was a regressive, dangerous leap into the unknown, an illusion of Britain going it alone outside the community. Both sides insisted that history was in their favour.

With just a week to go there was a big charitable show at the town's civic theatre, quite unconnected to the referendum and long planned to raise thousands for medical research. There were performances from local schools, a dance competition and a couple of professional jokers to hold it together.

As people milled about before taking their seats, Claude bulldozed his way through to hail Roger who was about to sit down. 'Hey Blue, I haven't seen you about campaigning to remain, but I assume we can count on your vote?'

The question was phrased in a menacing manner. Roger drew himself to full height, well above the fatberg facing him. 'Claude, I haven't been out campaigning. But I'm voting to leave. I am a Brexiteer.'

There was not exactly a sudden shocked gasp from those around, but Claude's face twisted in hatred. 'You're a little Englander, locked in some historical nostalgia, a fantasist who is threatening this nation!'

Roger bent closer. 'And you are a smug, establishment, puffed up selfish, blinkered, Euro-controlling traitor who would deny the British people a free and prosperous place in the world.'

It was only the second time Roger had spoken back to Claude. Claude's fist clenched, his neck muscles bulged. The lights dimmed and the show began.

Vanessa was embarrassed; neither enjoyed the show. They skipped ice creams or drinks in the interval and chose not to go to the bar. As it all ended, they made their way out as rapidly as possible to avoid seeing Claude again.

Brexit won the Referendum. There were city and regional and Scottish differences, but overall 17,410,742 (51.9%) voted to leave against 16,141,241 (48.1%) opting to remain.

A majority of one would have been enough, but the nation remained divided, often bitterly so. While a new campaign begins on the next day after the previous one ends, there were some in the media, establishments and among the self-proclaimed great and good who refused to accept it.

They became known as 'Remoaners'. Claude was definitely among them. And that Roger had backed the winning side - it was just too much.

During the next two and half years, there was an unexpected General Election and Britain behaved like a supplicant at the feet of the EU trying to secure 'a deal' that was not mentioned in the Referendum.

People got sick of it, even the media for whom it was the daily bread and butter of content. But before an outcome was achieved, there was a terrible winter with storms, snow on a scale not seen for many years.

Claude had long paid a team to watch Roger and Vanessa at home, when they went out, worked, shopped or visited family. Claude therefore knew before they did that most of their fence came down in an almighty wind.

It was not an ordinary fence, but the latest design of sprung steel around small wooden panels joined together in a long line. It relied on good posts to support it and stop it dancing free. Dangerously free.

A team of 'contractors' appeared within the hour, pretending they were looking for work after the storm. Roger authorised repairs at once, relieved their garden would be secure again.

Too late, Roger realised they were a bunch of cowboys, the fence was simply tied back up and appeared to be twisted and held back to a pair of holly trees by its own weight, not unlike an elastic band. The receipt for the cash showed an address that Roger realised later did not exist.

Most people hoped the worst was over; Claude banked on a sting in the tail of winter; he got a full week of crippling snow across much of the nation, including East Anglia. Indeed, it was all nicknamed, 'The Beast from the East.'

On the night that more high winds were forecast, Vanessa received a 'medical alert' text claiming that her mother who'd moved near to them after the death of Vanessa's dad, was experiencing breathing difficulties.

Roger spent a restless evening indoors, his lights flickering, his internet off, anxious about Vanessa and his mother-in-law. Their phones seemed to be dead.

About ten that evening, Roger took a call from one of his neighbours – at least he thought it was – who'd been walking his dog and noticed Roger's fence straining at the ties and threatening to spring out into the road. The fact that nobody but a madman would walk a dog at the height of the storm escaped Roger at that moment.

Cursing everything, particularly those contractors, he wrapped himself up and ventured out to see for himself. It was as he walked the narrow path along the house wall to reach the end of the garden and make his way back along the perimeter, holding a torch and looking down, that Claude, crouched in the shadow, cut the ties, his gloved hand carefully pocketing the cutters.

The fence was straining, indeed, but it was the other way. It was straining inwards. The line of panels suddenly freed of their restraints sprung towards the house, still fixed at one end but acting as a giant, flapping swat at the other.

Roger was smacked from behind, squashed against the wall, like a fly, bleeding from his head.

Claude smiled, nodded and blinked his piggy eyes. A brave observer out and about might have thought he was crying, but this was a tear of joy.

Claude's day was certainly made as he rolled away, recovered his car three streets off, punched on his favourite military band music and drove home.

The world felt suddenly cleaner. The Blue-Arsed Fly was finally still.

# A Chorus of Hallelujahs

*I am a camera, one of those handheld do it your selfie things so beloved of people these days.*

Jay smiled in the mirror. Jay was a superb high school drama teacher. There are drama teachers and there are great ones. Jay stood out. And on the day the Drama Department had to present their annual assembly, Jay had decided to break the mould and do a solo of the kind that exam students were constantly being urged to try.

A monologue that would turn heads, bring a lump to the throat and wow in a big way. Yes, Jay was nearly ready. Face made up with pure white, black eyebrows slightly above their natural placing so the character had a permanent look of surprise.

Jay was actually looking forward to it. Not that the annual departmental assembly was anything to be keen on. Maths, PE, Science and Art laid on assemblies with things to look at. English usually droned on with uninspiring readings that murdered the classics.

But everyone expected Drama to shine. And usually Drama did excel itself with some amazing student performances, both devised and scripted. Jay did rather resent the task, though, as it was surely senior management's job to tackle the tedium of the weekly assembly?

This year's theme was 'What can I do in my life with imagination and if I'm really determined and work hard and obey all the rules and suppress my ideas into the template and modify deep thoughts to toe the party line just think how far I could go.' Or similar.

Just time before the off for a final run into the mirror in the backstage dressing room, used only for the annual school show that the Head insisted on and as backstage for some events the school laid on.

Jay smiled again at Jay in the mirror. A sick, curled lip smile that spoke of darkness and secrets about to be shared that would give the younger kids nightmares for weeks. Bring it on!

*Shuffling through these hallowed corridors, my gown clutched tight as there is a bit of a chill pouring though the broken window outside the library nobody has yet repaired. Some people stare; others turn away. One speaks and stares.*

*I notice it's ten to eleven, according to the clock in the hallway, a big old fashioned thing in a polished dark mahogany case above a door behind which swings the pendulum relentlessly counting the seconds until suddenly it stops each time another one leaves the place.*

*The clock face, a little faded with the years and behind rather dirty glass, sports Roman numerals. Not everyone can translate them, these days.*

*In the Great Chamber I hear a Chorus of Hallelujahs. A heavenly host from on high. Sweet music, harmonies and uplifting words woven together in a divine revelation. It's the cleaner going about her daily flicking of dust from one surface to another.*

*She is from some foreign land, but then, aren't we all in this place? Smiling at me she completes her chorus. It brightens the gloom, just for a moment. I look down to find my footing.*

*When I turn back she is gone and her chorus with her. In her place is somebody I have seen before long enough to remember I do not want to talk to. I turn away, but she hails me with a chorus of caterwauling.*

243

*I am a tape recorder, the old fashioned reel to reel kind I used to have. I capture two of the people in long white coats in conversation.*

*'What's the time, Carlos?'*

*Looking at a phone from his pocket, '10.50, mate.'*

*Why does every male call every other male, mate, when it's clear most loathe each other? 'Hell, where has the morning gone?' retorted Carlos with a shrug.*

*'Down the toilet, mate.'*

*That reminds me someone is supposed to be making an important speech today. Mind you, a lot of people make speeches in here important and unimportant every single day.*

*Perhaps it's me. I am to make a speech! But what shall I talk about? Doesn't usually stop most of them. They just open their mouths and the speeches pour out.*

*'What was her speech about?'*

*'Oh she didn't say.'*

*'But she spoke for 45 minutes!'*

*'Yes but she didn't say what she was talking about. She just talked.'*

*Perhaps I'll play through a few of the tapes I've got secretly stored away. Old ideas are good. People don't remember they've heard them before but as they strike a chord in their minds, they tend to like them. Might even agree with them. Always a bonus.*

'All stand…!'

It's one of those barked orders that echo round corridors, upstairs and down and round the head, so everybody jumps to it. Or stands to it.

There is a procession! Whatever is it? A pompous jackass in fancy costume. What's this, a court of law, yes m'lud, no m'lud? Or is it the House of Commons, Speaker's Procession, hats off!'

Could be either. Or both.

The voice barked again. Somebody at prayers. Oh is this the chapel? But no, who'd be at prayers? As doors are flamboyantly locked, clearly it comes to me, this is the Commons and it's the Speaker at Prayers which means all those inside when the doors are locked stand to pray, each side with its back to the other.

The anteroom clock indicates ten to eleven. The date is blank. Perhaps it doesn't matter. Everyone knows the date even if they can't recall the time.

It floods over me, it's historical. When members wore swords in order to pray they had to kneel on the benches and could only do that when facing the back walls. Brilliant.

It will only last a few minutes and then somebody will speak. It could be me. I decide I will just start by drawing the attention of the handful who will be in there that I have had several decades of experience of this matter and while there are reports and surveys and recommendations, really we should not neglect the expertise that I hold.

Then a wet towel catches me a swipe across the face, sending me staggering. I am a whipping post. A punch to the other side of the head and I am surrounded by old men and women on crutches, frames and chairs pulling my legs off like a spider.

I am at school. Of course I am. A bell rings, kids and teachers respond like trained seals. 11.50, end of break, time to knuckle down again, knucklehead.

I am a dustbin, one of those old tin things that used to rattle when blown over with lids perfect for slamming down hard to make a point. Or several of them substituted for drums when we were kids.

Drums were the least of it. Bins for kicking around, stuffing with smelly rubbish that should no longer be in sight. The lorry would come round on the same day every week and strong men would shoulder carry a bin to it, tip out the contents and slam the empty receptacle back roughly where it was on the pavement.

'Stand here. Sit there. Don't move. Stop dawdling. Don't talk. Speak up.' Ah yes, all the familiar imperatives float about the rooms, school indeed. School as it was, perhaps as it still is, though I doubt it.

I am a rag. They wipe the wall with me, then the floor. They squeeze me out; then wipe the toilet bowl over and over. These are the best days of your life they say. But nobody says it while they're living it, of course.

I am making my way with some purpose. I could need to take food in. Or evacuate waste out, I'm not sure. My hair shirt begins to make me scratch.

In a white tiled chamber with sinks and cubicles a very old pair is washing their teeth. We used to brush them, of course, but that was when they were fixed in our heads. Now they come out for ease of cleaning.

246

It's a chorus of teeth, this moment as they rattle and grind, almost in unison. Another dodders in and adds his (perhaps her) strand to the key of something of other. Teeth at dawn.

Useful teeth – for biting, shaping insults, praise or love words. Words of hate. But now they're not so useful. They don't always fit, some don't stay in and some allow copious dribbling. Some are missing altogether, leaving a memory or pure imagination about what they used to be.

There is a feeding area. I suppose this must be it. Long tables and a selection of benches, raised chairs, gaps for the wheel chairs or for the terminal standers (people who stand rather than sit) and a few better chairs padded with cushions for ancient backsides.

I am a sponge, absorbing sounds, fragments of phrases, squeaks, curses, mutterings dotted with the occasional moment of sheer brilliance. Yes, this is the home of confrontational politics at its best.

There is a long row of arm chairs, a sofa and a few hard seats for the tougher frames. A line of men and women. I catch a chorus of bad breath as I stagger past them, one by one. Halitosis when they speak, stutter, belch, curse or hang open to supplement nose breath.

Tattered flags of newspapers are limp in arthritic fingers or lie forgotten on blanketed laps. One is actually being read by a straight-back man with lips that support what his eyes are reading as he goes along.

Unwatched muted screens flicker from the bays they've been parked in, their demands to watch me, watch me, totally ignored. A little clock in the bottom corner of each screen shows it is 11.50. Only one very old lady has been sat so close to one screen that her eyes must hurt.

247

'I've seen it! I've seen it!' she screeches unaware that nobody hears her. The white coated, grey faced assistants flitter about being busy, busy, busy. So, this is the old cranks' home, isn't it? Yes, has to be.

In what is laughingly described as the community lounge, a big woman in an enormous, garish yellow top and green trousers topped with bright green hair is exhorting the hapless people who've been left there to stretch those arms, flex those legs, twist that neck carefully.

Under her relentless cheerfulness there is a sense of being just a step away from turning all their necks in her ham fists over and over.

None of them moves. None appears to hear. If they did move, I recall from yesterday, there'd be a hideous chorus of knees. Knees cracking, complaining, struggling to support bodies. Not a pretty sound at any time.

Perhaps this is a hospital and I am a goldfish. I go round and round this fishbowl day after day in a kind of routine that once used to be thought sensible and solid but is nowadays given a label, such as obsessive, compulsive or anal.

I shouldn't be here. Hang on, isn't that what almost all prisoners protest? I am innocent. There isn't a guilty man here. Am I in a jail? Isn't everyone, in a way, even incarceration of their own making?

In the hope of avoiding the woman's ministrations, I turn to a chair by the piano, over the way. A broken nursery school clock has hands at ten to eleven. It sits on the piano top.

But there is a little, weasel-faced, wheezing man dressed all in black, with a dark Mexican moustache, dyed black hair like Elvis Presley and an oversize black suit as if he was Johnny Cash, looking bored.

His job appears to be to thump hell out of the piano keys and excite everyone in some old favourites. But they're favourites of people who have long since passed on. These half living folk are not interested in wartime, trenches and home fire singalongs – they want some rock and roll, surely?

At least that's what I want. If anyone of them did manage to sing anything, it would be a chorus of the tone deaf, so best that the paid staff just do their jobs regardless of the outcome.

I have reached the administration area. Here drugs are dished out, two people doing it to double check. But two people can be as wrong as one. Here the important paperwork is done.

And here is the office of the Head of House or Headteacher. Or the Chief Whip. Or the senior doctor. Or the room for a chance to talk to somebody who cares, if there are any. It could even be Room 101 where you face the worst fear you have.

I am a persistent fly so I enter the room. There is a chorus of swivelling eyes as twenty people look at me, the finest minds, sharpest intellects and clever boffins of the age. Every one of them as crazy as a wasps' nest. Ten to eleven on the wall clock, each second marked by a loud tick.

I am a bird's eye in the roof, slowly fading away, my images evaporating, my technology defunct. I release an unintentional chorus of spittle and farting and somebody wipes my face. Can't be looking too much like the living dead, can we? Not when visitors are due.

Today it might be students. They bring a lot of them round, school-kids or medical trainees, some of each. It could be family, or people who claim to be family, probably just to see if

*you're dead yet to get their hands on whatever you leave
behind.*

*Alternatively it could be friends, those you have forgotten.
But you don't know why they're friends and by the look of
abstract blankness on their faces they haven't a clue either.
Perhaps they're other denizens?*

*Equally the visitors might be the bosses or the media who
would love a story about this place. Worse of all, there may be
no visitors at all except those shadows that congregate in our
minds in the absence of other activity. From beyond the grave,
people we have known and are calling us to step across that
great divide.*

*Whoever they are, we can't let them see a chorus of
drooling, can we?*

*They might get upset or feel nauseated.*

*I am a chainsaw. On the blade, engraved by a
craftsperson, it says, 'For you, my lamb'. I hold it here, at my
gargling throat and reach for the switch….*

The applause was deafening, kids jumping about, fisting the
air, high-fiving and behaving as if England had just won the big
match. Senior management smiled benevolently, clapping
politely and tolerating the unseemly cheering.

Jay acknowledged Jay in the mirror. That was quite
something, Jay. Well done. Be careful to pack the chainsaw
safely in its bag.

The door opened to admit a mousy secretary screwing up a
sheet of paper in nervous hands. 'They're ready for you, now.
If you'd like to follow me?'

250

'Ah, Jay, if I may call you Jay?' boomed the Chair. The rest of the puppets sat round nodding like toy dolls. 'Sorry to keep you waiting.' They all checked watches and the wall clock. It was 11.50, of course.

The Chair generously indicated a wooden chair by the Table. Jay sat, smiling, looking around at the selection panel.

'And what, let's start with this, Jay, what do you think you might bring to the medical unit in this institution?

# Howling Darkness

I first met Adam Mann when he was referred to me at the revolutionary clinic I had set up to promote my theories on Howling Darkness Syndrome (HDS) and other original takes on the various conditions that are the human lot.

He struck me as a fine case study who'd be very helpful. At least to me.

I'm someone who has made a career out of debunking the serious side of others' work by coming up with lots of pseudo mumbo-jumbo. My notorious Seaweed Puree therapy for psychosomatic skin disorders and my theory about Sleeping All Day and Working All Night for the Unstable (SADWANUN) both ran for several weeks in the more zany corners of the media.

In that significant year when I met Adam, the little spare room above their family garage was crammed to capacity three days before New Year. Rammed from floor to ceiling with boxes bulging with tinned beans, biscuits, pasta, potatoes, long life milk and packages of food with very long shelf lives. He'd even drawn a map to find what they'd need when hunger struck.

There were sufficient toilet rolls, cleaning materials, soaps and spare electric heaters to survive a nuclear winter. Of course, nobody considered that power supplies might be cut off as well as supermarket doors.

He'd been worried about the family running out of essentials ever since the media began hyping up y2k and the potential that the switch to a new century had for disrupting computers on which the nation was already addicted.

Press and TV loved to ramp up fears of babies and pensioners starving in a cold winter; young people fighting over a few grains of cereal, business deals hanging on a bowl of rice. So he was at the forefront of the domestic stockpiling that gripped millions as the year 2000 dawned.

It was projected that as 31$^{st}$ December 1999 moved inexorably into 1$^{st}$ January 2000, many older computer programs, where four digits were abbreviated to two to save memory, would read 99 as 1999 but not 00 as 2000.

Those vulnerable computers would fail as a consequence, locking supermarket doors, jamming television signals, isolating hospitals, turning off traffic lights, spamming government systems and shutting down global banking - wreaking a societal havoc nobody could live through unscathed.

A further level of panic was fed when people realised that 2000 was in fact a leap year, 366 days instead of 365, although computers had handled leap years previously. Lifts in tall buildings would seize up, farm animals would be unfed, salaries would be unpaid, manufacturing would cease and food rationing imposed.

Screaming hysteria was reached when 9 September 1999 came, since early computer systems had used a row of 9s to close a program. Now martial and curfew laws were dusted down ready to be imposed in every country; the armed forces and police would distribute food on a need to eat basis; looters would be shot on sight.

Armageddon beckoned.

But Adam was not going to put his wife and children through that. Oh no.

And I was going to milk it for all it was worth. I set up the y2k Bug Resistance Course (Y2KBRC) to equip the vulnerable with resilience and backbone. It sold quite well until some of the mainstream health companies emulated me and marketed their own courses with far more generous resources than I mustered.

Adam's kids thought he was mad, certifiably insane and joked about toothpaste, tomato ketchup and spare underpants stocks declining while running about like headless chickens. But they didn't live through or after the last war as his parents and grandparents had done.

He pressed on those precious kids, with the swivel-eyed intensity of a lunatic waxing lyrical about the virtues of higher taxes, that it would be fatal to reveal to any friends and neighbours that they'd stockpiled supplies or they'd have to fight them off. He tried hard to acquire weapons to defend his family.

Teenagers being what they are, of course, I gather that at least half a dozen people living near them knew. One family was inspired to emulate the Manns and make their own deep provision; another relaxed, knowing that they could share, borrow or steal to keep themselves alive.

For most others, Adam Mann was a worrying joke. The blind faith in technicians' ability to solve the Millennial Computer Problem (MCP) was compelling. However, it turned out there was no problem and most systems were more robust for having been prepared for meltdown.

For Eliza, Adam's long suffering wife, it was folly to fill the room with supplies on the off-chance of a computer failure. On the other hand, if Adam was right and there was hunger and rioting, the Manns stood a better chance of survival. I called that the Optimistic Overview Test (OOT).

For me, the story illustrated just how the howling void of the permanently anxious, the howling darkness that threatens to engulf him or her, would make a great chapter in my next planned learned book.

Black dog – he once read that Winston Churchill called his depression his 'black dog'. While liking the term, despite his fear of long-fanged hounds, Adam didn't suffer depression. He was on the obsessive compulsory spectrum (OCS), yes, but towards the tendency to hyper-tense psychiatric anxiety (HTPA).

Adam didn't fear earthquakes, tsunamis, out of control guillotines, alien invasions, nights of the living dead, pandemics of incurable diseases nor environmentally dead winter. He was just anxious one or more could occur and damage his family.

While he didn't dread choking to death in smog during an abnormal heat-wave, being broken into pieces by a tidal surge or discovering a rare brain, heart, liver, kidney and blood disorder he was certainly concerned at the slightest possibility of damage through any failure of his weak human body. Therefore, he was not a hypochondriac; his was a classic Nonspecific Medical Anxiety Projection (NonMAP) diagnosis.

My first question on meeting him, posing as the friendly man sat dressed in elegant comfort on my plush sofa while I indicated my patient should sit and take off his shoes, was, what was your last dream about?

I dreamed I was on the edge of a very tall building, he said. I couldn't look down, I was sweating like a pig, my heart was racing away, begging for a heart attack, but I felt an overpowering surge to throw myself off. When you approached me – I imagine it was you – I warned you don't come any closer, I'm a jumper.

And what did I reply?

You said, don't worry, I'm a pusher.

Interesting! I let a natural pause hang in the air. It's what we in the trade call Delayed Response Exacerbation Technique (DRET) before asking if he found large periods of most days deeply worrying?

Yes. It wasn't worries that a plane would drop out of the sky, it was that a plane may drop with one of his loves on or near it.

Did he regularly feel apprehensive, on edge, a bit nervous about everyday things?

Doesn't everyone? My first thought on waking, assuming there'd been sleep worth calling it, is what's hanging over me today? Is there danger in the cooker and frying pans? Does the door mat mean me harm? Is the fridge singing a veiled threat to me in a minor key? Again, doesn't everyone?

Everything around, does it ever feel like it's on top of you? Is it larger than life? Larger than, dare I say it, normal?

Of course! With time always so short, the demands to work and earn to look after the family so great, to anticipate every mishap, slipping on pack-ice, an accident in a sawmill, falling down a black hole, attack from a gang of juvenile drug-crazed delinquents, robbery with extreme violence, a careless moment on a gallows or blackmail by MI5 is to be under a tidal wave.

What about relaxation and down-time? What about me-time for yourself?

No, not for me. Too much to do, see, stop, expect, prevent, save and rescue.

256

Are there any physical indications of the stress, such as racing heart, headaches, neck tension, dizziness and churning in the stomach sometimes leading to excessive toilet requirements?

Only racing heart, headaches, neck tension, dizziness and churning in the stomach sometimes leading to excessive toilet requirements. Often.

So do any of these terms apply? On the edge, panic, irritability, snapping at people, uptight, low tolerance for others? Faster breathing, trembling, the mind jumping around, always alert to potential disasters and dangers, especially towards others?

Yes. All of them.

A certain amount of stress and anxiety is natural, normal and actually a good thing. Do you experience it more dangerously and frequently than most, would you say?

That's a stressful question. How can I measure that?

Do you avoid doing things where you are fearful; you may be out of control or can't keep those you love close and safe?

I don't go to any social gatherings where I might be mocked, ridiculed, insulted or physically harmed. Getting my kids out of the lower deck on a sinking ship; holding them back from entering a moving washing machine, stopping them lean over a balcony high up, putting medicines and poisons out of reach. And keeping myself out of small spaces, away from clowns and with my feet on the ground.

Let me help you look closely at some causes of your Generalised Anxiety Syndrome, or GAS as we laughingly refer to it.

257

Gas?

You may have stressful periods in your work, social life, home life, relationships that elide together. You may have financial, health or sexual worries. You could be facing major surgery. You may be bereaved or have been bereaved. You may not cope well with new or changing circumstances.

Or, equally and simultaneously, you may have a gene-based propensity to look on the dark side (GBP2LOTDS), to see the worse outcome and to expect constant setbacks and nightmares. You follow?

My grandfather, he was too young in the First World War, but feared the age level being lowered to take him. He was too old in the second war, but feared as they raised the top age, he'd be called up.

Has this influenced you?

Well, of course it did. But it doesn't explain my worry about leaving enough money for her old age if I should go before my wife, or my grandchildren falling victim to some horror I didn't stop from happening. Or some death in a fight that I couldn't win and chaos descends into the screaming void.

We call it the howling darkness or void (HDv). Screaming is the first level of misery; howling is the post-sanity level of abject dejection (PSLAD).

Isn't that what your book is all about?

Yes, and I hope you will invest in a copy. People arrive at the point of being anxious about being anxious (AAbA). You've reached that point, I believe. You're in a vicious circle. Nothing makes you more anxious than being anxious. And when you're not anxious, it makes you anxious.

But dreaming every single possible thing that could go wrong does not insulate you against things going wrong.

I'm worried I'm going over the paid-for time.

Don't worry. This is important. The book will give you coping strategies to replace avoidance. It will structure your time better and focus your mind on the positives. It will rebalance your psychological well-being.

How much is it?

Don't worry about that, it's a tiny detail. Embrace the ambition of owning the solution. What does your wife say about all this?

She's got religion now. She says, do not be anxious about anything, but in everything by prayer and thanksgiving let your requests be made known to God. She wants me to have the peace which surpasses all understanding.

That's laudable. You could do worse. But buy my book and we'll go from there. Oh by the way, did you worry about this session before you first came here?

Yes, I did. I worried that you'd be a con artist, a fraudulent taker of my money and I'd fall for it. I don't always see dangers, despite having anxiously anticipated them in advance.

Well, that's half the battle won, then, my friend.

At no point was Adam Mann ever considered a suicide or self-harm risk. His anxieties were not of that order. Dreams of being in dangerous places where he could die (battles, high mountains, down mine shafts) were not totally taking over his mind, compelling him to wish them into existence.

259

Rather, he was focused on fears about loved ones more than himself because he loved them in a way that made them an extension of himself. I called it the Displacement Anxiety Complex (DAC).

From his comment about Eliza I concluded from my wide experience that of all the separate parts of his world, he feared losing her more than any other, including his left arm.

When they were first together, he'd get in a state about her ditching him for someone else. That was a natural male fear, but he'd carry it to an extreme by following her discretely, asking her friends and sisters about her previous relationships.

They played the sharing-the-past game that all couples play, quite early on. Eliza soon realised that Adam couldn't take it. It wasn't straightforward jealousy about her past; it was complex anxiety that things could have been different with a different man – she'd got pregnant, diseased, emigrated or he'd have murdered her in a drunken rage.

It really was a severe case of the What If Historical Anxiety Condition (WIHAC), where the 'what might have happened but didn't' becomes more overpowering and unsettling than the present or even the future.

Finally, as they settled into their marriage he stopped experiencing immediate loss as his main fear. Certainly once children came along, they became the prime worry. Though, during one session he did confide to me that when he was working a hundred miles away, he'd imagine he'd arrive home to find her old boyfriend sitting in his lounge chair.

Adam's mind then entertained several imaginary outcomes. In one, the boyfriend made an either/or offer for Eliza – marriage or an affair. Adam told him that the third option was that he pissed off back to the hole he crawled from, never to reappear.

In the second, the man was already married to Eliza and the children were his – he demanded of Adam what he was doing in his house.

I called this Anxiety Transfer Syndrome (ATS) in which the sufferer is the victim, the weak link, the outsider and the cuckold. All at once. It was slammed in the peer review journal, *New Human Dimensions*, so I cancelled my subscription.

Funnily enough, the day Eliza did leave Adam began ordinarily enough. It was a Wednesday in early summer. People had breakfast, went to schools and work, argued, shopped and cleaned. There was no warning, no clue and no prophecy.

About four hundred yards from their house a sinkhole opened up in the garden of a bungalow occupied by an elderly couple. It started small – a neighbour walking a dog noticed it on her way out. By the time she returned, it had grown to swallow the whole garden and path to their front door.

Unable to ring their bell to alert them, she rushed home to call for help. Even before she reached her own house, the hole suddenly enlarged itself with a rumbling and clouds of dust in a voracious hunger that gulped a car in the street and the whole of the front of the bungalow.

By now others were alerted and emergency calls started to flood in to the rescue operators. The hole moved rapidly, for a moment going in four directions and then after a moment in one only – towards the railway line.

The suburban service that fed into London was always busy, even mid morning. There was too little time to make the calls necessary to stop the next train. It was not going that fast, but with a massive hole beneath the rails it wasn't going anywhere but down.

The front dropped into the hole with the remainder crumpling into it and the very back splaying out away from the track, across the road and crashing into a lorry carrying sheet metal that swept off the road and into the side of a four storey apartment building under renovation.

What would later be described by almost all media channels as the domino effect – I roughed out a plan to offer counselling for people suffering Domino Anxiety Syndrome (DAS) later – came into play as the building rocked under the impact.

A gigantic cloud of dust was dislodged from the roof area, swept down the scaffolding and landed on the road beyond the crippled steel lorry.

A sudden gust of wind shifted it to the junction with another road, engulfing the traffic lights which caused a delivery van to skid on the spilt fuel from the lorry and a fire to erupt from the cigarette of a man standing on the pavement.

The fire caught hold in a split second, taking more cars and some of the screaming people. By now a major alert had been recognised by the powers that be who activated their major incident procedures. Fire engines en route, hospitals on standby and armed police racing there, just in case.

Eliza was hanging washing in her garden when the noise started and she stood craning for a better view because she assumed a terrorist attack was under way. She had a moment to be glad that Adam wasn't at home or he'd be in major panic mode by now.

An almighty explosion as an old Ford Fiesta blew into a thousand bits sent metal shards, three wheels and parts of two bodies into the air. Eliza stepped sharply aside to avoid a large piece of shrapnel descending towards her but stepped badly on the garden path and twisted her ankle.

She went down with a cry of pain, smashing her head on the brick wall that Adam had built. If this'd been a year ago, the wall would've collapsed under her. But last winter when the country was battered by horrendous gales, Adam had strengthened the wall with metal posts, a double layer of bricks and wire mesh.

It didn't give an inch. Eliza's neck was broken and her head shredded against the wall. She bled out slowly.

Nobody could have predicted that sequence. Even Adam in his wildest struggles in the howling darkness of anxiety, could not have dreamed all that occurring in that order.

It gave me my greatest product, a home tuition course for the treatment of Multiple Anxiety Disorder, MAD for short.

Oh, yes, I've just received an email from the Society for Psychotherapists and Analyst Practitioners (SocPaP) who are threatening to deregister me and kick me out of their club for unprofessional conduct bordering on the charlatan (UCBoC).

I'm not fussed. I'm not registered with them anyway. I'm freelance.

# Time to Stand and Scream

The dog-walker was paused across the street while her pooch performed on a grass verge when he emerged from the bungalow, stood for a moment to draw breath before letting out an almighty scream, a from-the-depths-of-his-body scream.

It was a silent scream.

John Peredes stopped screaming to draw more breath. He noticed Gail, the dog-walker. 'Oh hi, Gail. I was just silent screaming. What is this life if we have no time to stand and scream?'

She nodded with a smile. 'Been to see your old mum, have you? How old is she now?'

'She's 89 and as sharp as a scimitar mentally, but physically is not safe putting one leg in front of the other.'

'Well, at least she's there mentally. My dad is quite well advanced in his dementia. He doesn't always recognise me.'

And so began a conversation held in almost identical terms up and down the country between people sharing the common condition of needing to look after elderly parents while they themselves were getting on a bit too and also having children of their own to help with, grandchildren, maybe even great grandchildren.

His was the generation trapped between the oldies and the youngsters, pulled both ways. A rock and a hard place. It was a phrase John used a lot, to himself.

Peredes loved his old mum, of course; she was only sixteen years older than he was and daily asserted she was ready to go if the good Lord would only take her, she knew she was a burden to everyone.

Her son usually had to count to five before going through the ritual of saying, 'don't be silly, everyone loves you...'

What he had stopped loving for some time were the incredible waves of righteous rectitude, the puzzlement that nobody shared her views, the frustration that she could do less and that nobody, least of all John, could read her mind.

She didn't say it like that. She chafed and ranted, she snapped and snarled at him, usually after forgetting the 'thank you' word when he'd sorted the shopping, arranged a plumber, renewed her house insurance, listened to a rerun of a much-loved tale and failed to answer 'why don't they do this or that, or why do they do the other?'

She sometimes transferred how she felt onto him. 'What's the matter with you?' snarled the moment he walked in.

'Nothing.'

'Well, you don't look it,' she snapped back.

It wasn't just the small age gap between them, but there was a closeness during her early widowhood and the shared years of his schooldays, teenage years and all the activities he'd been involved in ever since.

When his kids were little, she never stinted on the help, getting involved in things, babysitting happily and frequently. She made, cooked, sorted, repaired, listened and did her best for years. She often turned up with a paintbrush, if she thought they needed radiators or a door painted.

She was feisty, refusing to take no for an answer if something had to be achieved. Nowadays, though, stubbornness was an unattractive trait.

After a fall one afternoon and a night spent on the floor in her outhouse to the kitchen before he called the next day led to her accepting an emergency alarm call button round her neck with bad grace to the point of making him want to strangle her with the cord.

Tough old bird that she was, she spent three days in hospital under protest realising at once what was wrong with the entire NHS and getting upset at the treatment of an old woman in the bed next to her who's son didn't visit often enough.

It was from a genuine desire to leave some of her assets to him and his sister, Marina, having paid 'more tax than anyone else' all her working life that made her determined not to go into a home.

Over the years she formed an unshakable view that all old folk homes were terrible, dark places depicted by Hieronymus Bosch. Allowed no possessions in such hell pits, all old people had their dignity stolen, were bullied to join jolly communal activities, play bingo and – heavens above – talk to a lot of old fools who were deaf and daft.

When she wearied of her food – an uninspiring palette from her wartime childhood – she proclaimed all there was to eat in those places was the ultimate gastronomic horrors of gravy, mashed potatoes, garlic and salad.

She graciously allowed the family to find and engage a cleaner one morning a fortnight and a gardener one hour every two weeks. Both of these well-meaning, perfectly reasonable people revealed their 'uselessness' after a week or two, after which she soldiered on, for once aware that John

266

didn't agree with her and was in no mood to find replacements to suit her better.

He was running her home and his – usually putting her demands first. She needed a new carpet. She wanted to move a flower bed nearer the lounge window. If only she could get that leak fixed, that light altered and that cupboard sorted.

If he and Angela took her out, she spent most of the journey commenting on people's gardens (better than hers because they had the help they needed), other drivers (only women knew how to drive) and why on earth was that woman wearing that colour?

It was getting more difficult for her to enter and exit the car, to shuffle about, one hand clutching a stick, the other Angela's arm. John walked with a stick of his own and was not safe to support his, let alone her weight. They bought her a collapsible wheelchair to go on outings, but she refused to be seen in it – what would people think!

In a country, particularly a town, of aging hobblers, sitters, motorised cart drivers and white hair, who would comment on another old woman in a wheelchair? But she'd have none of it.

Nor the rollator they bought for her to safely and more easily access the dying extremes of her garden. No, that was for old people! And she couldn't bear to see how her garden was giving up the ghost because she couldn't deal with it, anyway, so would rather chafe at her inability to make it down the garden, even using the specially fitted hand rails.

When one of her grandsons installed her a new hose and had fun trying out the spray gun effect, he was told in no uncertain terms that he'd killed 'all' the flowers through overwatering them in the summer heat.

John's visits gradually became daily, though he was still self employed working part time. Perhaps it was the familiarity, the expectation that he'd over-think her medication as she did, anticipate what she wanted to say and what her needs were, that made some visits such a hard slog.

Saint Marina's twice annual descent from the Olympian clouds of Ireland was the hardest of all. The build-up was horrendous. Mother's expectations shot through the roof – what they weren't going to see and do together; such progress in the garden they'd make and endless sparkling conversations where everyone would be put right and the world would be happy in the order they ordained.

The come-down was an obsessive mix of frustration, disappointment and puzzlement that Marina hadn't agreed with every view, spent too much time flogging herself cleaning the kitchen and/or toilet and toiling in the lost war of keeping the garden under control. Neither had she shown signs of improving her mind reading skills.

John prepared the ground; he cleared up the pieces after she'd gone back.

He acquired the patience of Job listening to how it was when he was born, when Marina was a toddler, when his late grandmother went into hospital two decades ago. He smiled at those tales told endlessly, grumbles made in a loop and accepted that we all will grow old one day and may all be in the same boat as his mum. If we live long enough.

Oh, but he did find it all very tiring sometimes.

\*\*\*\*\*\*\*\*\*\*\*\*\*\*\*\*\*\*\*\*\*\*\*\*\*\*\*\*\*\*\*\*\*\*\*\*\*

**Boxing Day 1946**

The town, still struggling in its post-war bleakness and drab greyness, offered little entertainment for anyone, let alone young people.

Daphne went to the pictures in the afternoon to get out of her parents' house and because she wanted time talking with her friend Mildred. Christmas Day had been a lengthy ordeal with little to celebrate and next to nothing to celebrate it with.

By mid afternoon, it was already dark and a handful of the gas lights in the street had been lit, throwing flickering shadows across the broken pavements.

Shoulders hunched against the North Sea chill rolling in, they walked arm in arm, no longer seeing the shells of war bombed buildings, the piles of rubble and the gaps in some streets like a toothless oldie waiting to suck on dried up gums.

It was Mildred, excited to go to a dance that evening who argued it would be more fun if they both went. Besides, a single woman alone at a dance was not the acceptably 'done' thing.

A former warehouse near the sand cliff top had survived both world wars and had recently been painted in several shades of clashing cream and vomit green. Someone had whimsically named it the Palais de Dance and ran one do a month.

The pair paid their shilling apiece and entered, hanging their coats in the cloakroom. Then they braved the hall itself. A band made up of an oily haired crooning chancer in his twenties, supported by a trio with ages totalling 190 on drums, piano and trumpet/sax, did their best.

Wall flowers clung to the perimeters. Most men were propping up the bar. It was beer for them or spirits for the

269

ladies. Still not late but there was already the air of the last dance, time to put the lights out and go home.

Most of the younger men had recently been demobbed from one of the services; some older men had worked keeping home fires burning, making weapons, providing food or serving the community in teaching, medicine or transport.

A few of these were looking out for a companion for their crowning years; the hungry youngsters were looking for fun with the possibility of settling down.

Ben Peredes saw her before she saw him. He noted the little blonde in a red dress. She later admitted she'd wanted to wear brown, but Mildred had been persuasive. Ben too had almost not gone, as dancing and drinking were anathema to him and his two left feet.

Soon Daphne and Mildred were spoilt for choice for a dance and a drink, or just the drink. As the evening wore on, some of the blokes offered a walk home.

But Ben, uncharacteristically, pushed himself to get to them first and found it was easy to talk, to laugh, to do a hog-tied shuffle round the floor, to share a drink, tales from home and the war years – he in the Navy; she finishing her childhood and growing up.

Gradually the competition melted away. Mildred found herself someone for the evening and only the singer tried it on as the last dance was called, offering to give the blonde a ride home, if she knew what he meant.

They were married the following September. Many years later John worked out that he was actually at that wedding, though scarcely showing yet.

*\*\*\*\*\*\*\*\*\*\*\*\*\*\*\*\*\*\*\*\*\*\*\*\*\*\*\*\*\*\*\*\*\*\**

Marina arrived five years later. A difficult, touch and go birth was followed by a challenging childhood for the whole Peredes family. John was usually the model child; Marina suffered the illnesses and the short fuse.

That said, their childhood was invariably described by anybody who bothered to think about it, as ordinary, quite dull and uneventful.

Infant schools, junior school, the 11-plus exams (John scraped through; Marina passed with flying colours) and Grammar School - the traditional education of lower middle class children in a small east coast town in the early 1960s.

By the time the hippies, drugs, sex and psychedelic music, art and fashion rocked up, the siblings were well into it. And their mother went along, too, throwing herself into the zeitgeist but not in a cringe-making way.

She opened a popular little pet supplies store, took an Open University degree as her own education had been destroyed by German bombs forcing her to be evacuated and volunteered practically and enthusiastically for every charity she could find.

But Ben Peredes missed all that, having been dead for some time - killed by a drunk hit and run motorcyclist, hell-bent on being somewhere else when he felled Ben crossing the road too slowly.

Daphne suddenly was not only a widow in her 30s but had to clear off business debt, sort out paperwork when it was still almost impossible for a woman to do anything and raise two teenagers on her own.

271

That she did it, that the three of them turned out pretty sane (with just a few wobbles) was a tribute to her maternal instincts and her grim determination to put the children first to make up for the life she argued had been snatched from them.

John was always grateful for that. It meant that he could attend university and later developed a career as an educational psychologist while Dr Marina eventually became a Professor of Sociology in Dublin.

And throughout it all from helping hands with money (Daphne gifted them property to fund their studies) to being involved with friends, experiments, further studies and closely with them when they became parents, there was never a moment's doubt but that Mother would step up to the plate and place a hefty wedge into it.

Even when a smaller or no contribution of help and advice would have been more suitable, thought John's wife, Angela, and Marina's husband, Todd.

And it was only in his sixties, after years of impossibly making up to his mother for what she'd lost as best he could while reflecting the fact that his own wife and kids came first, that he began to grow weary with the effort.

Bone weary.

\*\*\*\*\*\*\*\*\*\*\*\*\*\*\*\*\*\*\*\*\*\*\*\*\*\*\*\*\*\*\*\*\*\*\*\*

Many people over excited themselves when medical progress promised to keep human beings alive, not exactly forever, but certainly for decades after what might be deemed a 'natural' span.

Never mind how that sort of unproductive life was to be funded, how healthcare for so many ancient people was to be

272

managed and how young generations were to cope with a world of nodding grey heads, many demented, most carriers of multiple diseases and difficulties.

Every time he heard it, John reflected daily on which filling he was in that media labelled 'sandwich generation', caught between the needs of elderly parents and their own kids.

The sandwich sagged a little lopsided when children became parents themselves. It was often a four or even five generation beast. Lately, John had felt crushed by the weight around, below and above him.

Marina worried about not doing enough, but her lifestyle meant she really could only make those two annual visits and phone every week wrapped up in copious commiserations. Of course, if he wanted her to come more, she would. Of course.

He was invariably unable to drum up enthusiasm for more regular visits and didn't think the old lady would appreciate them. It took weeks for her to calm down from the trips that were made.

John adored his grandchildren, often marvelling how they could be both like him and yet different; such fun and yet so exasperating. He and his wife helped when they could with them, facilitated work for their children that way and did loads of things with the little ones.

He did find it physically draining. Nothing he could put his finger on. Nothing he could really ask the doctor about.

The usual aches and pains of advancing years – what Prince Charles described as 'bits dropping off' were present as he approached his seventieth birthday. His mother increasingly seemed unable to grasp that he was anything less than a young man, if not the boy she had raised.

Even that was wearisome.

*************************************

**Easter 1977**

It was a conference dedicated to educational psychology. It was an excuse for a handful of worthy delegates to go to a fancy hotel in the Midlands and eat too much, drink voraciously, talk lots of jargon and claptrap and generally feel much better informed.

John was to make a short presentation in the after lunch slot where those short of sleep catch up and people look ahead in their minds to dinner, the evening and night.

He saw her in a small circle at the midmorning coffee break. Tall and dark haired; elegant and poised, she was listening politely to drivel from a bloke obviously trying to impress her.

She looked up for a moment, perhaps sensing John's eyes on her. She looked away, but had clearly registered him.

He found his legs moving towards the group, his stomach turning but a definite determination in his mind that was not always part of his nature.

Ignoring the whole circle, almost to the point of rudeness, he held out his hand to her and kept it there till she took it.

'Hello, I'm John, John Peredes and I couldn't help noticing you during that last session...'

It was a lie, but the line allowed her to giggle in response, 'wasn't it awful? Who was that woman? Do they assume we don't know anything about educating teenagers?'

'Absolutely! I sensed you shared my thoughts.' John would have agreed the session had been sheer brilliance if she'd said that.

Finally taking his hand for a shake, she smiled at him in a conspiratorial way, 'I'm Angela. Where are you from?'

The jaw of the guy who'd been talking almost visibly dropped. He looked around at the rest of the informal circle and switched his focus to a small redhead with very white teeth.

The rest of the event was lost to John as he and Angela spent every spare moment talking. When they had to endure a speech, slides or discussions they sat together, nudging and making faces.

Once he returned to the office to report the event and 'cascade' down to colleagues, he rated it the best thing he'd ever been to.

John and Angela were married a year later and she secured a post in his area. His mother seemed to quite like her, included her in all that she did, but John sometimes felt a sense that Angela wasn't quite what Daphne would have chosen for him.

But she didn't choose. He did. It was the most positive thing he ever did.

*******************************************

He pondered and fully intended for ages to write an account of his mother's life and times as a homily to her achievements and for his grandchildren and others to understand that what old age did to her was not a reflection of her whole life.

It was to be the kind of address people make at a funeral, where the deceased is often en route to beatification. Indeed, he thought it would come in useful when that occasion actually arrived.

He never did write it. Marina dismissed the idea as fanciful, knowing he wouldn't – there were days, about one in five, when he could barely bring himself to leave the house, let alone recall and set down trivial details.

And for Marina there were still issues in their early years around the time of her father's death that were unresolved. In fact, they were unmentioned.

Daphne was of a generation that didn't discuss emotions, didn't expose private business and feelings with others. Nor with her own children, Marina often stormed. Marina would encourage no fond anecdotes of Daphne in her heyday.

When her daughter went into the world of sociology, the middle aged lady buttoned her lips even more. 'It was just not what we spoke about. I couldn't bring your father back. What good was there in opening all those wounds?'

They never agreed. And John was regularly in the middle. An exhaustive place to sit for long.

*********************************

In the 1990s there was a bit of a flurry when an old man was found dead in his bungalow not far from the Peredes' home. He'd been battered and strangled in what was described as a frenzy.

Outpourings of sympathy swamped the town. Poor old man. The old bugger – whoever he was – didn't deserve that.

Probably thieves on a scam that went wrong. Possibly someone from his past set on revenge.

When his middle-aged daughter was arrested and charged with his murder, the frenzy of gossip and speculation spread from locals to the media, even the national outlets.

A woman killed her own father!

At the trial it was established that the old man had dementia and was incredibly difficult to support, as attested by all his carers and his daughter. Over the years, her mental condition had deteriorated under the pressures generated by keeping him in his own home.

She got five years for manslaughter on the grounds that she had simply snapped, had not planned it and was a sick woman herself.

As the fuss died down, she vanished behind prison walls, the bungalow was demolished and rebuilt and people's lives moved on to the next tragedy engulfing others.

It stayed with John, though. How much would a man get for murdering his old mother without mitigating mental illness? How soon could he show mental illness to the outside world? Did silent screaming outside her house count?

Few in his family or his tiny circle of friends found it funny when he said he might do it. Nobody thought he was even capable of such a thing, if they considered it seriously at all.

And of course he wasn't remotely able to do it. Blood is thicker than water, and all that. She had birthed and raised him. She had devoted her life to him. It was a duty to honour your father and mother.

It didn't say anywhere that if they were difficult, couldn't move, hear, see or remember as well as they did, then it was ok to wash your hands of them.

No, of course not.

So girding himself, he soldiered on.

\*\*\*\*\*\*\*\*\*\*\*\*\*\*\*\*\*\*\*\*\*\*\*\*\*\*\*\*\*\*\*\*\*\*\*\*\*\*\*

Like a cancer that starts as a bruise, problems don't just heal themselves. John was vaguely aware that things couldn't continue as they were. But that was life. Things do carry on, exactly as they were. Or they only get worse.

After an early summer evening, 2018, during which he'd complained to Angela of even more tiredness, world weariness and loss of appetite than usual, he had a very early night.

John Peredes passed away in his sleep.

Following one initial scream as Angela informed her, his mother never uttered a sound again as long as she lived. And she had seven long years alive after that.

Time enough to sit and scream. Silently.

# The Alcatraz Stretch

Wherever they went during their Californian holiday, the Websters were styled variously 'the whole bunch', 'the tribe', 'the gang' or 'goodness, you're a big family!'

Sometimes they'd be asked, 'You Australians, you guys?' The response to being told the Websters were actually English varied between a lot of head nodding and sheer puzzlement. English? Are there such people?

And this in California, the home of the Big. Dad, Vernon, was a building surveyor in his late 40s but here more like a kid fulfilling his lifetime dream of being in the Sunshine State. And being proud that his big brood could share it with him.

His wife of twenty odd years, Ceri, was less relaxed. She was enjoying it, knew it was an experience, but worried about their savings that had gone into it, about keeping four kids safe and how strange so much was, even though like most Brits she was steeped in American movies and books.

They'd often been thought an odd couple. Vernon was ten inches below average, but packed some extra weight. Ceri stood ten inches above the average and was sparse on her frame. He took risks in the heat; she would rather stay in the safer shadows.

The sun burned him a bright red set off with blisters; Ceri's skin remained pale and interesting. Adoring movies, it was their draw that both brought them together and drove his desire to relive several of his favourite scenes.

Mel was their eldest, a tall, somewhat awkward girl on that hideous cusp of teenage at 12 years of age and starting to find her dad, her mum and occasionally her siblings grotesquely embarrassing. She was aware of the looks she got, particularly from young men, but wasn't yet ready either to provoke or enjoy them.

At 9, Martin was already taller than his peers by some way, good at athletics but neither confident nor able to push himself at school or home. By contrast, Lucas, a shorter 7 years, dumpy, energetic roller-ball forever on the go, pushed at boundaries.

Little Annette was their youngest. At 4 going on 5 she'd remember none of this trip in the years ahead, but Vernon felt the others would, so it was worth it. The early signs of being more like Ceri than him were showing, and he just adored her for that.

They bought a two-day, queue hopper pass for Disney in Anaheim and in Hollywood with photos of the iconic white letters in the background he had them standing in the footsteps of the greats in the walk of fame. They'd driven the Californian coastal highway in a hired limo, with Vernon having to master automatic driving pretty quickly.

Once they reached San Francisco Vernon knew he was at the apex of the US mountain he'd always dreamed about.

He had them all on the trams at least three times a day and, grinning broadly, crammed them into a people carrier taxi to recreate the chase scene from *Bullitt*. Twice.

They'd admired the Golden Gate Bridge so often everyone was sick of it. Ceri had vetoed a second run round the *Dirty Harry* movie sites. In Chinatown he waxed lyrical about *Joy Luck Club*. Ceri and the family played on games in the hotel room while he took a taxi alone to explore the city's features including Nob Hill that was in Hitchcock's *Vertigo* (1958) and others in Woody Allen's *Play It Again, Sam* (1972).

This was living the dream - California dreaming indeed. And especially San Francisco. The movie titles rolled off his tongue – *San Francisco* (1936), *48 Hours* (1982), *Dark Passage* (1947), *Harold and Maude* (1971), *Mrs Doubtfire* (1993), *The Conversation* (1974) and even up to date with *Blue Jasmine* (2013). Vernon prided himself that he knew them all.

They learned at the start of the holiday that most Americans staying in hotels don't eat breakfast in them. They go to breakfast hotspot hotels where the bargains were. If they weren't staying in a hotel, they'd still often go out for breakfast. Breakfast was big business.

And it was in the queue for breakfast at the Sunny Daze Hotel (they were staying at the Holiday Inn), that the family encountered Racey Kravitz though they didn't learn his name till later in the day.

At over six foot he was stood in front of them in line. Waiting for the doors to open, people started random conversations and the tall man turned around to see what was behind him, the children's high pitched-chatter a sign of hunger.

'Hi, you guys', Kravitz growled at them.

They nodded and Vernon acknowledged it with a British, 'Good morning', ready for the inevitable question about them being Aussies.

But it never came. The tall man was more interested in the needs of his stomach as well.

'They always keep you waiting like this, sons of bitches. They enjoy the power. I seen it before.' He stared off into the distance, over the heads of everyone else, even Ceri.

With no sign of the doors opening any time soon, Vernon craned his neck up and took it on himself to talk to the guy.

Ceri kept her eyes on the children, holding Martin and Lucas apart and picking up Annette when she started to get restless.

'You could have breakfast at the Hilton. Or downtown, any place. There are breakfast places all over the city. And they're all the same, keep you waiting in line.'

'Well, it must be soon, or the kids will start eating each other,' suggested Vernon by way of a joke.

The man stared down at him with something approaching pity through watery eyes in a lined face that had been around the block. His wispy grey hair stuck up, his hairy ears were enormous, his chin was firm and needed a shave. This man had to be in his 80s, Vernon realised, yet he stood tall in a posture that spoke of defiance.

'I hope they like slop,' he said shaking his head, 'because that's all they got here. Slop. Breakfast slop.'

'Well, you're going to eat it!' Vernon cried, a little surprised.

'Slop, I tell you.'

'Don't you want to eat somewhere else, then?'

'Oh they're all slop. Everywhere is slop.'

On that, the doors opened with a flourish allowing the line to surge forward inside to gorge themselves on slop.

Ceri knew it would become a family joke. Slop. Breakfast slop everywhere. She knew it the way Vernon kept on sharing it with the kids, 'enjoying your slop, kids? Like sloppy eggs, Martin? More bacon with your slop, Mel?'

Once they left the breakfast, the slop joke was temporarily forgotten as they made their way to Pier 33 Landing to catch

282

the boat to Alcatraz. Vernon had already told them about *Point Blank* (1967) amidst a host of movies made on and about 'The Rock'.

A film of that name came out in 1996 and there was *Escape from Alcatraz* (1979), Dad enthused to his kids before realising that he may have already told them about Alcatraz films.

It was actually a good thing they'd been staying several days in San Francisco they learned two days ago when they booked tickets for the former prison. It was a highly popular location and you had to book a time slot on a particular day, often weeks ahead.

They'd struck lucky and got a party ticket. Vernon failed to stop himself from repeating for the millionth time as they marched towards the line to board the ferry - the Island had been a federal penitentiary from the 1930as to the 1960s. Mel sighed loudly.

He confirmed that Al Capone was a famous inmate, sentenced for tax evasion, not murder. The 'Birdman' of Alcatraz was there – film named after him in 1962. There were 14 separate escape attempts involving 36 inmates. Twenty three were caught; six were shot dead and two drowned.

Five disappeared but were never seen again. Close as the island is to the city, how dangerous the waters are. When his memory dried up, Vernon read from the leaflet they'd been handed, focussing on the prison time not the wealth of history before or after.

It was a fair but tough prison. By now his whole bunch had heard enough. Annette didn't understand any of it and Mel would have preferred somewhere else where she could sit and soak up the sun. The boys just wanted a swimming pool.

The sun broke through. Yesterday had been a bit obscured by fog. They joined the line, Ceri checking their tickets against the signboards overhead.

'I hope you guys haven't paid top dollar for this!' growled a familiar voice behind them.

They swung to see the tall 'slop' man from breakfast, which made the kids giggle. Ceri glanced at him; then looked around her. Vernon smiled warmly and wondered how to phrase a question about whether he'd enjoyed his sloppy breakfast.

'I said, I hope you guys haven't paid top dollar,' the man repeated, showing no sign of having seen them not two hours ago. 'We Americans can't bear to pay top dollar for anything.'

Vernon shook his head rigorously, 'No, no, we got some discount as we are members of the AA – the Automobile Association in Britain, it gave us something off. Every little bit helps.'

'You don't never wanna pay top dollar, never,' the tall man reaffirmed as if Vernon had just admitted to paying over the odds for their tickets.

The conversation died. Vernon turned back, stretching his neck after the big tilt up. The kids had long lost interest in the weird man; just standing in line was an unwarranted burden. 'These people love standing in line, don't they,' Mel muttered.

Suddenly the queue moved forward and they left the man behind and scrambled to find seats on the top deck of the ferry. During the short ride, Vernon found it necessary to dig up yet more fascinating facts about the prison island, till Ceri muttered, 'I expect there'll be guides there, Vernon'.

In fact there were lots of guides and for the actual Cellhouse tour they were given headsets and a little device to

284

hang round their necks with all the words for a truly informative experience.

But first, as they moved off from the quayside to the toilets and then upwards, they noticed a large crowd congregating - old men, a few with old woman accompanying them, several in wheelchairs, greeting each other with much slapping on the back, bear hugs and hysterical laughter.

It was Martin who spotted him among them, a head above but to the side. 'There's Mr Slop!' he yelled, pointing rudely and with a little jump.

Sure enough, their breakfast, top dollar stranger was very much part of a rendezvous of some sort. 'Yeah, that's a reunion of inmates and guards...' a voice told them.

It was one of the volunteer guides who'd noted the family staring across. 'They come every year, for an alumni reunion, those who served time and those who guarded them, all buddies now.'

The Websters could only stare and think about that. A reunion! Would those two groups really want to meet up? Obviously, yes.

'They're all getting on a bit now,' the guide noted. 'Perhaps a year or two more and the Alumni Association will have to call it a day.

They pushed it out of the forefront of their minds as they made their way round the bits of the old imposing fortress open to them and accessible with the children scampering about, letting off steam.

They took photos of each in turn in a cell that was open for the purpose. They stared moodily out the barred windows across the bay to the city as inmates must have done. The city sounds carried across the water, adding a further torture for inmates and perhaps guards too.

Vernon wanted to lecture about a similar feeling he'd got on the Greek leper island of Spinalonga, where people afflicted by a hideous infectious disease could hear others across the waters, but couldn't join them. But it was neither appropriate nor welcomed by the family right now.

In the old exercise yard they sat on steps – out of the wind they burned hot in the sun, in the wind it felt pretty chilly. The yard was all grim and foreboding but what a lesson of social history, as Vernon felt but didn't utter once he'd caught Ceri's warning glance.

Vernon enjoyed it more than most, as usual, but Mel would remember much of this particular experience and she'd seen some of the movies Dad went on about on the DVD collection in their house. Ceri had gleaned something from a few moments, when she wasn't fussing about Annette's toilet, food or safety needs.

Martin and Lucas found the cells and the bars cool, the dusty refectory a bit weird and the showers boring. The yard was good for a bit of a run and a bundle over an empty cola can to kick around till they were stopped by both parents and a volunteer guide simultaneously.

It was coming down the final slope towards the ferry landing stage for the trip back to the city that they came face to face with Mr Slop. He stood with his mouth open, staring at them all, but particularly at Vernon.

Stifling groans or giggles according to age, the Webster family stopped in front of the man. 'Hello, there!' Vernon cried out, 'nice to see you again.'

'Mister, you ain't ever seen me and I ain't ever set eyes on you in my life, but I see you coming down the hill and I just know who you are!'

'You do?' Vernon responded, wondering how he could politely tell Mr Slop they'd had two encounters already that very day.

As the man reached out and took Vernon by surprise with a man hug, crushing the Englishman to his American chest, the boys found a stone to kick about, Annette pressed to be picked up by Ceri and Mel sighed and sat on a rock by the pathside, her fingers itching for a phone she hadn't brought.

'My name is Racey Kravitz. I did a three year stretch in Alcatraz. I was sent here from lots of other jails, because I always seemed to get in with the wrong kinda people, you know? That's what led me to me being there when that son of a bitch storekeeper in that robbery got taken out. Pardon my language, ma'am'

Now he had Mel's and Ceri's interest. Vernon was instantly hooked. 'Yeh, I got eight to ten because I was just a kid. One year older and I'd a got the chair. Paulie got it. But then he pulled the trigger. They used to say everyone in a group was equal in guilt, common purpose.'

'I got noticed on account of my tallness, you see. That's why they called me Racey because, man, I could run. And that was a bad thing for me. It was hard being tall in prison. The sons of bitches guards thought I had it coming. And if you get sent here they call you one tough muther. But I kept my nose clean and after the stretch they sent me home. I come back every year to see the guys.'

Other visitors were struggling to get past them in the pathway, but the former inmate didn't notice. 'Look, shall we... er, move on? Vernon suggested, waving at the ferry station.

287

'Yeh, great idea. Let me buy y'all a cup of coffee'. Refusing to take no for an answer he strode towards the facility, one arm round Vernon's neck leaving Ceri to shepherd the family and follow. As they walked, Vernon told him all the family names and where they came from in England and what his work was and how much he loved America and movies.

In return Kravitz explained he'd just had a great hour with a former guard only a couple of years older than he was who was very nervous being stationed on the Rock back then but quickly graduated into a Grade A Asshole. How they'd laughed about it today in a bizarre reminiscence that defied logic.

Once he'd stood them coffees, colas, cookies and a beer for himself, he stretched out his legs and slapped Vernon on the back heartily. 'Now, I am sure you can see it now, and you, lovely lady, you can see it?'

They were at a loss. He smiled at them. He looked at Mel and waved at her parents as if to say 'what a pair of dopes, hey.'

Mel put down her cola. 'Well, you and Dad look as opposite from each other as it's physically possible to look. You should be a double act on the stage. Be a laugh a minute.'

He slapped the table and roared a strangled chortle. 'Hey, you got it. But we ain't opposites, no, Mel, we are the same. Can't you see it? The eyes? The nose and the chin? Man. We are kin.'

'And the height difference?' It was Ceri, surprising herself with the interjection.

He shrugged it off. 'A few inches, a couple of pounds, different countries, different bringing up. But it's there, we are

288

kin, brother. My father and mother sides both came from England way back.'

'Related as English family origins, you mean?' It was Ceri again.

'No, Ceri, I mean we are blood. We are so identical that somewhere a few generations back, we come from the same man! You got Kravitzes in your family history, Vernon?'

'Not that I know of, Mr Kravitz.'

'Call me Racey. I don't know we got any Websters in the line, but hey, that's not proved, that's all. It don't mean it ain't true.'

It was madness. 'A bit like the movie, *Twins*,' suggested Ceri.

'No lady, we ain't twins. We are family, though.' He had clearly never heard of that particular movie.

Vernon, impressed that Ceri remembered the film, smiled at Kravitz. 'Well, I suppose we'll never know. But thanks for the drinks and we ought to be getting back now ...'

'Sure.' The big man stood and led out at once. The family followed.

All the way back to the city, he regaled Vernon and Ceri till she got bored with what it was like in prison. The regime. The hours. The grown men crying at night for their moms. The kitchens. The work they did. The exercise yard. The danger other inmates posed.

Back on Pier 33 it was the natural time to shake hands, say good bye and move on with their lives. Vernon thanked him for his hospitality again, for his shared experiences with Alcatraz and for being such a nice guy. Ceri thought if he went on any longer he'd be talking up the Special Relationship between the USA and the UK.

'Don't say goodbye, Vernon. This is a stroke of luck, meeting like this. How often do you meet people related to you on Alcatraz?'

'Well, it might be a bit of a stretch to go that far, Racey,' Vernon ventured.

'No,' the big man snapped back. 'A stretch in Alcatraz - that was the stretch. This connection we have is not a stretch, it's real.'

Suddenly they saw in his face and eyes a dark something of the long years in prison, the hard life and anger lurking behind the affable old man façade. Ceri's unease passed to Vernon, Mel took a step back and the boys stared, instinctively standing closer together. Annette turned into her mother's shoulder.

'Why don't I give you our address in England and we can write when we get home?' Vernon suggested, wondering if he had the bottle to give the man a false address.

'Why don't we meet up tomorrow for breakfast? They got a lot of slop houses in San Francisco, but I know a good one where they don't charge top dollar.'

He had that air that few people would argue with. Ceri rummaged in her bag for a notebook so that he could dictate the name and address of the eatery he'd chosen, the Carbino Lite.

And with a round of handshakes from Racey to all the kids, even Annette, a warm hug for Ceri and a bear grasp for

290

Vernon, they settled on 7.45am the next morning, their final one in San Francisco.

Back in their family hotel room the children expressed a desire not to eat with Mr Slop, nor to see his face anymore, really. Ceri concurred. Vernon wasn't keen on having a meal with one of the demented, either.

So, after sleeping on it, Vernon got them all up early on another bright, breezy morning and they trekked two blocks to the Hollywood Barns, a ramshackle greasy spoon with tables inside and out the back.

They tucked into their breakfast with loads of jokes about slop while both Ceri and Vernon kept a wary eye out, expecting their ex-convict friend to suddenly appear before them hoping they hadn't paid full price for that.

He didn't show. Vernon ticked off a few more minor sights from his list; Ceri started their packing and with a taxi the 13 miles south to San Francisco International airport, Kravitz receded from their minds.

An airport meal that was definitely slop and overpriced at that preceded their piling onto the night flight to London Heathrow. Vernon amusingly called it the 'redeye' but the kids knew what he meant.

And so they left the US after an amazing holiday and 12 hours later turned up at their five bedroom semi in the London suburb of Barnet. Life returned to routine and follow up – bills to pay, calls to return, friends and family to see to gloat about their California trip and a plague of laundry to be overcome.

A couple of weeks later the new school year began and 'slop' at breakfast became an in-joke with decreasing potency until Mel made omelettes as a surprise and then it really was slop again.

One chilly autumn Monday morning, two school friends called for Mel and she left with them engrossed in conversation and didn't notice anything or anybody else. Half an hour later Ceri left with Annette in a push chair for reception class and the boys fresh in uniforms headed for their primary school.

Only when they had walked a few yards from the house did Martin say that he'd just seen Mr Slop! He was disbelieved, especially when cross examined by Lucas who was told the American was staring at them like a zombie.

It was Vernon that Racey Kravitz had travelled across half the world to see. Vernon dashed out, a few minutes late, briefcase in hand, locked the door and pressed the release on his car door, his mind full of the client meeting he had at 11 and the mountain of paperwork to do before and after it.

'Hi there, Vernon.'

The voice stopped Vernon in his tracks; he dropped his car keys. 'Here, let me,' growled the unwelcome visitor bending down to retrieve them for him.

'You look in good shape, Vernon. In fact, you look so much like me, it's just amazing. I wonder people aren't stopping to point it out, how alike we are.'

'Racey... er, um... what a surprise!'

'Thought I'd keep it a surprise, Vernon. Give you a bit of space after San Francisco and our Alcatraz day out to feel when you see me again that yeah, we're definitely very closely related.'

A handful of people scurrying to work, parents on the school run with kids and some teenagers dawdling to get their education paid them no attention. Only one old woman observed and smiled to see two such different people locked in a bear hug.

'Let me look at you.' Kravitz released him. 'I am looking in a mirror!'

'Er, Racey, I do have to get to work, I have a crazy day. Can we meet up later?'

'Sure, I'll take you all out for a meal. And we can plan when you're going to introduce me to your big English, I mean, our big English family.'

Vernon gulped and managed a nod, thinking rapidly. 'The weekend would be better, I think. You know, school and all that... the kids will be delighted to see you. Ceri, er, um...'

'That's swell. The weekend it is. I'm staying with an alumni association of ex cons in the east end of London. Can you find us some place that doesn't serve slop and doesn't charge top pound? My money will have to go a long way during the next six months.'

'Six months?' asked Vernon, already knowing the answer in his heart.

'Six months to get to know all my ancestors. The hostel will be a fair bit. How many bedrooms you got here, Vernon?'

As he muttered 'five' Vernon pictured three nightmares in quick succession. One, going to an estate agent at lunchtime to see how quickly they could move house; two, Ceri's face when she knew Mr Slop was staying and three, him looking for a divorce solicitor.

# Cedric's Left the Building

## 1. Heading for a New Business

When their father set up the first known legal cryogenics business in the UK, his grown up children, Lisa and Donald, were happy to join him.

They had few other ideas, Lisa having studied secretarial skills as advised by a teacher; a working life in light engineering works interested Donald not one jot. The siblings were in their early twenties, a year apart, close but not excessively so.

Donald was a good-looker; Lisa had a certain animal charm about her, but neither had yet partnered up. Both could hold a conversation and tended to like the same things – crime stories, loud music and fatty food. They were neither tall nor short, not overweight yet and not too thin.

Neither did well at school, but they got by. Reports suggested they both coasted rather than pushed themselves hard. As secondary school, ended the problem of what to do with their lives became more urgent. But they instinctively knew that Dad would come up with something.

So when their entrepreneurial-minded father, Albert Forester, dreamed up the idea of a lab and facilities where people would pay to have their bodies cryogenically preserved so that at some distant future date when medical science had progressed enough, they could be brought out of the hibernation and possibly cured, they jumped at the opportunity.

People could, in effect, live for ever. It was a heady prospect for many; a dystopian nightmare for others. But it was potentially a sure-fire money spinner. There would be an initial fee of several thousands to assess, check and prepare people before death, then a fee to freeze them with a recurring annual service charge to keep them in their comas.

Albert set the prices to accelerate each year so that relatives would say, well, we've come this far, we might as well carry on. After all, Granny's heart attack might be reversible now; Granddad's cancer might be curable.

Our future ancient ancestors could walk again, out of their time, at sea in a world that'd changed beyond recognition. They could possibly be as barking as a bag of frogs. That is, if they could actually be resurrected.

What stories they would tell, though! And what a boost it would be for families wanting to show off their great, great somethings to an amazed bunch of jealous friends. Dinner parties would never be the same again.

In this Forester future, people could potentially be on this earth forever and day. Amen!

And Lisa and Donald could be part of that. Pioneers of social well-being, bringers of hope to millions who feared never seeing their loved ones again! Surely they would win the Nobel Prize, at least?

When Donald came home one day in their research and planning phase and announced he was convinced they needed the buzzword 'ethical' in it somewhere, regardless of the actual ethics, they all got very excited. And so, Forester's Life Ethical Academy was born – FLEA for short.

The science was looking theoretically possible. The family bought the anonymous warehouse facilities on a mini industrial estate. They had a water-tight spreadsheet and business plan. Start up capital was raised.

Planning and tortuous licensing hurdles were cleared and a high court judge eventually gave them the green light. Lawyers trousered a fortune to draw up the legally binding agreements they'd need and a handful of doctors were lined up to declare clients legally dead before any processes could begin, for an agreed fee.

They hired consultants to wage the public relations war for them. Albert would handle the scientific angles, Lisa the administration and finances while Donald would use his baby-boy looks and charming ways to chat up old people as future customers.

It certainly looked promising. It was only later that they realised the criminal potential in their monster that they'd overlooked in the first rush of altruistic enthusiasm.


## 2. No Head for Heights

They used to say of Cedric, commonly known as Sadric – indeed, he would say it of himself – that he had no head for heights.

Well, he had no head for anything now.

In fact he hadn't got a head at all. Not for heights, thinking, communicating or living.

Nope. Cedric was dead. Headless.

Strictly speaking he had the head, but the body was deep frozen and the head was now marooned.

There'd been a bit of a cock up in the cryogenic FLEA labs. The body had successfully undergone the cryogenic procedure. But its head got separated somehow and now it was too long since his passing to give old Sadric any chance of resurrection into this world.


## 3. The Grand Launch

When they were fully and double-checked ready, Albert approved a big party around their first signed up, paying client. They invited hundreds. The new labs and working areas were cleansed spotlessly to within inches of their lives.

The PR people had worked overtime to prepare the ground. They'd gerrymandered a survey claiming that 79% of all ages with 93% of the over 80s thought it was a good idea and would certainly consider it for themselves or their loved ones.

They'd lined up local, national and international media. The whole event was planned to stream live to audiences of millions. One Japanese TV company asked if they could hide discrete cameras to capture the whole process from arrival to freezing – real time reality TV at its most cutting edge.

While still negotiating the TV company donation, Lisa'd also hoped for a celebrity to declare the facilities open, but in a bout of hostile media comments they could only secure a third rate, perma-tan newsreader from the local TV who said he 'wouldn't get out of bed for less that three thousand' but settled on one to anchor the show.

Mrs Chamberlain was wheeled in to the *Chariots of Fire* music, oxygen mask obscuring much of her face; canisters strapped to a trailer behind her bed and three nurse-costumed actors ministering to her every need. The minor celebrity flapped about feigning concern and making what he thought were jokey faces to cameras.

Her hapless son, Sidney, Sodney or similar surrounded by the fish out of water that was his extended family, ready

297

stuffed into his wedding suit that fitted him thirty years ago was pushed in front of a barrage of cameras and microphones to sob how much he loved his old Mum and longed for the day when her multiple conditions would be cured and he could hug her again, just like he did when he was a little boy.

One cynical journalist pointed out that perhaps by then, Sidney would be at least 150 years old or was he going to be cryogenically suspended as well? This seemed harsh, sending Sidney off into manly sobs yet again.

Another one asked why not put the whole family under, so that the baby Mrs Chamberlain's granddaughter was nursing could be cured of whatever she didn't yet know she had? This was even worse, so the PR people asked her to leave at once on account of the distress she was causing. Great television that made.

Mrs Chamberlain's performance was textbook. They interviewed her through her mask getting very little sense out of her, but it was extremely moving, nonetheless. Apart from the journalists, there wasn't a dry eye in the place. Her GP told the viewers that she perhaps had a only few weeks of life and FLEA offered the best hope of futures for her and her precious ones.

He managed to hold in his mind an image of the cheque he'd banked last week to keep a straight face.

Outside, a bunch of several hundred protestors made so much noise that the PR people rushed to get some sentimental violin music on to drown it out. The alleged 'celeb' explained that the protestors were religious and other zealots who'd been the sorts to stand in the front of motor cars and jet planes when they were invented.

Apart from that it was a successful event in marketing terms. Three people got themselves the worse for wear on the free booze with dozens more approaching the point of vomiting or violence, so Albert had the bar switch to charging, which solved the problem.

He himself made the speech of his life, lauding his children's vision and the selfless attitude the Forester family had been born with for this very moment to bring hope of cheating death for ever. With curing illnesses and replacing worn out parts, why not? His rhetorical flourish got a round of applause supplemented with a recording of a stadium crowd.

He said that for those afraid of burial underground or being incinerated, cryogenics was the only alternative with the added bonus that in the future, however many years that future was from now, a fully healthy lifestyle should be available.

Of course there was a cost to pay for highly skilled and trained staff and state-of-the-art equipment, but it had been reasonably and fairly calculated to spread opportunity and they had instalment plans in place as well.

Moving to stand next to Mrs Chamberlain, on the grounds that personalising the description of the actual process would make it more easily relatable to future customers, Albert explained.

'Mrs Chamberlain has signed the legal Agreements. Her family have done likewise. After her passing, she will be brought here – in fact we are building a dormitory where clients can come to die in respectful dignity, if they wish.

'Her body will be frozen to prevent brain damage, cooled in an ice bath to reduce temperature incrementally. In the lab her blood will be fully drained and replaced with a specially formulated anti-freezing fluid to prevent ice crystals forming.'

'She will then go into a pouch, like an Arctic sleeping bag, to be cooled by nitrogen gas to minus a hundred and ten over some hours. Finally, she will rest in one of our patient rest modules suspended in liquid nitrogen indefinitely. Or until medical science catches up.'

Some unspoken thoughts added, 'or till the money runs out' or 'until somebody can figure out how to wake her up.' But a smiling Albert called his daughter Lisa to explain a new service coming up.

'Yes, ladies and gentlemen,' beamed Lisa, particularly for the benefit of a man about her age who looked very cool without the freezing, supporting a dear old lady who'd already signed up herself.

'We are developing an extension to our customer offering – we call it neuro-cryopreservation- where we will separate the head and freeze it, but not the diseased body. That will be cremated and returned to the family.'

She moved quickly on. 'In the future a new body could be cloned or regenerated or replaced with artificial intelligence. There are leaflets explaining it in your packs on the door as you leave. Together with a voucher for a whopping 15% off the annual fee for three years!'

Looking round, probably only half of the attendees showed signs of feeling sick.


## 4. Not in the Room

The elephant in the room was sometimes that people used to comment or joke about Sadric that he wasn't in the room. That he'd left the room and there was no point in trying to talk to him. He could hear what you say, but it didn't always mean a lot.

Gradually he not only left the room; he left the entire building.

Ladies and gentlemen, Cedric or Sadric has left the building. Please don't look for an autograph. Nor a selfie. Nor an answer to any questions you may have. He's just not here.

Well, he was here physically, of course. You could see his head over there in the mini-freezer, on a shelf in the corner, awaiting guidance from one of the carers. His body, on the other hand, was tucked up in minus 196 degrees Celsius.

But he was not at home. There's nothing going on upstairs. Not really.


## 5. Business Grows Exponentially

Lisa loved the word and the concept. Business growing exponentially, taking off, going viral, becoming 'must have.'

FLEA started slowly with just three clients and none yet dead. Costs were mounting and income was thin.

Then Donald came across a man who looked about 90 but was actually in his fifties. His festering skin was ravaged with burns after an accident in his kitchen. He had diabetes and multiple sclerosis and had fallen, bringing down a pan of boiling water from the cooker on top of him.

James Collins nearly died. He lay in a coma punctuated with waking spells of hellish agony till he was discovered by chance and blue-lighted to hospital. There they found he had lung cancer as well. They gave him a week to live.

Donald just happened to be in the hospital foyer when he saw the sobbing family unable to leave the building through distress and caught the gist of their problem. They were all ushered into a side room by staff anxious that they were upsetting other patients and visitors. Donald allowed himself to be moved in with the family, as if he was one of them.

He clipped his official looking name tag on his jacket – 'Donald Forester, Health Director, Forester's Life Ethical Academy'. He expressed his sadness at the family plight with a suitably grave face.

Nobody knew who the hell he was, but the fact he was in there with them, nicely suited, his badge shouting keywords like 'health director' and 'life' and 'ethical' enabled some of them to stop their sobbing to listen to him.

He spoke warmly about the future hope of medical science, about how curing cancer was a matter of time, and perhaps not long at that. When he gathered, like a good 'mind reader' doing a show, that their beloved James Collins had other conditions including multiple sclerosis, he nodded and said, 'Of course, I know, we anticipate that will be cured in the not too distant future....'

Donald could actually sell piss pots in a urinal and soon had the female members of the family in his palm, in a manner of speaking. He told them that with cryogenics, a relatively new but exciting science, there was hope of a healthy future with no diseases.

He secured an appointment to see James' daughter at her home and before long, persuaded them all that as the first client at LIFE with a substantial discount (about 2% in reality), their beloved sufferer would be preserved as he was until heaven dawned. One day.

They signed on the morning that James passed away. A well-rehearsed procedure immediately kicked into motion and it went remarkably smoothly. Their first client was in his snug, protected, bomb-proof casket supported by five layers of back up generating capacity within days.

Albert went public and without revealing the name, publically announced that LIFE had its first client and was ready for hundreds more who's loved ones cared enough to sign them up.

The very next day there was another signing, two days later they signed two more and within a week, they had eleven on their books. By the time they reached the first 25 in hibernation and nearly four hundred signed up, it suddenly started to become fashionable.

That PR firm was worth every penny, Lisa, Donald and their father agreed. And when their minor celeb from the opening was diagnosed with early stage Alzheimer's and in a moment of lucidity and a big discount for the pictures of him for posters and adverts, they were truly on their way.

## 6. The Head Will See You Now

For Cedric, no longer with us in any meaningful way other than his severed head, it wasn't always like that, naturally.

In the 1960s he'd enjoyed the most amazing career as a general ideas dogsbody for the BBC. Tallish, quite dapper and with perfectly coiffured hair till he grew it longer and relaxed his suited dress code into a kaftan and headband, he was one of those who fitted in while remaining a complete oddball, a very strange person indeed.

He popped pills like sweets, drank to excess and smoked anything that was going. Everybody did. Nothing odd about it. When anyone challenged him on the amount of substances he was abusing his body with he claimed they helped his creativity. His work depended on them.

Despite no official title, he was expected to come up with game show ideas, write quiz questions, research likely star roles, source theme tunes and sometimes make the coffee. But he was astonishingly good at it. His head seemed to be constantly full of ideas.

His work was used on both TV and radio and as the satirical political mockery of *That Was The Week That Was* and the absurdist surrealism of *Monty Python's Flying Circus* became almost everyone's idea of top of the hit parade, he was allowed to experiment into the wilder reaches of dark side performance.

His classic, his very best piece and the one for which he might be remembered by a few people, was a live audience game show called *The Head Will See You Now.*

Based on a simple idea, as all the best ones are, it had a succession of boxes, caskets and baskets, buckets, cases and other packages that people had to answer topical questions to be given the right to open.

In some were severed heads of the great and the good, the infamous, the weirdos and a few historical anachronisms. Good clean fun. If the head was facing the person who opened it, then he or she would win a prize, because the head could 'see you now'.

If the head was turned away, then a booby consolation was offered, such as a bucket of brains or giblets, a hanged dog, a kidney dish of teeth or a flagon of blood. There was a little bonus for anyone who could say who might have owned the blood, with three guesses available.

Each week the Star Prize was the head of last week's winner. If the contestant by chance found that one, then he or she could choose anyone else to have their head appear in the next show.

Losing contestants were invited back later in a roundup end of series event in which all the heads were from their loved ones and friends, where they had any. The audiences didn't rate that quite so highly.

The TV and cinema adverts promoting it had the voice-over saying, 'what happened here? Only Mr Blamer knows, and it's gone right out of his head….' with a gradual close-up of a headless corpse sitting in a comfy armchair, all to the accompaniment of Richard Strauss' *Also Sprach Zarathustra*.

Cedric found himself on talk shows, appearing in the rags and mags, as someone to be cherished for creating so many hours of harmless fun. Some thought he should be honoured with an award from the Queen for services to mass entertainment.

A few thought he might be committed to an asylum, but ratings couldn't be argued with. However, as time passed and the idea seemed a little stale, and all the best people's heads had already appeared in a box, the management decided to commission one more series.

When celebrities began to appear more than once, the show was dead. No more work was offered to Cedric, even though he suggested ideas less dark, not quite so stomach-churning and more upbeat, in tune with the 70s and 80s and 90s. No joy.

In the early 2000s to mark a new century, he was promised repeat fees when they said they'd make a show of his highlights as part of a history of mass culture before social media and the internet became King.

But even before they began searching for tapes of *The Head Will See You Now* terrorists started beheading people in a genuinely sick perversion of their religious beliefs and out of some madness that it would advance their cause.

Nobody would touch a show about heads now. His new idea of an old stand-up comedian making a living around contemporary Britain fell foul of the compulsory revulsion against sexist, gender and racist jokes that swept the nation, which Cedric had regurgitated years ago.

A footnote in a Sunday paper called him Cedric the Sad, or Sadric, and assuming he had long gone, speculated what sort of death he himself had met. The name stuck.

He was dead, really, but lived on, his savings dwindling and his body getting weaker. When they diagnosed a new strain of smallpox, even from his isolation unit he signed up for FLEA, investing his remaining cash into the hope of a better tomorrow.

## 7. Lisa's Romantic Catch

As the man who'd bravely supported the dear old lady at the launch came into the office to say that his grandmother was fading fast, Lisa took the case from the special needs helper-greeter they'd hired on the advice of the PR people.

'Hello, I'm Lisa Forester. Welcome to Forester Life Ethical Academy.' She offered her attractive hand. Well, she stuck out her mitt – it was others who had called it attractive but she could have dreamed it.

Taking it, he looked into her eyes, 'Yes Lisa, I saw you at the launch party. Grandma had signed up then and we didn't think she'd last this long, but now I'm afraid we may need to call on your services.'

'Of course, we're all thrilled to help, to prepare her for future medical miracles.' She fished in a drawer and produced a fat, glossy wallet of brochures, information and instructions.

'Now, you paid the deposit and she signed all the consent forms. Would she like to pass in our new specialised ethical, green passing dormitory surrounded by every care to ease her way?'

'No, she's going to die at home. Granny prefers that. I'm Mark, by the way, Mark Stephens.' He grinned at her and there was immediate warmth, a rapport there that anyone would have remarked on. If anyone had been there to see it.

Once Mark had parted with the next payment, signed more forms and confirmed the date the doctor had advised, all was set for their next customer.

'Just one more thing, Mark, is your grandmother wanting the neuro-cryogenic option of head preservation only, or is it whole body?'

'Oh, whole body. She and my mother are very clear about that, Lisa.'

'Yes, most people are, I find. However, in fact it would work out a little cheaper as we do not use so many expensive chemicals with just the head ...'

'Oh I think we can afford the full works, Lisa.' He smiled at her and she twinkled in response. 'And just one more thing from me, Lisa.'

'Yes, Mark?'

'Will you have dinner with me or is that not allowed?'

Taller than her, a man of some means clearly, short cropped off-blonde hair and piercing blue eyes, she felt warm in his company. He reminded one of their staff of an officer in a concentration camp, but she didn't repeat that.

'Oh, I think any evening will be allowed and would be very agreeable, thank you... I'll write my private address down and you can pick me up.'

'Better be soon, before she goes, don't you think?'

And so began a relationship that grew from macabre beginnings to become as intertwined as that between Sweeney Todd, the barber and Mrs Lovett, the pie maker.

Once they reached the dessert, Mark who'd asked a lot of questions about the business, took Lisa's hand in his and said, 'I have an idea to expand the company rapidly.'

She'd assumed he was going to propose marriage, but what he had in mind was a business partnership.

'Your dad deals with the science and the mechanics of the processes. You handle finance and admin. Donald is the chief salesperson, in effect...' She nodded. He got the picture.

'Well, does Donald ever come across clients who change their minds? They get so far and then chicken out?' She nodded big. 'These are what you might call people who get cold feet without the ice bath?'

'That's good, Mark. Yes, we get a lot of them. A few want their initial payments back, but we've covered that in the small print. But if they don't go through with it, we get no more revenue from them.'

Thoughtfully, he drained his wine, checked the bottle they'd shared was dead and looked around dramatically to ensure they were not overheard.

'Lisa, what if these cold feet cases are asked to sign a termination notice which they think is terminating their contracts with FLEA, but hidden in 20 pages of small print what they are signing is a termination of themselves notice?'

'How do you mean?' she asked, the truth already starting to dawn.

'The cold feet case has signed the termination, so FLEA is protected. The old dear is taken into the new specialised ethical, green passing dormitory surrounded by every care to ease his or her way. The cold iced bath begins the process and within an hour or two the case is very cold indeed.'

Lisa checked her glass, her mouth suddenly very dry. 'Some water, please,' she asked a passing functionary. 'Go on, Mark.'

Mark obliged. 'You now have a number of options. Go through with full freezing head and body, store it away for a few years till everyone has forgotten and then turn off the machine. Cremate and return to family. Or not.'

Lisa smiled. The water arrived, she drained a glass.

'Your second option is to do the above with either head and/or body. The third is just to cremate the whole thing and say the frozen corpse is safely stored in a canister with the name on and create the paper trail to support that.'

Lisa considered it for ages. Looking at Mark, knowing she couldn't wait to tear the clothes off him tonight, she said finally, 'Let's do it.'

'And Donald and your dad?'

'We'll persuade them. I feel a sudden financial crisis coming up; we have to up the income. Leave that to me. Join us, Mark, join us.'


## 8. Cedric's Backstory

Cedric had not had a totally bad life, at all, despite being a fully signed up hypochondriac. Fear of heights was the only thing that held him back he always claimed and as he'd never have jumped off a cliff or tall building, so he must be sane, he often joked.

He reckoned that's why he'd missed the enduring dizzy heights of fame not realising that they are neither enduring nor worth having.

Freddie thought when they met to discuss his future that Cedric had nothing wrong at all. He therefore became one of their early cold feet cases.

He'd had two wives – one, he'd lost when he was riding low and the second when he was grovelling low. The first was carried out in a box; the other walked out of her own volition.

No children had blessed him and with a sense of relief he'd lost touch with any relatives he could vaguely remember. For a song he'd bought a big house in Hemel Hempstead in the 60s and done it up over the years. It was now worth a shed of money, especially with such a demand for homes there from London commuters.

The sale of that house would fund his freezing. A solicitor drew up the papers to make sure the money was invested with regular payments going to Forester's. Everyone assumed that recessions, boom and busts being what they are, it would last 20 years.

By which time, Freddie assured him that all his ailments would be cured. The Head alone option might be better, slightly cheaper and with so many health conditions Cedric should consider a body transplant in the future rather than trying to keep his present carcase going.

## 9. Keeping It in the Family

At a family dinner to introduce Mark the following week, Lisa worked at the itchy patches she'd sowed in her father's and brother's minds about their cash flow and how Mark was so brilliant he could come up with a solution.

In the end it was agreed remarkably quickly. Father and son were happy. Mark would join them as Chief Operations Officer and would process all cold feet cases from start to finish. Other employees would be kept in the dark.

As they shook hands all round, Mark told Donald, 'You just to have to keep finding the cold feet as well as those happy to jump on for the ride. We'll do the rest.

Donald nodded - he could do that. Albert nodded, too – he could see Mark as his son in law. The future was in safe hands.

## 10. Cedric's Heart Rules His Head

At some point in the 1990s, Cedric got religion. It came about when he was preparing to pitch to one of the US cable channels a great idea for a TV show called *At the Crossroads of Dead Time* where the theme was time and where  the contestants always ran out of the stuff with hideous consequences.

High on something he'd picked up in the street outside his hotel in Carson City on the way to the grand offices of Hermann Cable, the Young at Heart Network, Cedric felt optimistic.

The offices turned out to be a small reception room and a shabby, over-crowded office like a ready made set for some show about a clichéd rundown private eye. It was ten flights up a construction that may have been truly magnificent, about 1904 or 5.

Wheezing and grasping at the wobbly rails, Cedric slowly climbed. When he finally collapsed into the reception area and gasped his name to a woman who would have received her 100 year telegram from the Queen if she lived in England, he was ordered straight through.

Pausing to draw breath and surreptitiously swallow a bit more of what he'd bought on the street, he entered to find a man who looked like the receptionist's father, Mr Hermann.

'Welcome Cedric. I heard a lotta stuff about ya. Welcome to the Young at Heart network. You look like it was an effort to climb up here?'

Cedric nodded, but said nothing.

'Now you got 120 seconds to make your pitch and it had betta be good or I'm opening this window and tipping you out for the short cut down so you won't get so tired. We're young ideas here.'

Hermann was actually as far gone on something as Cedric, but carried it better. The host moved stress balls about the desk while Cedric spoke in warm terms about *At the*

*Crossroads of Dead Time* and how clocks and every timepiece known to man would be set against contestants, each one a little different time from the next.

Demographics, possible ad revenues, future stars who'd be made – he glossed over those angles. Instead, noticing that Hermann was starting to slide into a drug-induced coma, he described in graphic detail the consequences of contestants running out of time before completing impossible, comical and humiliating tasks.

Garrotting by angry women, electric chair, chainsawing limbs, poison sandwiches, eating other food that guaranteed to choke, dangling heads down in water, the playing with fire game where spontaneous combustion was inevitable and the roller game where a series of ever heavier trucks rolled over the contestants' bodies.

'Get outta here,' Hermann cried when he realised Cedric had finished. 'What the hell are you on? That kind of stuff went out with *The Head Will See You Now* and Japanese torture television. We need modern ideas.'

And with a remarkable and totally unsuspected energy and alacrity, the movie mogul leaped up and grabbed Cedric by the throat with one hand and the shoulder by the other and slam-dunked him into the wall by the window.

Cedric was pinned, his face squashed into the dirty brown wall while Hermann wrestled with the rusty metal window, which he finally flung back in triumph.

Now Cedric really started to panic. With a totally puny struggle pushed aside, he found himself gulping air as the street and pavement ten floors below slowly came closer because Hermann was easing him out the window.

When Cedric's ankles were the only fragment of him between life and death in about 5 seconds, a voice from below reached Cedric. It was a man he'd not noticed before but who'd seen him and his predicament.

'Hold on, hold on…' the man shouted as he ran to stand right under Cedric. He's never going to catch me, went through Cedric's jangled mind. And then, this would make a great TV show followed it.

The man below was shouting up. 'Today you will be in Heaven if you welcome Christ into your life. Remember my chains. Thus spoke St Paul in the book of *Colossians*. Remember my chains. If you remember his chains as you say the prayer you can be saved right now.'

Cedric, even at that moment, understood the man was mad. But as Hermann released him a fraction lower to the point where he'd surely not have the strength to haul him back in, he murmured the prayer.

Up to now in his life he'd allowed his mind, his head to dismiss any sentiment or emotion about the efficacy of faith. Now he said the prayer.

He shouted aloud every prayer he'd ever heard of and a few more he made up on the spot. A bunch of watchers had gathered round the lunatic and were holding hands up to Cedric to pray for him. It looked for all the world like they wanted him to jump, they'd catch him.

He shrieked the prayers.

There was a heated exchange of words in the room, and Cedric felt himself being hauled up, banging against the aged cladding and clouting his face on the window sill as Hermann and the secretary hauled him back into the room.

He lay on the floor panting hard, just beginning to feel the pain from his bruises. He was saved.

The secretary leaned down to him, spreading the joy of her breath and yellow dentures. 'Thank you for coming into Hermann Cable, the Young at Heart network. We'll be in touch. Now Mr Hermann, time for your medication, I think.'

## 11. The Crime Spree

The first cold case went well and nobody appeared to suspect a thing. The family of the old man seemed not to realise that he wouldn't come home from a little rest in FLEA's dormitory, but they understood they had to keep paying for a little while and just hoped for the best.

When they signed for an urn of ashes in the parcel post with an explanatory note that Percival had succumbed to a heart attack but FLEA had treated his head, they were puzzled. His body had been cremated and 'please find enclosed his ashes'.

Oh and by the way, FLEA's invoice for services was also attached, with a seven day paying request written in bold purple letters. The Foresters didn't intend to bleed the grieving relatives dry, but costs had to be met.

The second and third were just as simple. Mark suggested carrying out a range of cold feet solutions, so no patterns emerged to excite the interest of any criminal or tax investigators. He installed a row of fake canisters. Some contained heads only, a few stored complete bodies and two were empty.

The fourth case gave them pause for thought. A 15-year old girl enduring a hideous pattern of degenerative diseases that would only get worse so that her body would eventually deny

315

her breath and crush her to death. The girl had to go to the High Court through a panoply of advisers to get consent for the process to be carried out.

The PR people argued that all publicity was good. The idea of a child being processed was anathema to many; an act of supreme heroics and hope for others felt some people. The judge ruled in the girl's favour and FLEA staff braced themselves to carry out what they needed to do.

Lisa was secretly relieved when the child changed her mind, very near the last minute. She was therefore surprised and alarmed when Mark started discussing her as a cold feet case.

It led to a full scale family row. Donald sided with Lisa but Albert argued that to maintain their integrity and secrecy over the other cold feet cases, they had to go through with it.

With no decision reached well-wishers paid for the girl to go on a bucket-list visit to California to see Disney and Universal Studios against medical advice. She passed away on the second day and was buried in Orange County, so the discussions became academic.

The Foresters didn't take long to resume their above board and behind the scenes activities. As greed is a product of criminal addiction, they increasingly administered cold feet treatments to clients who did not want to pull out. Their lifestyles reflected their income, but Mark kept urging caution in their spending, using a range of savings accounts for his own share.

Without intending it, Cedric became their eleventh cold feet case. He worried and fretted about the idea of his head and body separated, even in suspended animation. It made him ill. If he wasn't frail and vulnerable before, the thought of it was definitely a signature on his death warrant.

He began to fear the money would run out – then what? Would they just pull the plug or would they continue to store him as one of the Undead for ever or until a disaster like plague, volcano, tsunami, earthquake, Biblical flooding or takeover by aliens or artificially intelligent giant rats?

He swallowed pills to calm down, tablets to reduce his blood pressure and sat a lot under a blanket trying to pray for guidance.

Finally it dawned on him that the whole madness was ungodly. It defied the way things were created to be. So he rang in his apologies and asked to be released from the contract, shaking and sweating.

Lisa was totally understanding, soothing and reassuring him that all was well, no problems. Of course he wouldn't be frozen against his will. His head could stay on his body alive and dead. Her brother Donald and assistant Mark would call on him at home to bring the agreement to an end with a termination form he had to sign and all would be over.

They called at his house late at night in a black, unmarked van. When Cedric saw two smiling men in black coats and gloves, he knew his number was up. These were neither Grim Reapers nor Angels of Death. They were the Devil incarnate.

His trembling fingers signed a scrawl on the termination form. The prayers died on his lips as a syringe brought soothing darkness to Sadric. His life didn't flash before his eyes. He just caved in, unaware of anything as they bundled him into the van for his journey to the ice bath.

## 12 Cedric's Nightmare

When he came round, Cedric was lying naked in a metal bath being filled by ice from a dispenser. Harsh, clinical lights glared above him.

To say his mind was unbalanced is to understate it. He was slipping in and out of sense and nothingness. The cold soon ceased to be a problem. He felt nothing. There was no pain. Just the lights above and a numbness that held him down.

He was fast leaving the room. Soon Cedric would leave the building. No more ideas from Sadric. In the distance he caught a faint sound. Lord Jesus was coming to collect him. It grew louder, a party like used to follow early recordings of *The Head Will See You Now*.

Closer. A group of technicians were celebrating Robbo's birthday and had already put away a deal of booze, obviously against all the rules. Cedric opened his mouth to tell them so, but nothing actually moved.

They seemed to be dancing, one precariously balanced on the dissecting table. They gathered nearby, staring at the bath next to his.

As he moved further out of the room, Cedric was aware that they'd taken a woman's head off and were dancing with it, throwing it to one another like clowns playing ball. One dropped it, triggering giggles and jokes. Another checked the clipboard.

'No, listen. This one should have kept her head....'

'Bloody hell. If you can keep your head when all around are losing theirs...' roared somebody. 'It's a cock up. Better not make any more. Now who is this?'

'Oh, this one is Cedric, famous once for a TV show about heads!!'

318

A fresh burst of laughter and rude comments engulfed them. 'He'd better lose his head, then', suggested one voice.

'Says whole body, here. I think.'

'Well just to be sure, we'd better take it off.'

'Shouldn't that be just to be sure we keep it on?'

They were having a whale of a time. Cedric was hauled out of his ice and laid on the metal table ready for the next stage.

Albert's appearance sobered the crew remarkably quickly. 'All right, everyone?'

'Oh yes, fine, thanks, Albert.'

'What! Hell's teeth, that was Cedric! You've taken his head off! Can't any of you read instructions?'

Cedric tried to raise his arm to attract Albert's attention to rescue him, to get him out of there. He had to escape. But he had no head to think the idea through.

Cedric had now truly left the building.